FORGED IN THE REALMS OF TIME

This story had been in my mind wanting to be heard. About two girls who meet and instantly their destinies sealed . The enchanted bracelet's had always been the key. While waiting for my first story, 'A forgotten Island In Hawaii', to be finalised and published, I was back in chemotherapy, and met two lovely women that I thought of as sisters. They were in sink with each other at work, and I later found out, as friends too. They became the main characters in this very novel. From there it became so clear. That Distance means nothing when a friendship is so strong. These characters, my beautiful, caring, nurses, kept my mind on making this the book - my novel of all novels . I hope this story, with all its twists and turns, immerses you completely into its fantasy world. Or, is a metaphor of something more alive and real, I'll let you decide...

The real Hannah and Shelly

FORGED IN THE REALMS OF TIME

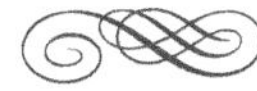

Y'VONNE CLEMENTS

Paperbark Book Co + Publishing House

Contents

One

Bound By Two Bracelets

WHO WOULD'VE THOUGHT THE HOUSE YOU LOVED AS A CHILD WOULD BECOME YOUR WORST NIGHTMARE.

"Are you ready yet, Possum?" I loved it when Mum called me that. It meant that she was in quite a merry mood.

As I'm running down the stairs, she calls again, this time calling me Hannah. I ran into our kitchen, where I saw a school bag. A shiny and new one, complete with that fresh bag smell, sitting there, waiting for me as if it were as excited as me, for the first day of school. But I was also nervous.

"Turn around and let me look at you." Mum said, with a calm yet slightly unusual tone. "You're all grown up in your school uniform!"

I guess she is feeling as though it won't be too long, before it's time for me to begin my journey into adulthood, even though I'm only starting primary school today.

Mum asked me if I remembered what she had told me at breakfast.

"Yes Mum, my little lunch is in the red container, but don't lose it. My lunch will be at the tuckshop, and I must line up to ask for it, and tell them my name."

Mum was very excited for me to go to school. I wished I felt that excited. I loved all the new clothes, even the school-branded shoes and socks, and especially the new coloured ribbons, for my piggy tails!

Mum walked with me to school and showed me where to put my bag. She took me inside where all the other children were playing. Some looked nervous, waiting with their mothers and fathers, to meet our teacher. This place certainly differed from my house.

"Hannah, this is your teacher Ms. Lee. Say hello Hannah". Mum said, as she gave me a little nudge forward.

I tried to, but my voice was only a squeak, so mum squeezed my hand with her cranky look. I spoke again, this time getting my words out, loud enough so that Ms. Lee heard me.

"Hannah, you will sit at the front desk, so that I can hear you clearly," Ms. Lee remarked, in a confident tone.

Mum grabbed my hand, and said, "You sit here, always, unless Ms. Lee says otherwise. Now don't get into trouble, and don't embarrass me." She whispered, so that Ms. Lee couldn't hear her.

I replied, "Ok Mum", not really knowing what she meant.

The other children were being hugged and kissed goodbye. I guess my mum was in a hurry. Maybe? Ms. Lee asked all the parents to say goodbye, so that the class could settle down to begin. My school days had started... Mum had told me not to get into trouble, but what did that mean? Ms. Lee had a very loud voice, like mum when she was angry. She told us lots of things that we needed to do, but still, I didn't know, what not to do.

There was a girly girl sitting next to me, with pigtails like mine. I thought maybe she would know. I asked her if she did and felt something hit my hand. And my, it was hurting! I looked up to see Ms. Lee with a piece of wood in her hand, and a furious expression on her face. As I rubbed where it hurt, she reminded me to speak only when asked. I wanted to cry, but I wasn't sure if that was trouble either.

Ms. Lee went back to her big black wall and began drawing on it! Now I was really confused. Mum had given me some chalk to draw with, and some paper, but when I ran out of paper and drew a picture on my wall at home, she got furious at me and smacked me. Is drawing on walls here aloud?

"What letter is this?" asked Ms. Lee.

Lots of children answered, but Ms. Lee remained unimpressed. Were they all wrong? "Put your hand up when you want to speak!" Ms. Lee exclaimed.

Wow, I was so glad I didn't know what letter it was, even though I'm so eager to learn how to write. Ms. Lee kept drawing on the wall and asking the same question. I knew to stay quiet now. There is no way I'm going to say anything that could get me into trouble. Maybe that's what Mum meant too.

A loud bell rang, and Ms. Lee spoke, "You may leave the room by two."

Luckily, the girl next to me asked me to go with her. Everyone was getting their food out of their bags, and I realised that this must be what Mum meant, when she mentioned a little lunch.

The same girl who asked me to walk with her out of the classroom, came up to me again, and said, "We have to go downstairs."

I followed her, and we sat down on the bench seats beneath the classroom. "I'm sorry you got hit, but my older sister told me she was mean, and not to talk in class. That's why I wasn't game to answer you. My name is Shelly."

Shelly continued to talk to me and said that we needed to eat quickly so that we could go to the toilets before the next bell rang.

"I'm Hannah, and I don't have a sister, but I wished I did, to tell me not to talk in class!" I replied with a little giggle.

I was much happier now that I had someone to talk to. Shelly asked me if I wanted to be her friend. I've never really had a friend before, other than my favourite teddy at home. When I told her yes, she gave me the biggest hug. No one has ever really hugged me like that before. But now I know what one is, and I could tell from that very moment, that we would be friends for our entire lifetime.

The bell went, and we went back up the stairs. Shelly told me never to run, or we would get into trouble. Now I knew what trouble meant.

Ms. Lee taught us lots of things I didn't know. We were each handed small black slates and chalk. I sat still. Ms. Lee then came over to me and asked, "Why aren't you drawing your letters from the blackboard, Hannah?"

"I'm not allowed to draw on anything but paper, Ms. Lee," I replied.

I heard some children laugh, and Ms. Lee hit my desk with a ruler while telling the class to be quiet. I was still shaking from the bang of the ruler, as she turned back around to me.

Speaking a little nicer this time, Ms. Lee said, "In my classroom we use these, and you have a duster to rub out anything, when you need to correct your work."

"Thank you, Ms. Lee," I replied, still shivering in fear of what the rest of the day would be like.

I watched Shelly draw her letters. She was great at this! I had drawn a few too, when Ms. Lee came up and hit my hand once again. This time I cried. She told me that I must always use my right hand. Mum and Dad had never told me that. Shelly grabbed my knee and smiled. I just wanted to run away. I wanted to be anywhere else but here, in this classroom with that nasty Ms. Lee.

Another bell rang, and we were told to get our lunches from the tuckshop. Shelly grabbed my hand and showed me where to line up. When we got to the front of the line, she asked for both mine and hers. I'm glad she did. I don't think I want to talk to anyone else today in case they are like Ms. Lee, too. We found a seat, and Shelly asked me if I knew how to get a drink of water. Mum never sent me any, so I'm not sure what she meant by how, so I just told her no.

Shelly showed me how to use the strange water taps, and not fall in the trough underneath. While getting a drink, Shelly asked me how old I was. I told her it was my fifth birthday last week, and then she asked what I got. I told her, very excitedly, about my new shoes, and these pretty socks, and my shiny bag.

"Mum had bought a cake and put five candles on it for me to make a wish." I told Shelly.

Shelley then asked me what I had wished for. Of course I told her. I explained to her that dad had given me a picture book, that had all the different places where people lived. Some had snow, like where Santa

Claus comes from, and others had mountains, full of jungles and wild animals.

"I wished I could have been there!" Shelly said, with as much excitement as I had when I told her about the book.

"If I had known you, I would have asked for you to come to my birthday too!" I replied.

Shelly hugged me again, and this time, I hugged her back.

We stayed friends throughout our primary years, but one day, at the end of grade seven, Shelly said she was leaving. She was crying when she told me, and I asked why. Shelly told me that her dad had a new job to go to. That all of them had to leave. I cried with her, as I didn't want our friendship to end. I asked Shelly if she would be here for Christmas, but she sadly said no. Her Dad had to be in the new town, to start in two weeks.

"Mum is having a goodbye party, and she wants you to come. Will you? Please come!" Shelly said, between the tears that still rolled down her face.

My mind was a mess, but I told her I would, even though it was the last thing I wanted to do. Life without Shelly??? We had so many plans, of what we were going to do when we were older. To travel together, and to do so many other things. I couldn't believe that my best friend would be gone soon.

Shelly just kept sobbing, and I sobbed just as much while hugging her. She told me her mum said we could be pen pals, so that we could keep in touch.

Two

Living Without Shelly

I had already given my Christmas present to Shelly. That meant the most to me about Christmas! Shelly gave me one too, and in a mysterious tone, she said to put it on at exactly midnight. She said it would be a different time zone where she was going to be but said that she would keep her watch on my time and put her identical present on at the same time. I was so intrigued about what this identical present could be. I waited impatiently for Christmas to come around.

When Christmas Eve finally came, and I opened the gift, I couldn't believe how beautiful it was! Then the phone started ringing, and I knew it was Shelly calling, so I ran downstairs before my parents awoke.

"Hello Shelly!" I said, squirming with excitement.

"Hello", Shelly said, then without taking a breath, she blurted out, "You know the house we love? With all the fairies, and pretty lights in the tree? That lady sells things at the markets. She said hello to me and asked me where my soulmate was. I asked her what she meant. She told me when she sees you and I together, that we have some white light around us. Then the lady gave me these two bracelets and told me what to do with them."

I told Shelly how much I've been waiting for Christmas Eve to come, finally getting a word in. But she soon cut me off again, telling me to put my present on. So, we both did, at the exact same time. When we did this, Shelly said that a light started to shine, from within her wardrobe door. It didn't scare her, but she said that she would walk over to it and open it. She told me that I should go to my room, and check if there's a light in my wardrobe too. I did. And there was! I walked into the light, and then there was Shelly!!

We both took a second as we couldn't believe this was real, then she hugged me and at that moment, I knew it was Shelly. I asked her if she knew this would happen, but she didn't, and then we both broke into laughter over it. It was so good to talk with Shelly face-to-face again. It had been too long. If this was a dream, then I hoped that I wouldn't ever wake up!

"I wonder if I can come through to you...?" Shelly mentioned.

We tried holding hands with our bracelets on, and the light surrounding us shone brighter. We walked in the direction I had come in, and we were back in my room!

I whispered to Shelly, "We have to whisper, as Mum and Dad are next door to my room."

We squeezed underneath my bed to muffle our voices. Shelly started telling me how much she likes it where she lives now, and that the people there, speak with an accent, but sometimes she can't understand what they mean. I asked her if she was happy living in a new town.

Shelly told me that it was different because it's cold and raining all the time. "We do more indoor things at school, than outdoors. We go to an enormous cafeteria to be served hot lunches, and I have two friends called Vala, and Francesca." Shelly continued, "They have shown me everything. They have other friends though, and I feel uncomfortable when their friends are with us. They understand that though, and we went to the movies together without the other girls." Shelly then asked, "Who is Jake?"

I told her how he went to school with me on the bus, and how he's a nice boy, but doesn't talk much. Then told her how his parents had moved him here, and that he misses his friends, too. I thought it best not to make Shelly sad, by telling her that he lives in her old house. "He said he can't wait to be old enough to go back to his old town."

Shelly said that she was glad I had someone to talk to, then said, "How bad was that last drunken episode with your parents?!?"

I answered her but hated having those things brought back into my mind. They had a huge fight, and I heard one of them fall down the stairs. I was going to go out and see if they were ok, but then I heard them both yelling again. So, I put my pillow over my head, trying to ignore it. I really can't wait to run away. I wished it was easier said than done...

Shelly hugged me, and we giggled as her jumper got caught on the mattress wire that was sticking out. Shelly then mentioned that maybe I could walk through alone - through the light in the wardrobe.

Shelly touched her bracelet. The light was still shining, and we slowly walked through. We were both now standing in Shelly's room. The sun here where she lives, was setting. We heard her mum call out to her for dinner. I laughed and said that this was a funny time for dinner. Shelly told me how it was Christmas Eve in her town. I laughed again, thinking that I was having two Christmas Eve's. Her mum called out to

Shelly again, so we both stood beside the cupboard door, and the light came back. We hugged, and I sadly stepped back in, and walked back into my room.

Now Shelly and I knew that even the distance couldn't keep us separated. I stayed awake, replaying the adventure in my mind, that no one would ever believe!

"Hannah, come and see what you have for Christmas," Mum called out.

I ran down the stairs, and Mum and Dad were finishing breakfast. She told me to look under the tree. I didn't do it enthusiastically, as most times, it's not anything to get excited over. It was probably a hand-me-down from mum, I suspected, as that's what I usually get each Christmas. I opened my present. It was a ticket to see a band I liked!

"How did you know I liked them?" I said, in disbelief that I was holding real tickets to see my favourite band. They have done nothing like this before.

"Your dad won them in the raffle at the hotel," Mum replied.

I shouldn't have asked or expected anything else. I thanked them and finished breakfast.

"We are having a roast for dinner tonight." Mum continued.

I thought great, but half knew that they would start drinking soon, and that the roast dinner would most likely not happen. I felt happier though and walked to Jake's house to show him what I scored.

As I passed Castle House, the lady who lived there said hello, and she said my name! I wonder how she knew it?!

"Would you have time to chat, as it's Christmas day?" she said in a soft and kind voice. "And I have no one to celebrate it with."

I felt sorry for her, as she seemed nice. I went in through her pretty garden and sat on the stairs with her. She told me that her name was Esmeralda, and that she had no family here. That must be so lonely, I thought.

With a far-off look in her eyes, she said, "This was my grand-parent's house, and their parents before them, but they have all since passed away, many years ago. Now, it's just me. My name is Esmeralda." Esmeralda continued, "I once had a soulmate just like you, and Shelly".

I gasped! She knew Shelly's name as well!

Esmeralda held my hand, and said, "Don't be frightened. I gave Shelly those bracelets, knowing you two needed each other. When I see you and Shelly together, I am reminded of how I was with my soulmate, Margaret. We were inseparable, and the day she had to leave, I cried just like you."

I wondered how she knew that! She was still holding my hand, saying that the bracelets only work when a friendship is true. Then asked me if I had fun last night trying them out with Shelly. Now I was curious. How did she know that? Esmeralda told me that she and Margaret had made those bracelets when they were young.

She continued, saying, "We had found a book of spells and magic in the attic. We told no one, in case they took it from us! But it devastated us that her parents were taking her away. We read all the different strange words, as best we could, and did everything it said to do. Then these bracelets appeared. As we put them on, we felt the power in them. When I had to say goodbye to my friend Margaret, who was in her bedroom packing, she touched her bracelet thinking of me, and the light appeared in her cupboard, and of course, she opened it and the next thing we knew, she was in my bedroom with me. As time went on and we learned more about our bracelets, we learned that there was no limit to their powerful use."

My heart skipped several beats, thinking of what she meant by that.

"Don't fret, I will tell you, so you don't have this fate befall you, or Shelly," Esmerelda said, trying to calm my thoughts with her words.

My tummy was churning. Esmeralda continued, telling me her and Margaret had visited each other often. But one day, when Margaret was coming to see her, travelling through the light, that the light shone for but a moment, then disappeared. "I tried to go to her, but the bracelets had stopped working. We did not have phones back then, so all I could do was write a letter. Her mother replied to me eventually, saying that Margaret had gone missing, and that the police still had no clues as to her disappearance. I have stayed here, in this house. Waiting for over 50 years. One day, I opened the wardrobe, and her bracelet was on the floor." Esmerelda continued, "I added up how many times we had used them. It was 20. If only we had known then, what I now know. We would have never used the last one."

I had tears rolling down my face. Esmeralda hugged me and said that she knew when she saw Shelly and I, that it was meant to be. Her passing on the bracelets, to us.

"I feel your life will change soon. Be very strong." Esmerelda said, and then asked, "What are your plans for your future?"

"After two more years of school, my goal is to find a job. I would love to be wealthy so that I can see the world! I have this book with pictures of different countries, and I know I want to travel to so many of them!" I shared with Esmerelda.

Esmerelda replied, "Well aren't you an ambitious one! And that's what it takes to make dreams come true!"

"I do very well at school, and my teachers say that I could do anything when I'm older." I replied.

Esmerelda laughed, saying that I was a lot like she was. The she went on to tell me that her parents named her after her -great-grandmother, a famous actress. "So, I wanted to be an actor." Esmeralda said.

"What was your favourite movie you played in?" I ask Esmerelda, assuming she made it.

Esmerelda laughed. "I was the '*Queen of Hearts*', in a making of Alice in Wonderland. It was a silent movie, made from the book. I have had others since then, but that was my favourite. I believe the book of spells that we had found in the attic was my great-grandmothers, and I have always been interested in white magic ever since. But even white magic used wrongly causes great tragedy. Now I am old, it will eventually end up with a new owner."

I realised how much time had passed while talking to Esmerelda and I said goodbye. "I will call in again if you like?"

Esmerelda said that she would like that very much, and that we would have an afternoon tea party when I next visit. I thought, why not, if that's what she wants to do. As I went to leave, she told me to always keep my window open. I found that quite weird to say to someone leaving, but that is exactly what Shelly always said to me, too. Maybe Esmerelda knew my parents? I ran home, to my room, and cried, feeling like Esmeralda cared.

As I lay with tears rolling down my face, my wardrobe begun to glow, and Shelly walked through. She told that me she could feel my pain and knew that I needed her. She cried with me, expressing her wish to go out, but she was afraid of being seen and our secret being revealed.

Shelly knew her mum would be home from shopping soon, so she had to go. So, we hugged, and then she was gone again.

Three

Christmas With Esmeralda

Shelly and I used our bracelets very carefully, knowing what the outcome could be. Shelly was able to continue school. She was studying to be a teacher. She had grown to love where she lived. Our lives were becoming different, but I just knew in my heart, that no matter how many years went by, our bond would never change.

I had started work in a publishing office. It was interesting work. I have a position of editing. I had achieved straight A's in English throughout my schooling, so editing seemed easy for me. I had been there for 5 years when my boss decided to hold a celebration and take all the staff out for a special dinner.

When I walked home, I saw Dad's car parked badly, and knew he had been drinking again. I went in hearing the normal fighting, and just headed to my room to get ready.

As I left, I yelled out "I'm going out and will be home late." No answer, so I closed the door and left.

I had a great night at the staff party. My boss, Mr. Winston, offered me a higher position in the company. This was wonderful, and the pay rise will come in handy. Everyone congratulated me and were all genuinely happy for me. We were a good team and had a good reputation. I often wonder what it would be like to write my own story though, instead of reading others.

As I walked home, I saw that Esmeralda was on her veranda with the light on. I called out her and said hello, and she called out saying that she was there if I needed her. Funny thing to say, but I said thank you, as we were good friends now, and I often spent Sunday afternoons reminiscing with her.

When I reached home the lights were out, but the car was gone. I thought, probably went to the hotel. I went straight to bed and slept like the weight was getting lighter on my shoulders.

I awoke to a strange noise and went down to the kitchen to see what was going on, unbeknownst that this is where my life would change forever. My mum was sitting there crying. I asked her what was wrong, and she said that dad has packed his things and left us. I was not even sure how I felt about that, or what I should feel about that! I asked if I could do anything for her, but she was angry and told me to just leave her alone. I never went against what she said. So, I went and dressed and left quietly, realising that I never told her my good news.

I walked down the road, and as I walked past Esmeralda's house, I remembered what she had said. Surly she wouldn't have known what was about to happen. I loved her old castle house, with its crooked roof and old gabbles. The flowers seemed to bloom all year around, and the scent was beautiful. It brightened my mood up, and I headed into my new position with great excitement.

My first client was a very well-known author, I was a bit overwhelmed. I edited a lot of his bestseller books. When I first introduced myself, he had said that it was nice to put a name to all the comments. I replied saying that I hoped I never offended him. He laughed saying that it was a breath of fresh air, for someone to be honest instead of telling him that everything was perfect.

"I wouldn't have wanted you to be my school teacher though!" He said laughing.

"You wouldn't want to have met mine either!" I replied.

I asked him to take a seat, and while we discussed his new book, he asked me what my thoughts were on illustrations for the cover. I told him my ideas and he said it was perfect, then asked me if I had ever written a book.

"No, but lately, I have been thinking about a fiction one." I replied.

He offered to help me if I went ahead with my idea. I was so taken back by the offer, and I stayed on cloud nine all day.

As my day came to an end, my boss came in to congratulate me on a job well done and told me that I had made quite an impression on my first client today. I thanked him and expressed that my client had made such an impression on me too. When my boss asked me why, I told him. He was speechless and said that I should not let that opportunity pass me by.

Walking home, I saw Esmeralda wave. As I walked through her gate and up the stairs, she said, "You had a good day, didn't you?"

"How do you do that?" I replied.

"Your aura changes colour, and other times, I just feel the vibes in the air." Esmerelda replied.

I told her what I thought of writing about, and she said, "Why not? Nobody would know if it's fiction or not, and who better to tell it than you."

I told her I wanted to call my book, 'The mystery of Esmeraldas Ghost'. Esmeralda then said that if I couldn't find peace at home to write, that I was welcome to write it at hers. I hadn't thought of that, but I grew up studying at home, blocking out everything around me, so I'm used to writing in most situations. I was now on a mission to write my book.

Arriving home, Dad's car was back. Along with the never-ending arguing. I decided to write my book at Esmeraldas after all. I grabbed everything I needed, then headed back to Esmeralda's house, not bothering to say anything to my parents.

Esmeralda was inside, but she had left the porch light on for me. She called out asking me to come in, before I even knocked. I laughed to myself, thinking how she knew I was here, when I just been in and out of my house without even being noticed. That's twice now, that I have had the feeling that I didn't belong in my own home.

"Pop your stuff down and take a seat at the dining room table." Esmeralda called out.

I was getting used to the fact that she could see through walls, and it made me giggle of the thought. It felt like ages since I giggled. Then my mind started missing Shelly.

When I sat down, I realised there were three settings laid out. When I went to walk into the kitchen, Shelly walked out! I rushed over to her, and our tears and hugs felt like they lasted as long as it had been since I had last seen her. We both started talking at the same time, just like we always did, and laughed. Could this day be any better?

Esmeralda brought out a full roast dinner, fit for a queen, while telling me that I never got to have that Christmas dinner I was always told I would get. "So, let's pretend it's Christmas!" Esmeralda said.

With that, the room turned into bright coloured lights, and decorations began sparkling everywhere. Even a Christmas tree appeared, with a very big parcel under it. When we asked what it was, Esmeralda said that it was for us girls, to open after dinner. We were so excited to know what it was.

Shelly told me that she was back to stay. She said that her dad's job had ended, but her sister Mary would stay as she had a man in her life back there.

"Mum and Dad are buying their old house back. They are staying in town until it's all settled." Shelly said.

She then asked me about my life, and I told her all the good things that have recently happened.

"I will be back in a minute." Esmeralda said, as she hugged us both.

We suddenly realised everything had gone quiet in the kitchen. We went to make sure Esmeralda was ok. She wasn't there, but she left a note that read:

'I will always be with you both. Open your present!'

We went to the Christmas tree and began to open our present, not understanding where Esmeralda had gone. Inside was the big book that she had always spoken about, and a letter. We opened it, and it was the deed to her home along with another note, that read:

'You are both now the caretakers, and owners of castle house. Go to the solicitors and ask to see my will, and signed papers to my estate. Eternal love, - Esmeralda.'

Four

Do We Own Castle House?

Shelly and I made the appointment to see the solicitors. We were both still mystified at why Esmeralda would do this, and where Esmeralda disappeared to. Neither of us believed she was gone. Shelly rang me early, to say that she would meet me there, as she had something she needed to do with her mum first.

As usual, I left home on this beautiful, cool aired morning. Without even seeing my parents. Walking to work was so exciting now, except I half expected to see Esmeralda sitting on her front porch, waving hello. It felt quite sad not seeing her there. Her flowers and birds were still just as beautiful though. I closed my eyes and felt her presence, and smiled as the feeling of happiness enveloped me.

Walking into work, I saw a big bunch of flowers on my desk. Whoever would have sent them? Everyone had smiles and began giggling as I read the card. The card read:

'A little thank you for your help yesterday. Looking forward to our further meetings.'
- Mr. Ray Sallinger.

This was the candle on my cake! I now knew that I was going to write my book! The office went quiet, but phones kept ringing. I saw my boss after his client left and asked for the afternoon off.

Mr. Winston looked at me in shock, and said, "Yes, Of course, is everything ok?"

I assured him that it was better than all right.

He laughed, and said, "That's my girl! Nothing ever defeats you!"

I went back to my beautiful smelling office. Struggling to focus, I decided to leave, and go to the park. It was so quiet and relaxing there, that I was able get my scrambled brain clearer headed before the solicitor's appointment. I still couldn't make sense of the scenario though. No one would understand what the bracelets could do either. Letting myself think for a moment, was any of this even real? I started seeing my life in a whole new way.

Slowly making my way down to the solicitor's office, where he would either laugh at Shelly and I, or give us good news. I thought to myself, either way, I still had Shelly back, and an amazing job within great company, and workmates I loved.

I saw the sign, hanging from the roof ceiling, and then I saw Shelly, walking from the opposite direction. We arrived at the door at the same time, which made us giggle. We used to arrive at school at the same time too. Shelly was in the same mood as me, excited, but uncertain if this was real.

Together with all our courage, we walked in, and I said, "Hello. We have an appointment to see Mr. Brian White."

The receptionist said, "Hello..." And with a smile, she continued, "My name is Zoe. Please take a seat. Mr. White won't be long."

We sat as if Ms. Lee was watching us. Shelly giggled then tried to restore her composure by telling me what she and her mum had been doing. I told her about my flower delivery at work, and we both held in our elated happiness. Normally we would have hugged and giggled, but we had to be professional today.

The meeting room door opened, and a well-dressed, very good-looking gentleman walked out, and said, "Come in, young ladies."

This was it! We held our heads up, expecting to be laughed at, and took our seats opposite Mr. White. He asked, 'the question'. We showed him the letter and held our breaths.

He read it. Then read it again. "Are your name's Shelly Bryant, and Hannah Adams?"

We acknowledged that we were and showed him our school reports to provide proof of our names. We didn't have a licence, and Shelly's birth certificate was packed in a shipping container. My mum had no idea where mine was. So, school reports were all we had at this point. Mr. White rang through to Zoe and asked her to come in. He gave her the reports, asking her to confirm with the school headmaster their authenticity. He also asked her to contact births, deaths, and marriages, and have copies of our birth certificates sent over. He asked for our parent's full names, date of births, and the place where we were born. Zoe took notes, and then asked Mr. White if that was all he needed. He nodded, and Zoe left the room smiling.

Mr. White asked us to wait one moment as he walked over to the safe, and then popped out of his office. He seemed very professional, but also very pleasant to speak to. Time felt as if it was going super slow. When he finally came back, he had a very disturbed look on his face. As he sat, he asked us who had told us about the will. I had thought he might find the date unusual. Shelly explained to him that when we cleaned Esmeralda's home, it was in all the old paperwork. We thought that sounded easier than trying to explain Esmeralda and her ways, who has now vanished.

"Give me a moment while I read this." Mr. White said.

We tried hard not to be anxious, or looked scared, but we are here now.

Mr. White looked at us over the top of his glasses, and said, "This is a very unusual will." As we sat staring, he continued, "It appears in order, but the date stamp is from my predecessors. I would prefer to have all your paperwork before I continue. My secretary will make another appointment with you after the paperwork arrives. I will keep your letter with the will, if that is ok."

We nodded at Mr. White with a yes and said goodbye. He walked us to the door mumbling to himself, then said, "Miss Bryant. Miss Adams." As he opened the door for us.

We heard the door close behind us, and as we looked at each other we were lost for words. Zoe asked us what day would be suitable for the next appointment and mentioned that the paperwork should arrive by next Monday.

"Tuesday morning, please." Both Shelly and I said, at the exact same time.

Zoe giggled, and said, "You are in sync with each other." I replied, "Yes! We seem to do that all the time!"

"We will see you at 10am, Tuesday." Zoe said, as she offered us her business card.

As we left the office, I asked Shelly if she was in a hurry to get home to her parents, but she said that they were going to the real estate today, so they probably wouldn't be home.

So, I said, "Great, let's go to Esmeraldas!"

While walking to Esmeraldas, Shelly and I talked about what kind of jobs she was interested in. Shelly said that she still wanted to be a teacher.

I said, "Maybe Ms. Lee has left. You could teach the new children."

Shelly said that she would really enjoy that. I told her to just make sure she tells her students what they can't do, so that they don't get into trouble. Then we both burst into laughter, remembering our first day.

"But look at you now!" Shelly said.

I thought about it, and with pride, I told her that I am so happy at work. I have saved up enough to buy a car but was hanging onto my savings in case I needed to rent a place of my own. You know, with all the predictable unpredictability between my parents, and the usual fighting between them.

Shelly said that she would move with me if I had of rented my own place. I asked Shelly about her sister, and if she would ever come back here. Shelly thought about it, but then said that she didn't think so, as both her sister, and her sisters' partner, had great jobs, and they are saving for their own home. I couldn't imagine anything worse, living with a male. I'm quite happy not to have a boyfriend. Shelly understood why I thought that way.

As we reached Esmeralda's home, and walked through the gate, the gardens were still blooming, and their scents still intoxicating. We were half expecting Esmeralda to open the door, so we went in and checked the kitchen and the dining room for her.

My writing stuff was still sitting where I had left it. But with Esmeralda not home, my curiosity began to wonder what might be upstairs. We walked down the hallway to the stairs and saw some old pictures of people hanging on the walls. As we began to head up, one of the old stairs creaked. We both grabbed each other in stillness for a moment. This house seemed so different without Esmeralda's presence here.

We continued until we came to the upper hallway. There were different doors lining the walls. All closed. We were unsure if Esmeralda was going to walk out of one of them. Not knowing if she might be back or not. Cautiously, we opened one at a time. Peering in. Each room was decorated in very old, dust covered, draped curtains, stained covered old bedding, carved old timber furniture with clumps of dust settled in every nook and cranny of the hand carved shapes. There were layers of dust on top of everything. We had opened one door to a very old bathroom that only had a carved clawfoot bathtub, and a rusty old shower head hanging above. The rest were bedrooms, all similar in style. I asked Shelly which room she thought was Esmeraldas. Shelly just shrugged and was more intrigued in continuing exploring this old home.

Two of the bedrooms had a wardrobe in each, and we decided to look in one of them. There were clothes, but they were very old and very musty. I thought this might have been her friend Margaret's room. We went into the next one, and it had a similar wardrobe with carved doors and a set of very old dresser drawers, that matched. Some very old, but expensive shoes, lots of exquisite, beaded ball gowns, and very expensive looking coats. We opened the other side of the wardrobe, and for a faint minute, I thought I saw a light. It must have been my imagination playing tricks on me.

Shelly had opened the drawers and said it was nearly empty. Just some very old nighties, lots of stockings, and underwear. Then in the top one was Esmeralda's pearl necklace, along with some other very old, expensive-looking jewellery. This shocked me for a second, as I had seen her wearing that pearl necklace, though none of the dresses looked familiar.

We made our way back downstairs, and to the kitchen, and opened the cupboard. This was where we had put all the dining sets that we had washed up. But when we opened the doors, there was Nothing! We checked the cutlery drawer, and nothing again! We could not understand where everything had gone. Then we noticed that the Christmas tree and lights were all gone as well. We raced out hoping the book was still in its box, and breathed a big sigh of relief when we saw it was still there. I said to Shelly that I was starting to think that I had dreamed this all. But this book still being here, that made it real. Right?

We sat at the table deconstructing all the latest events, trying to make sense of what was going on. I asked Shelly how she got here, the night of Esmeraldas Christmas dinner. She said that she was on her way to my house, and Esmeralda called her. She said Esmeralda had told her that I was coming over, and to wait for me to arrive so, that she could surprise me. The last time we saw Esmeralda, she was walking into the kitchen.

We looked around and saw a cupboard beside the old cooker. It dawned upon me how Esmeralda could even cook a whole turkey in that small thing. Shelly walked over to the cooker and pulled the knob handle, and it opened. We weren't sure what to make of it. There were shelves but no food. Again, I thought I saw a flash of light. There was nowhere else in this room to go to. Or any other way to leave it.

Shelly noticed the light string and told me to try it. I pulled it and it clicked, but no light! I was sure that light was on the night of the roast dinner. We went around all the downstairs area of the house and tried the other lights too. None of them worked. This mystery just kept evolving.

As Shelly and I sat thinking, we heard noises upstairs. It was nearly dark though, and we needed to leave. But we wondered if there could be a doorway in the wardrobes. We climbed the rickety stairs again, and walked into the room that we thought might have been Esmeraldas. There was no light, but we opened the cupboard door to check anyway. Nothing. We looked around and noticed that the top draw was open again.

"The pearl necklaces! It's gone!" Shelly said.

We called Esmeraldas name a few times, waiting for some sort of response. Silence consumed the room, so we headed back downstairs. Shelly and I decided that we would hide the magic book until we could take the time to read it. Shelly said that her mum would find it in the hotel room. I thought Mum would never come into my bedroom, but I would still need to get it up the stairway, without being seen with it.

"Pack your writing things back into your suitcase and put the book under them. Then she won't know any different if she sees you." Shelly said.

It was a heavy book, but worth the effort to keep it hidden.

"Any trouble, call me!" Shelly said, as I zipped the suitcase up.

We closed the door, and the aroma of roses hit us. I felt I could feel Esmeraldas' presence.

Walking home, I saw Jake at the corner store. He did say hello, but he seemed lost in his own thoughts, I waived hello, and walked up to him. I asked Jake if he had a new home he was moving to. He looked at me strangely, and asked how I even knew.

"A friend of mine used to live there, and her parents decided to buy it back when it hit the markets. You did tell me about it too, but only briefly though." Then I continued, "My books are getting heavy. I'll see you around."

Jake replied, "Yeah", but had no smile.

My gut said he needed help, but my mission was to get this book safely hidden. I made it home and the car was gone. I took all my writing books and things out of my suitcase, then stuffed some clothes on top of the old book and put my suitcase back under my bed. I looked in the kitchen to see if there was any food. I found some eggs and made myself an omelette, quickly cleaning up my mess, before I was trapped in between another disagreement walking through the door.

Just as I closed my bedroom door, I heard the car pull up. One day, I will be gone. When that day arrives, I won't have to feel the way I do right now, ever again.

The night flew by, and morning came.

Back to work, where my flowers were still waiting for me. My mood always felt proud and grateful there. When I walk through that glass door, with that name plaque saying, Book Publishing Office, it's like I'm in a whole new world. A world where everything is perfect.

I had a look at my diary and checked what I had booked for Tuesday. Hopefully, I could rearrange my appointments. My boss wasn't in this morning to ask, but I knew he wouldn't mind. My day flew by, and I was able to sort Tuesday out.

I gave Shelly a call and she said that she was out with her mum but would meet me at Esmeraldas. This time, I took some takeaway and cold drinks, and walked through the park. Again, I was overcome with that feeling of not being alone. I walked through the gate at Esmeraldas and saw Shelly sitting on the porch.

"Oh no! I brought dinner as well!" Shelly said, laughing.
We sat out in the intoxicating garden, where I used to have afternoon teas with Esmeralda. I was wishing she would join us. Then I heard a rustle in the trees, and a light breeze floated over us.

Shelly looked at me and said, "Did you feel a presence just now?"
"Yes! I was thinking it was Esmeralda!" I replied.

Shelly said, "I wish I knew how to make cups of tea like her."

We then heard a noise inside and we went through the front door to look around. I said that it was probably a stray cat, and we scared it. We decided to go and sit in the dining room, and as we walked in, sitting on the table were two cups of tea. Neither of us were scared. We both knew it had to be Esmeralda.

We had the weekend to ourselves, as Shelley's parents had gone to catch up with family and said they wouldn't be back until next weekend. Shelly said we could stay at the hotel and go to a movie.

We closed Esmeralda's house and walked to the theatre to see what was playing. My eyes couldn't believe what I saw! The theatre was having a movie marathon tomorrow, in honour of 100 years of film. They were running the black and white silent movie, Alice in Wonderland. I took my time to take this event in. Shelly asked me if we should get tickets.

I said, "Definitely!", and walked with her, knowing she felt there was a reason. But knowing she was happy to wait until I could tell her.

When we got back to the hotel, I knew we could speak knowing that no-one would hear our conversation.

"Now, tell me what startled you!" Shelly said.

I told Shelly about Esmeralda, and that she said she had played a role in this particular version of the movie. We both took a minute, as it was now 1975, and that sounded impossible!! As I spoke, we could both feel her presence again. It was always like a soft gentle touch.

We turned on the television but fell asleep, somewhere in the middle of a movie, but awoke to the noise of static on the screen. Looking at our watches, it was after midnight. We snuggled into bed and later awoke to the sunlight streaming through the window.

Being Saturday, there was no traffic noise. It was quiet, and we were in no hurry to go anywhere or do anything. Shelly and I talked about what we would do, if we owned Esmeralda's castle. We both agreed that we would live in it. I mean why wouldn't we! I was too scared to get my hopes up, but to finally have a home, of peace and happiness, would be my absolute wish.

Later that morning we went to the cafe and had brunch. We had a few hours to fill in, so we decided to look at some furniture at the local warehouse. We had lots of fun trying out beds. If we were really going to do this, we both decided to keep the dining room as it was. Oh, and get the electricity put on.

Time had flown and we headed to the theatre for the movie night.

As we entered, we had that feeling of Esmeraldas gentle presence. This was going to be so interesting! Then, 'The Queen of Hearts' came on, and we were mesmerised! But it was Esmeralda? We watched the whole movie, and when the credits started to roll, there was her name.

Five

Living With A Ghost

Monday morning came around. When I got to work, I asked my boss for Tuesday off.

"Is everything alright?" He asked.

I told him that everything is ok, but there were some financial things I needed to get sorted.

He said, "If there is anything I can do to help, you know where to find me."

"It's ok, I've got it under control, but thank you." I replied.

My day was quite busy, but I tried to get ahead in case I needed another day off. Shelly called me to tell me that her mum and dad were staying away a few extra days and asked if I wanted to stay with her at the hotel again. I told Shelly that that would be great, and that I would duck home and get clean clothes after work before, before I headed over.

When I arrived home in the afternoon, it was the first time in ages that my mum was home. She was sitting in the dark.

"Your father has been in a car accident and is in the hospital." Mum said.

I asked mum if it was his fault. She said he had run off the road and rolled the car. I said a quiet prayer for him in my mind and was thankful that no one else had been hurt.

Mum then asked, "Are you going out? I'm feeling a little lonely."

Those words hit me hard, that's how I had felt all my life in this house. I had no words to answer her. Not anything that wouldn't upset her more. So, I turned and walked away to get my things, and headed to the hotel.

Walking down the road felt different today. I walked past our soon-to-be home and waived at Esmeralda. Well, at the presence of her anyway. I know she's there even though I cannot see her. My new life starts tomorrow, in that very house. I was walking on air and had a beautiful soul walking with me. Other people would never believe me if I told them that I walk with a friend from the past. When I thought more about it, I realised Esmeralda always knew when there was some- thing sad, or bad, happening in my life. My teachers used to ask me if every-thing was ok at home. They used to say, 'your parents don't seem to come to any of the parent interviews.' I hated having to give excuses for that. Shouldn't it be the parents giving the teachers excuses for a child's absence, or work?

School holidays were always spent at Shelly's, and we would pre-tend I was her sister. I remember being asked what my father did for work, and I used to say that I wasn't sure, but he worked away a lot. Strange how that was normal to me, but that's what made me into who

I am today. It gave me my broad imagination, and that was my bedroom friend.

As I arrived at the hotel, Shelly had been watching out for me. She was so excited about how we would be able to live together in the castle house. I told her the thoughts I had while walking here, and she said that her parents always knew. She said they used to say that I had no home life, and that they used to tell her that she should ask me over more. I told her how special it was that life gave me her as my friend. Shelly said that maybe it was Esmeralda. In a weird way, that kind of made sense.

Shelly and I started watching a movie. It was called, 'The Legend of Fisher's Ghost'. When it was over, we both agreed that they should have just asked the ghost for afternoon tea! We laughed so hard our bellies hurt.

I asked, "Do you think Esmeralda found her friend Margaret?" Shelly said, "I do hope so. I would never want to lose you like that!" I hugged her and told her that we were meant to be eternal friends!

Feeling famished, we went to the local burger store up the road. Jake was there and I introduced him to Shelly. He said hello, but he was still as sad as the last time I had seen him. I asked if he wanted to sit with us and he nodded.

We sat outside at the tables. I asked Jake how his work was going. He said that it's been great, and that his boss had said that he would be the next in line for a promotion. This seemed to brighten him up. I was so glad to see a slight smile appear. I told him what had happened at my work as well, and the author I was currently working with. He said that he had read all his books, and mentioned how amazing it must feel to know that I was a part of his written art, being that I was the authors editor.

Shelly told him how she was going to be a teacher. "I like helping children learn, and have my degree being posted over to me now that I've graduated. Then I will be able to teach children here."

Jake said, "I work in a car factory, and seeing all of the cool cars makes me really want to own one myself!"

Shelly began to ask Jake where he was living, but I swiftly kicked her under the table. Lucky, she got the message and understood I didn't want her to continue that sentence, so instead, she asked him where he had gone to school.

He laughed, and said, "With Hannah, of course. That's how we met."

I asked Jake if he wanted to go and see a movie with us. When he asked which one, Shelly mentioned that there was an old American Indian one called, 'Broken Lance', that we should watch. Jake asked if he could bring his friend, Brad.

"Of course, how could we say no!" I replied.

I was glad that Jake had brightened up, and I looked forward to meeting his friend Brad.

After the movie was done and dusted, and we said our goodbyes, Shelly and I wandered through the park back to the hotel. We grabbed an ice cream from the old man with a pushcart. I think both of us were just wasting time until our fate was told tomorrow.

The movie was great, and Brad was lovely too. He told us that we could call him anytime, then gave Shelly and I his number. I don't know why, but when he did that I kind of felt shy and clumsy out of know where, and almost tripped over my own feet.

As Tuesday came around, Shelly and I were up and ready at the brink of dawn. The excitement was so much that we decided that a good breakfast at the cafe was in order. Our tummies felt like our exam days, but a gentle feeling was with us too, and both knew that it was Esmeralda.

Now, we were finally at the solicitor's office, the reality of it all started to kick in. This was it! We held our bravado and went in. Zoe greeted us and asked us if there was anything we wanted while we waited. Both of us asked for a black coffee at the exact same time. Zoe laughed, then told us that Mr. White was running ten minutes late and would see us as soon as he was finished his current meeting.

While we were waiting, Shelly's phone rang. It was her mum. She told Shelly that they could move back into their old home as soon as they liked now, as the tenants were all moved out. I remembered I hadn't told her about Jake. But I thought right now wasn't the time to bring that up.

As we finished our coffee, a gentleman walked out of Mr. Whites office, and looked directly at Shelly and me. He tipped his hat to us as he said, Ladies, then left. Then Mr. White called us straight in.

"Sorry for keeping you waiting. Mr Jeffries, the man who just left, is a specialist in signature forgeries. I had to have verification of the signatures on the old deed and letter you gave me, as it is a very unusual situation." Mr. White said. He then read out the will and said that he cannot find any reasonable explanation, for Esmeralda knowing us both.

Mr. White continued, "But, after all the searching, your letter, and the signatures upon it, are indeed authentic. What I must explain to you though is the rates, and that previous caretakers were set up with a fund. So, there is also a financial will conjoined with the estate deed that you will need to sign on. I have spoken to the bank involved with this trust, and the manager has asked you both to see him once you are finished here. He will explain the terms of the trust."

"Sooo, does that mean that we are now the official owners of Esmeraldas Castle House?" Shelly asked.

Mr. White stood up, so we followed his actions. He shook our hands, and said, "Shelly. Hannah. This is your deed and the keys to Castle House." Passing us the paperwork and keys that were on the desk in front of him. "This is the name and details of the bank and the manager you will need to go and see. I will call ahead now so that he is aware that you are on your way. One day I will make sense of this." Mr. White then walked us to his door as he mumbled that he now believed in miracles.

As Shelly and I walked out of the foyer doors onto the footpath, we let out the loudest ohhh myyy GOSH!! Then walked in silence, as we let it all sink in. It felt so surreal. We own Esmeraldas' old mansion! We own CASTLE HOUSE! We now have this piece of Esmeralda in our lives, and hopefully one day, both Margaret and her will be with us in that home.

When we arrived at the bank, the front of house lady asked us to take a seat and said that Mr. Hughes would be with us soon. Shelly was looking nervous about this meeting. I was too slightly, as I had no clue what this meeting would entail. Mr Hughes popped his head out of his office and asked us to come in.

As we sat down in front of his desk, Mr. Hughes said, "This is the most unusual situation I have ever dealt with. I have had all signatures, and birth certificates checked for authenticity, but for the life of me, I cannot understand how this could be. Do you young ladies know how the woman of Castle House would have even known to leave her estate to the both of you?"

We told Mr. Hughes that we had no idea how this came to be. In all honesty, we didn't. He continued to tell us that everything was all in order, and that he could only suspect that we had an ancestor, who must have planned the names of our births prior to our parents even becoming pregnant. He didn't believe that anyone could leave such an inheritance, to fate.

We signed the agreement and Mr. Hughes explained the account, and how it was set up. A majority of the funds were set up as a particular fund for property maintenance only, however, there was still a significant amount allocated for anything else.

"We will be contactable at this address until the house is ready for us to move into." Shelly said to Mr. Hughes, as she passed him a piece of paper with all the details. "Good day, Mr Hughes. It was a pleasure dealing with you today."

Shelly and I stood up, and shook Mr. Hughes hand, and he walked us out.

Since all the paperwork was signed with the bank manager it begun to feel more real. Not only did we have this beautiful old home, but we also now had the funds to fix it up too!

After leaving the bank we stopped into a restaurant to celebrate, then caught a Taxi home. To our home. Castle House. Shelly and I opened the door for the first time, officially as our home. There sitting on the dining room table was a beautiful bunch of pink roses freshly cut, smelling divine. We sat down and decided to write a list of things that needed doing. Deciding on power first, then an upgrade on the bathroom and kitchen. We knew if Esmeralda didn't want us to do something, she would let us know.

While I was visually taking in the room that we were sitting in, I noticed a door. I asked Shelly if she had noticed it before. She said no. I went to open it, but it was locked.

Shelly and I headed outside, and walked around the house, to where the door should have been. There definitely should be some sort of room through it, by the shape of the wall from the outside. There must be a stairway in that room too, as the room from outside has very high walls, and there were windows, both low, and higher up. Neither of us were tall enough to see in.

We continued to walk around the house. There were more beautiful gardens around the back, and another extension. This was very strange. It must all be connected by that one door we had found inside. We walked past an old gazebo in the garden that had an old metal table and chairs under it. Then we noticed another strange room that didn't match what we had seen inside, when we had explored a few days before. There were back stairs to this room, so we climbed them carefully to see if the door would open. Again, another locked, mysterious door.

We descended the stairs and kept doing our circle of this strangely made house. There were more walls with windows. Then we came to a large garden that took up much of one side of the yard. It had stepping stones covered in moss. The stepping stones took us back to the front of the house, where we had sat to have our tea parties with Esmeralda.

We headed back inside and followed the verandas around until we came to a stop. Yet another wall belonging to a room, a room we couldn't access. But we could see through this window! There were tattered lace curtains hanging. It seemed more like a room that would have a piano, or maybe an art studio.

We went back around the other way, until we came to a dead end in that direction. I thought it might be the kitchen underneath this flooring, then it dawned on me that maybe town planning might have a house plan from the original build.

Shelly and I went inside and added a few more things to our list. It was get- ting late, and without power we couldn't do much. Shelly said that she would go back to the hotel and make some appointments for us, and then asked me if I wanted to stay at the hotel again tonight with her, or head home. I told her that it might be best if I went home, to make sure that the book was still safely hidden away under my bed. Shelly said that she would ring me with our schedule once she got a hold of a few places for appointment times.

As I walked home, I remembered that Dad was in hospital. This meant Mum would be home, but it also meant that she had no car to get around in. My happy mood started to leave me, but I then I felt Esmeralda's presence surround me again. I walked into my house, and there was my mother, on the phone. She was shouting at someone, I assumed it was Dad on the other end.

I went upstairs and closed my door, then opened the window. I checked under my bed and saw my suitcase. At least I would not have to worry about hiding the book soon, as I would be in Castle House. I went back down to the kitchen, to hopefully make something for dinner, but Mum came in and yelled at me asking where I had been.

"What do you mean? I've been coming in and out of here like a ghost." I'm sure I heard Esmeralda laugh as those words rolled off my tongue in Mum's direction. "When I'm not here, I'm either at work, or with Shelly."

She gave that stare and told me that I was too old now to be playing make-believe! I went to argue with her, but stopped myself, and instead I asked how Dad was. I shortly realised that that was the wrong question to ask. She screeched at me saying that he was living it up in the hospital, while she had to catch buses everywhere because of him crashing the car. Then she went on about how they won't fix it on insurance.

I decided I might go to the hotel for the night after all. I could buy a burger on the way for dinner instead too. This scenario was only going to escalate if I stayed, as she had no way to get to the pub and drink her anger away. So, I told Mum that I was going for a shower and meeting some friends in town. Trying to get upstairs before something became my fault. She huffed at me and went into the lounge to watch her shows.

Luckily as I walked past the phone, it rang. I picked it up before Mum heard it. It was Shelly, I quietly told her that I would be there in an hour and then hung up before Mum even noticed I was on a call. Now to get ready and out of here, before her show ends.

I was just about packed and ready to head out the door, when I heard a bottle break in the kitchen. Then Mum' voice followed, screaming out for me to come and clean it up. I quickly locked my door and made a b line for the window, climbed out, and dropped to the ground. I was off!

I stopped at the burger joint and saw that Jake and his friend Brad were there. We talked while I waited for my order, but I didn't stick around once it was ready. The hotel wasn't far, so I ate my burger on the way.

When I arrived at the hotel, I knocked at Shelly's room, and was surprised to see Mrs. Bryant as she opened the door. She hugged me and told me to come in. I was overcome with that warm feeling again, as Shelly came bouncing out of the ensuite.

Shelly's mum watched us with such love and care in her eyes, and said, "Ooh just look at you both!" Holding her hands over her heart, "You two could be movie stars with that much charisma!" We both giggled at her, as she was usually very biased and forward with her words. It did feel nice to have someone say nice things again to me though. I told her that I had missed her so much, then hugged her.

"Mum, do you mind if Hannah stays the night, as we have lots to talk about, and organise." Shelly said.

Her mum smiled and said that it would be a pleasure, just like old times. She said that I could stay whenever I wanted or needed.

I told Shelly that Jake and Brad were at the burger shop, and that they said to say hi. Mrs. Bryant teased us in a way that I think she thought we were keen on them. I told her that Jake used to go to school with me though, during the time that they had moved away. Hannah asked me if that was why I had kicked her under the table, the night that she was about to ask him where he lived. I forgot to tell her about that, and I laughed and told her yes, but I also told her that there was more to that story. I went on the tell Shelly that he used to live in her home, but I didn't want to make her feel bad, so I kept it to myself.

Shelly's mum interrupted my conversation, and said, "Oh dear. The real estate told us that Apparently the father of that family had lost his job. They were behind in their house payments to the bank, and as it fell behind too much, the bank made the decision to take the house back. The bank then had it sold to recoup some of the loss. The family was evicted. I heard they are living in a homeless shelter run by the church.

This was terrible news and we all felt so bad for them. Mrs. Bryant said she hoped their dad would find work so that they could start again. Now I knew why Jake was so sad when I saw him. Shelly hugged me, assuring me that something good will happen for them. I hoped so as, I felt bad for them having such a hard time when we had been having such good luck.

Six

What Can We Do To Help?

There was a moment of silence, as we sat in thought.

"I rang town planning for you. About the house plans. They said that there wasn't any for the address of Castle House." Shelly said.

"That seems strange." I replied.

We both felt Esmeralda touch us. We agreed that she was telling us not to worry about that. My thoughts then moved onto Jake and his family. I thought about what Jakes dad might have been doing for work, before he was fired.

Shelly saw the look on my face and asked me if I wanted to go for a walk. Her mum told us to take a key if we did. This reminded me to put my bedroom key on the duchess, so that I wouldn't lose it. Shelly asked why I had a key. As we walked out the door, I told her what had happened when I went home.

"I can't wait for you to get away from there." Shelly said.

We grabbed a soda from the cafe and kept walking. We saw the boys ahead of us, but we were happy just chatting about what we needed to do, with our soon-to-be home. We saw the boys turn down the next street, and I realised that that was the street that the church had their refuge on. Shelly and I decided to turn around and head back to the hotel, as we didn't want them to see us, and have them feel even worse.

The next morning, I woke early, got dressed, and tried to sneak out.

Shelly rolled over, and said, "Good morning."

"I'm going into work early to get some tasks finished. In case we need to be at the house for the electricity connection." I informed her.

"Your work ethics are so good that I'd hire you!" Shelly replied. We both laughed.

As I was walking away, I started to think about Jake's dad again. I stopped for a coffee and toast.

While I was sitting there, Jake walked past, and said, "You're up early."

I explained why, and he told me that he gets the bus from the corner. This was my opportunity to talk to him about what was going on.

"What does your dad do?" I asked.

"He's an electrician, but the company folded so he's looking for a new job." Jake replied.

I said to Jake, "I'm so sorry to hear that. Can he do odd jobs on his own?"

When Jake told me he thought so, then asked me why, I told him that I might know someone who could possibly need some private work done. His bus arrived, so he asked me to let him know more next time. I now knew how Shelly and I could help!

When I arrived at work, the cleaner was just leaving, "Good morning, Hannah. You're an eager beaver today."

"The early bird catches the worm." I replied, as we both laughed at our funny sayings.

It was nice to get work done with no phones ringing. Time flew by. Before I knew it, in walked my boss, with a big smile, saying, "Good morning."

I said to my boss, "I'm sorry, I need Thursday morning off, so I'm making sure that I am caught up with all my tasks."

He told me how lucky he was, to have someone who puts in the effort to have their work finished prior to taking a day off. Instead of the usual, catching up on tasks when someone gets back. I laughed and told him that I was the lucky one. Not many people love their jobs. He laughed and told me that I could take the whole day off. He said that the main person I needed to see was booked in for Friday anyway. So, I thanked him and looked up my booking for Friday before heading out. There it was. Mr. Ray Sallinger. Why did my heart jump when I saw his name?

While walking back to the hotel, I bumped into Mr. Bryant. He greeted me with a big hug commenting, "My goodness! Where has that little girl gone?"

I blushed, and he laughed. We got to the hotel door and Shelly came out. She hugged her dad and then me. I felt like my world was back. Shelly asked her dad how everything went. He said that everything went smoothly and that her mum was over at their old house now, unpacking some boxes that had finally arrived. Shelly asked him when they were able to move out of the hotel. He told us that it would be once the power gets turned back on over there. Apparently, the electricity company was heavily booked. I told her father that I knew of an electrician who needs a job. Mr. Bryant suggested that I should get in touch with him, as he might be able to hire him privately for a few things.

I asked Shelly if she wanted to come for a walk. As we headed off, she asked me what that was all about. I filled her in, then asked her what she thought.

Shelly said, "I'm not sure Jake's dad would want to meet the people who now live in his old rental. Especially when they are still living in the refuge."

I thought about that but told Shelly that Jake would eventually find out, regardless of us telling them or not. It was best we tell him, and he can ask his dad what he thinks about it.

We walked into the burger joint, and saw that Jake and Brad were there. We greeted them, then Shelly and I went to order. Shelly suggested that she would chat with Brad so that I could tell Jake who Shelly was. Then if he's seeming ok, we could tell him about the work for his dad.

We walked over to the boys, and they shuffled over so that we could sit with them. Shelly started a conversation with Brad. I swallowed the lump in my throat and turned to Jake.

"Jake, I need to tell you something." He listened as I explained everything. Surprisingly, he was very calm said that he was glad it was

Shellys family moving into their old rental, considering it was their old home to start with.

Jake stood up, leaned over, and shook Shelly's hand, "I'm glad you are back. Hannah never shuts up about you, and now I can have some peace."

We all laughed together, and knew that from this point, a new bond between Shelly and I, and these two boys, was going to grow. In between eating, Shelly and I spoke about how things had evolved so strangely for us. We didn't mention that we could feel that Esmeralda was with us though. Jake only knew I had some friend called Esmeralda, even though he had never seen her himself.

I told Jake about the company that was too busy to get our power hooked up. Jake assured us that his dad would love some work but wasn't sure if he'd want to work at that house. Shelly gave Jake her dad's name and number to pass on anyway. We all hugged and went on our own missions. It felt great that all secrets between us and them, were out.

It was already dark by the time we arrived back at the hotel. Mr. And Mrs. Bryant were chatting between themselves when we walked in. Their smiles warmed my heart, and I knew my new life was getting better every day. Shelley told them Jake's dad might be calling about the work. Shelly's mum asked if Jake was the boy of the evicted family. I told her he was and added that he's very happy that they were the ones that had bought it. Shelly's mum thought that it was so grown up of him to think that way. To not be jealous. I told her that he has been a great friend to me from the moment Shelly had left town back then.

Shellys dad joined the conversation, "It was unfair what the bank did to them. We were lucky I could get my old job back, after being made redundant at the company I was working for, before coming back here. Otherwise, we could have quite possibly found ourselves in the same predicament."

Shellys mum suggested that Mr. Bryant put a recommendation in for Jakes father, at the electrical company.

Shelly and I hit the beds. It had been such a big day. It pondered on me that Shelly hadn't told her parents about Castle House yet, so I asked her why she hadn't.

Shelly laughed, and said, "Just in case we wake up, and it was all a dream."

Both of us having the same dream? I guess that could happen. It would be typical of us too, considering we always seem to say the same things at the same time.

The next morning, Shelly and I woke at the same time, with the warmth of the sun, shining through the hotel room window. We noticed a note sitting on the end of Shellys bed.

'Good morning, our little sunshine's. We are at the house and will be unpacking until dark.
Enjoy your day. Love Mum and Dad'

I looked at the clock and thought Jake's bus would have left by now. Hopefully all went well for them.

Seven

Good News For Everyone

Waking up on Friday morning was hard. Shelly and I had spent most of Thursday cleaning Castle House. Well, all the downstairs areas anyway. The electrical company never called, and nobody turned up either. Mr. Bryant was right about how busy they must be. I tried to be as quiet as I could while I got ready for work, but I was not doing a great job of it.

Shelly mumbled, "Good morning."

"Morning Shelly. Lucky you can stay in bed." I whispered, trying not to wake her parents. "Call me if you need to or leave a message with the receptionist if I'm in a meeting, and I'll call you as soon as I can."

As I was closing the hotel door, I whispered good morning, and goodbye, to Shellys parents, in case they were awake. I was too late to catch Jake at the bus stop again, but I stopped and grabbed a coffee, hoping that the walk and the caffeine hit would kick in and give me a burst of energy before getting to work.

As I walked through my favourite doors, I heard whispering and giggles. "Who did what, and to whom?" I called out, laughing. But those questions just seemed to make the receptionists laugh even harder. I walked into my office to get this slow beginning day, into a day of great flow. Luckily, I had that coffee on the way, as Mr. Sallinger was sitting in my office waiting for my arrival.

Ray stood up, and said, "Good morning, Hannah. Sorry for being early."

"Please, take a seat." I replied. Noticing I was still slightly giggling as I spoke and apologised instantly.

"That's ok. But please do share your thoughts." he replied.
I looked at him, slightly embarrassed. "You will think I'm silly." "Never!" He replied, in such a cheerful tone.

I told Mr. Sallinger about all the appointments that Shelly and I had been to recently. Then made light of how Shelly was nervous at our last meeting. Explaining I had jokingly said to her, that if we took all the seats we've been asked to, we would have enough chairs to fill our entire house.

This made him laugh so loud. "I wish I had you at some of my appointments. I have been asked many times to take a seat, and never noticed the funny side to that saying. You are a very special lady, Hannah."

I blushed, then remembered I hadn't thanked him for the flowers. "Mr. Sallinger. Thank you for the flowers you had sent to my office last week."

His reply startled me. "Please, call me Ray."

"Ok Ray. How can I help you today?" I spoke, smiling that I could feel comfortable calling him by his first name. I never really liked calling him Mr. Sallinger. It felt too formal for me.

He told me he was on his last chapter and would like to start the final steps towards publishing. I knew the story well and had already organised a book cover design for it. I proceeded to bring the file up on my computer, and he loved it!

"You nailed it! That is exactly how I had pictured this book's cover in my head. When could the final proof be ready for approval, and print?" Ray asked.

"It just so happens that I have made availability in my schedule for your book, and can have a proof to you for approval, next Friday, I can extend that if you need extra time to get the final chapter to me. Once your tick of approval is received, I can then send it to our print department."

"That's perfect! But did I hear you say your house. During the conversation earlier?" Ray asked.

"Yes, we inherited one." I told him.

"Congratulations! You are destined to have fun with a house of your own." He replied.

"Yes. It's very old. But Shelly and I, we love it!" I told him, with such excitement.

"Make sure you make a special area where you feel at peace, and focused, and start writing that book!" Ray told me.

I told him that that was on my to do list, but we needed to get the kitchen and bathroom up to a better standard first. He told me that

that's quite the task in front of us, and asked if we needed any help navigating it. I thought about that for a moment. How hard could it be.

"We will see how we go, Ray. If we get stuck, I'll be sure to ask for your opinions." I said, as I thought about the rooms that Shelly and I couldn't even work out how to enter.

Ray replied, "I like your positivity. However, if you get lost in the mazes, call me. I have built homes and completed renovations in the past."

"You have done a lot for your age." I said to Ray, curious as to why he mentioned mazes.

This made him laugh. "How old do you think I am?" Ray asked.

I thought for a minute and answered, "Twenty-eight?" "Wow, you're good." He was clearly impressed.

"When I reach twenty-eight, I'd like to think that I would have as many books published as you. But I'm thinking that these house renovations might take forever."

"Well, you have my number. Don't be afraid to call and ask me anything while you're not sure about. I always leave your company feeling exuberant, Hannah. I'm off to finish that last chapter. Goodbye, Hannah. I shall see you next Friday. Same time?"

"That's correct. See you then, Ray."

The rest of my day flew by, catching up with all the stick-it notes in my diary. I finally shut down the computer for the day, I realised that I hadn't heard from Shelly today. I closed my office door behind me, and noticed I was the last to leave.

On my way back to the hotel, I saw Jake and I waived him down.

He jogged over, and excitedly said, "Thank you so much for whatever you had said to Shellys dad. My dad received a call from the electrical company, and they offered him a job."

"That's wonderful. When does he start?" I asked. Jake told me that he started that day, and that he's doing Shellys house too. I swallowed hard, asked how his dad took it when he was asked about that? He said that he was more than happy to help. After all, Mr. Bryant had helped him get a permanent position with the electrical company, so he was more than happy to help them with their house. He said his father called Shellys dad to thank him for putting in a reference with the company, and that's when Shellys dad asked about doing the work on their house. I was so happy to hear all of this, as Jakes dad is such a nice person, and now I was also curious to see if Shelly and her parents had moved out of the hotel.

While I was walking to the hotel, I realised that I hadn't felt Esmeralda with me all day. I wondered if Shelly had. I went to knock on the door but noticed there were no lights on. So, I went to the reception to ask if they had seen them around today at all. The lady told me that they had left about an hour ago, in an ambulance. My heart stopped. I hadn't felt anything was wrong. I usually do if something is going on that I'm not aware of. I asked if she could ring a Taxi for me. I couldn't imagine what could have happened.

When the taxi dropped me at the hospital, I raced into the front desk, and asked if someone with the surname Bryant had been admitted via an ambulance. She told me that Mrs. Bryant was in room 3B.

Thanking her, I headed towards the lifts. As soon as I found the room, Shelly ran to me crying. Her mum had had a heart attack. Her dad was sitting beside the bed, holding her hand. I asked if there was anything I could do to help. Shellys dad suggested that I take Shelly back to the hotel, and he would stay the night at the hospital.

Shelly hugged her parents' goodbye, and we walked silently to the taxi rank. She had stopped crying. I didn't know what I could say, or if even talking about anything was even appropriate. I had never been in a situation like this before.

We went back to the hotel room, and I helped Shelly get sorted for the night. She still looked lost. I wondered if I should speak or let her think it through. I decided to sit silently with her. Holding her in my arms. We both fell asleep, but I was woken to the room phone ringing. I answered and it was Mr. Bryant, checking in to see how Shelly was doing.

"She hasn't spoken a word and is still asleep. How are the both of you?" I whispered, trying not to wake Shelly.

He said that the doctor had seen her and is still running a few tests. Then he told me to let Shelly know that her mum is doing well, and that they would both be home soon. I sat in the armchair, in the corner of the room, and finally felt Esmeraldas presence. As I sat there thinking about everything going on, Shelly awoke.

"Hey, was I asleep for very long?" Shelly asked, in a tired slur.

I told Shelly that it was already the following morning, and that her dad had called earlier to check in. I let her know that her mum was going well, and that they would both be back soon. I saw the light come back into her eyes, and then the tears began to flow. As Shelly calmed down, I asked her if there was anything I could do. Shelly asked if we could possibly go back to the hospital. So, we got sorted and caught a taxi there.

As we arrived, we walked into Shellys mums' room, and there was Mrs. Bryant, sitting up smiling at us. Her dad was asleep in the chair. The machines looked scary, especially with all the noises. Shelly asked her mum if she could give her a hug. Her mum raised her arms, and as Shelly wrapped her arms around her, my tears flowed.

A doctor came in and introduced himself. Mr. Bryant woke up and asked him how all the tests were looking. The doctor said that she would need to rest up for a while, as to not give her heart any more stress than it needs right now, but there has been no permanent damage. He then said that she must stay in one more night for monitoring, so that they can be sure all is well, but he saw no reason why she wouldn't be leaving the hospital tomorrow.

I could feel the relief in the air. Shelly offered to stay at the hospital so that her dad could go home. I could feel Shellys sadness but something also felt weird, and not in a good way. I didn't understand why. It lingered in the air around me, the entire day.

Later that evening, Shelly said that she wanted to ring her dad. I stayed with her mum and held her hand.

"Thank You for looking after Shelly. You girls have been twins in my eyes, since the day you first walked into our home. Please don't let Shelly put her interview off for the teaching position, regardless of how much she tells you that she wants to stay home with me." Mrs. Bryant said in a soft, caring tone.

When Shelly mum said this, I realised that the feeling that had been lingering all day, was the confusion Shelly must have been feeling about her upcoming interview. "I will do my best to make sure she goes, but you need to rest and not think of things like that."

Shellys mum squeezed my hand in thanks and drifted off to sleep.

As Shelly walked back, I walked out of the room to speak with her. She asked if her mum was ok. I told her that she is just tired, then asked how her dad was doing. He had told her that he got a hold of Mary, and she desperately wanted to travel over, but couldn't afford the fares. Her dad had put everything they had into the house, and while Shellys mum couldn't work, he would have to sort all their bills on the one wage. I asked Shelly if we could help, but she said that she offered her dad to help cover the fares and some of the bills while her mum was unable to work, but he refused to allow Shelly to help.

"Your mum told me about your interview." I mentioned lightly to Shelly.

"Yes, the school rang. They want me to come for an interview tomorrow, at 12pm. I'm not sure how mum will be on her own in the hotel though."

"Between us, we can all pop in and out to be with her. Shelly, she wants you to go to the interview. I wasn't going to tell you, but she asked me to make sure you went." As I spoke these words, I felt relieved, being able to bring up what her mother had said to me the way I did.

"It's at 12pm. So, you have an early lunch with her, and I can organise to be back here before you leave."

"That sounds perfect, Hannah!" Shelly said. "But tonight, let's get some rest back at the hotel, Mum will be ok here in the hospital."

It was early the following morning, and Shelly's mum arrived back at the hotel. I was still asleep when Mr. Bryant must have slipped out to pick her up. She had been given some medication and strict instructions. Shelly and I thought it best to give them both some time alone and decided to go and explore more of Castle House. I realised I hadn't been home for a few days. But I'll be back there when it's time to get my things.

We saw Jake with his dad at the burger shop. Jake waived us over. He introduced us to his father. I was surprised that he remembered me from years ago. I suppose if Mr. Hays is brainy enough to be a qualified electrician, remembering a name to a face wouldn't be hat hard, regardless of how much time had gone by since then. Me though, I wouldn't remember the name of an old classmate if they walked by.

"You've grown so much Hannah, yet still pretty as a picture." Mr. Hays said.

I blushed as I thanked him.

He then asked Shelly how her mum was doing. Shelly brightened up and told him that her mum was now home, and just needs to take it easy for a few weeks. "Have you met her?" She asked.

"Yes. I arrived at your house early that morning. Both Your dad and mum had a coffee with me. I'm truly happy your family is back in your childhood home. Things always have a way of working out." Mr. Hays replied.

Jake began to talk about how excited he was, that his dad had full time work again, and that he was able to get a job there too. He said that it wouldn't be long before the bank would be able to give them a loan for a house, and continued to say that he hoped that when that time came, that they could buy one around here.

"I need to say thank you to the both of you, for helping me get back to work." Mr. Hays said.

We both told him that we were happy to help, then asked if he knew a good electrician as we needed one too.

Mr. Hays laughed, saying, "Well, girls, where can I help you today?"

Jake also offered to help and said that he had his tools in his van, so Shelly gave them the address. Jake told me to jump in the van with his father and said that he would walk with Shelly to the house. I excitedly agreed, without even asking Shelly if she was ok with walking. Castle House, here we come!

As Mr. Hays pulled up in the driveway, he remarked, "This place has been here since the dark ages!" Then laughed at his own pun.

"Yes, we know. Do you think it will be an easy job to get the power back on? We are happy to pay whatever it costs." I realised after saying that, that he might have wondered how we could not only have this house, but the funds to get it back to a liveable state too. After all, I was only an editor.

I don't think it even crossed his mind. "I will look around for the power box if there is one. Is there a cellar?" Mr. Hays asked.

As Mr. Hays and I walked into the house, I wasn't sure which way to send him. He said that there would be a stairway heading down, into a laundry or basement. Shelly and I had only ever walked upstairs from the main floor in this home, and yet, we hadn't even come across any staircase heading downwards.

"Sorry, I'm not too sure which way the staircase you referred to would be. Shelly and I have looked around somewhat. Mostly upstairs though. What we do know, is that there is a lot of rooms and doors, that we have no idea on how to enter though." I replied to Mr. Hays, waiting for some sort of intrigued look to appear on his face.

Jake and Shelly walked in before Mr. Hays could say anything else.

With a dumbstruck look on his face, Jake said, "Who lives here, and why are you helping them?"

Mr. Hays walked off, looking for the staircase that might head down to a basement.

I walked closer to Jake so that I could speak quietly, then said, "Jake if we tell you, you can't tell anyone. Mine and Shellys parents don't even know yet."

Before I could finish, Jake's dad walked back in, which stopped the conversation. "I found your so-called laundry. There is an old-style electric box, so I would suggest you get a new one. It would be safe to have all the wiring in this old home replaced too. Are you doing renovations?"

"Yes. We were planning to do the bathroom and kitchen." I told Mr. Hays.

"You would be better to do that after having all the electrical wiring replaced. You could hire a generator until then. That is, if you needed power beforehand. I might be able to get some power in this room, but I won't be able to connect the kitchen power up at this point though, sorry." Mr, Hays said, looking rather intrigued at the lighting.

"No, that would be great! One room is better than none! If it's no trouble, of course." I excitedly replied.

"Come on Son. Help me get some tools out, but no touching anything for you in this house lad, it's a bit too old for my liking. I want you safe." Mr. Hays said, as he pat Jake on the shoulder on his way past.

Shelly turned to me and asked if I still wanted to live here. Is that even a choice? Between Castle House, or the house of my parents, I instinctively told her here. We laughed and agreed that we needed to go and buy a heap of candles, some torches and lanterns, a toaster, kettle, crockery, and cutlery. All the things we needed to be able to stay here. I told Shelly that we could put a washing machine in too, and just run an extension lead when we needed to use it. We also needed to think of getting some linen, and probably a new mattress, or two, or three. I could just imagine the mites in the old ones upstairs.

Jake returned saying, "Dad thinks this house is strange."

"Really? Why?" I asked.

"He said he found new wiring in some of the rooms. Nobody has lived here for as long as he remembers, and that's a fair while as dad grew up here. He told me to let you know that he will keep working until it gets too dark to continue." Jake said, while looking around, a little lost at what he could do.

We asked Jake if he had his driver's license.

"Yeah, I've had mine for ages." He proudly answered.

"Well, can you drive us to the city so we can go shopping?" I asked, giving him my go to puppy dog eyes that always seemed to work on Shelly whenever I needed her help.

Jake replied, "Sure! Jump aboard girls." As he opened the van door with a happy smile, he continued, "I'm your personal chauffeur for the rest of the day!"

I climbed into the van first, and as I looked up at the house, I saw a woman who was not Esmeralda. She was in an upper widow, but she disappeared as quickly as I saw her. It didn't feel right to tell Shelly, so I put it out of my mind for the time being.

During the trip to the city, we had the best time. Jake was even having fun, trying out the mattresses with us. He helped pick out a television, and at one point, he joked around saying that we also needed to get a fridge for his beer. I was thankful he said that because both Shelly and I completely forgot about a fridge!

After picking out everything we needed at the warehouse, we organised to have it all delivered. They only had a Thursday available. I was a little worried about taking yet another Thursday off, however Shelly and I discussed that if her mother was well enough, maybe she could be there for the delivery, and I could pop in to see her mother. That way it sounded like a more important reason for time off.

On the way back to Castle House, we grabbed some dinner, and ordered extra for Jakes father too. It was the least we could do for Mr. Hays, and Jake. Considering how much they have done for us already and are still doing for us.

As we pulled into the driveway, Shelly and I got excited to see that the house had lights turned on. Then I saw someone in that same upper window. I thought we needed to go and check it out. Just to be safe, as we wouldn't like to wake one night to find a homeless person standing in our bedroom.

Jake's dad was washing his hands in the kitchen when we walked in, and he told us he was able to sort the power in the kitchen, the lounge, and even the bedroom at the back. We told him how amazing it was that he was able to do that already and asked him to make sure he sends us the bill. Jake suggested that they could come back on their days off, and his dad was happy to agree.

As Jake was leaving with his father, Jake asked if he could come back tomorrow. Of course, were more than happy to have him come back and hang out.

After we said our goodbyes, I turned to face Shelly, and asked if she had felt Esmeralda today.

"No, not for days." Shelly replied.

"I think there is also someone upstairs, in the front bedroom. I saw her twice, but it wasn't Esmeralda." I explained to Shelly.

We decided it would be best to look for her. Better now than later. We grabbed our torches and headed upstairs. We couldn't see much as all the doors were closed. We went to the end of the hallway, then opened the door while saying *'helloooo, we are coming in.'* We shone our torches around but could see no one. I thought, maybe she hid in one of the other rooms. But it was too hard to search in the dark. We decided that tomorrow we would check it out further, and headed back downstairs, to eat our cold burgers, and unpack some of the things we had bought earlier today.

Before we knew it, it was getting quite dark, so we decided to head back to the hotel. Hopefully Shellys mum has been resting. I thought that we could help them with anything tonight if they needed, then head back to Castle House tomorrow. We switched out the lights and turned on our torches. As we were leaving, I shone my touch up to the window, and there was the lady, staring out again, watching us. Shelly saw her as well. We wondered who she was, and where Esmeralda could be.

Eight

Owners Of Castle House

We reached the hotel, and the outside door light was on. It felt nice. When my mum would leave our outside light on for me, back at home, the feeling was quite the opposite.

Shellys parents were watching television, but they soon turned it off as we walked through the door. Shelly and I looked at each other and knew it was time. Better to tell them what was going on now, before they happened to hear it from anyone else. About Castle House.

I asked Shellys mum how she had been feeling. She said she was good but was still feeling quite fatigued. Shelly asked if there was anything we could do for them, but her father said that everything needing to be done was all caught up with.

Then, Shelly began, "So, we have some great news to tell you!" As Shelly continued, I felt like holding my breath. I was so scared of what her parents' reaction might be. "....and we are hoping to move in soon."

"There's been no one living in that old house for ages!" Shellys dad exclaimed.

I politely said, "There was, but she was very old, and when we were walking to school, we felt sorry for her. We used to sit on her veranda, and chat with her. After you guys' left town, I spent more time with her. I even spent Christmas Day with her."

Shelly's parents looked sadly at me, and her mother softly said, "We knew you had a hard time growing up. It would have been nice for you having someone like her to talk to."

"Esmeralda was very kind. Then one day she wasn't there anymore. I thought maybe someone she knew stopped by and she left with them. Then the day you guys arrived back in town, I received a call from the solicitors. They said they wanted to discuss a will that apparently Shelly and I were mentioned in. We organised an appointment and were told that Esmeralda had left the property to us, and that there was also a trust fund attached to to be used on the upkeep of the property. So then we had a meeting with the bank manager, and it was true. But with everything going on lately, we decided to wait until things settled before we mentioned anything." I let out a deep sigh as I finished speaking. Feeling so much better that it was all out in the open.

"You mean to say, that you girls have dealt with this all on your own?" Shellys father said, looking at us as if we might say that we were only joking. " Well. I'm impressed! But I hope everything is in order."

Shelly said, "Yes dad. We know it's a big job, especially with the renovations that are needed. But we are up to the challenge."

"You know, there were stories about that house. It was meant to be haunted by the original owners." Shellys mum said.

Shelly said to her mum, "Well in that case, lucky it's big enough to share with them!"

"You girls are so strong together. It's like you were meant to be twins. You even have matching bracelets. They look very ancient. Wherever did you find them?" Shellys mother asked.

Shelly said, "Remember I gave one to Hannah for Christmas just before we left. You've seen mine before though, Mum."

Her mum thought about it for a moment, then said "Oh, how silly of me. Of course you did. Well, this is all very exciting. Us moving back into Shellys childhood home, and you girls gaining a home of your own." Then Shellys mothers tone changed. "I'm proud of you girls. But I must get some rest now."

Shelly looked at her dad, as if to ask if her mum was ok. He nodded, and then put his hands up to his ear, signalling for us to let her rest, then signalled for us to go outside.

Shelly asked her father if he wanted us to take turns staying with her. He told us that it would be a big help, even just for a few days, until her next check-up. We told him that we would all take different lunch breaks, especially if Shelly got her job and had to start work within the next week.

I asked Shellys father if it was ok to crash on the floor in the hotel tonight and Shellys father laughed.

"What, are the beds not comfy enough?" He replied.

"I would prefer to have it sprayed for creatures!" I told him, giggling.

Shellys father added, "And ghosts!"

We all laughed, and then Shelly told him how kind Jake's dad Mr. Hays had been today.

"He's a lovely man! Jake, his son, is nice as well!"

I looked at Shelly and saw a sparkle in her eyes. She blushed when she saw me looking and we both giggled. I had never thought about Jake in the way Shelly seemed to like him. He and I were great friends. Note to myself! Watch Jake to see if he is paying Shelly more attention!

"I'm very interested to see the inside of your rickety old Castle House." Shellys father said. "Is it safe inside?"

"We've only spent short amounts of time there. But when we walked around the outside, there seemed to be way more extended rooms coming off the house, than there are doors inside." I told him. It's like a big maze!"

He laughed, and said, "If only those walls could talk!"

"No thank you!" I replied, laughing.

"If you are home with Mum tomorrow, we can go and get some things cleaned up?" Shelly asked her father.

He asked us if we needed anything, and we told him that we had a trip into the city today with Jake, and that we brought some small things home with us. We also explained that we bought some furniture and that those would be getting delivered.

Shelly was now excited about her interview. She said that she thinks they will wait until the new term for her to start. I began thinking about how far we had come since we were only five, when Shelly and I first met. Like, we were never really apart, thanks to the bracelets. We have a ghost as a friend, a very much loved but strange home, and, by the sounds of it, we both have our dream jobs. I also have a family who cares about me. Shellys family. That thought reminded me that I still need to go home and get my things, especially the magic book!

I heard Shellys voice creep into my thoughts, "Hannah! Hannah!"

I looked at her as she shook me.

"You scared me, Hannah! Where were you?" She asked.

Answering her, I said, "Daydreaming in my happy thoughts. You do that as well sometimes. Do you see us as lucky, to have so many good things happening, even though your mum frightened us for a little there?"

Shelly agreed but said that she felt her mum was going to be ok, then added that we do really need to be close to her while she is so fragile. She continued " But we are so lucky. It's funny when I look back. I had to help you in the beginning. Then you forged ahead with everything you ever wanted to do. You followed your dreams and made them happen. And now, with our own place, we will be unstoppable as united property owners!"

We both giggle at that, as neither of us has a clue what we are doing regarding renovations, or anything homeowner related really.

"You girls will be the latest gossip around the town soon!" Shellys father added.

This reminded me to get to Mums before some 'old crony' at the pub tells my parents what's going on.

"Well girls, I need to head back in and get some sleep. We should be leaving the hotel in a couple of days and settling back into our old house again. I'll be here tomorrow if you need a lift anywhere, but one of you girls should really consider your next step as getting a license, and a car. Being property owners, you have standards to live up to now." Shellys father stated. His laugh made me so happy.

We all headed back inside, and Shelly and I laid the at the opposite end of the bed head, so that if we were whispering it would hopefully not wake her parents up.

I can't wait for my parents to be back in my childhood home." Shelly said. "Maybe Jake will stop by tomorrow."

I didn't tease her about her comment this time. It would be great to have some muscles to help with the furniture delivery.

Later that night I woke to a terrible foreboding feeling. I sat up to try and focus and understand what had happened.

"Are you ok? Shelly whispered.

"Yes, but someone isn't. At least I feel like someone isn't." I told Shelly.

Shelly instantly sat up to check on her mum, but she was fine, sleeping. I couldn't shake this feeling, but I had no vision of a dream. It was nearly sunrise. I asked Shelly if she minded me getting up early. Maybe there was something Esmeralda was trying to tell us.

Both Shelly and I quietly got dressed for the day and snuck out quietly so that we didn't wake her parents. I remembered to take my room key as well. Still dreading the confrontation with my mother, and possibly father as he might be home now. Maybe that's all it was. That feeling. Knowing that still had to be done.

Shelly said that she could feel my anguish, but not any sort of feeling like I had. As we walked through the park, the sun began to appear. It was a beautiful sunrise, and it made me feel ready for the day. We turned the corner to head up to our house. We were both surprised to see Jake's dad's work truck in the driveway. He saw us and waved.

Jake came around the side of the house calling out to his father, "Is that enough wire?"

"Yeah buddy, look who's here already!" Jakes dad replied.

We said hi to Jake and asked him if there was anything we could help with. Of course, he told us there wasn't because it was men's work, then laughed as he knew it would rev us up.

"Well, we will start cleaning so that we can move in." I told him.

Then Mr. Hays voice echoed from within the ceiling, "Be careful of the spiders! There are also a few mice!"

Shelly yelled back out to him, "We bought a large can of bug spray, for those horrid creatures! We had forgotten about mice though!"

"Probably trip over each other running more likely." I said, laughing. "We will leave you 'men', to your men's work."

I looked up out of curiosity, to look at the front upper window where I saw the woman, but there was no one there. Then headed inside, to clean the living area first. After we sort that I thought that we could then make our way to the bedrooms.

As we pulled down those disgusting curtains, I noticed that the windows were clean. It made no sense. But I was happy for the help from whomever did them. When we tried to get the old rug up, we realised how heavy rugs were and instead decided to pack up all the old decor and put them in the hallway. We were able to drag the large lounge rug part way across the room, and the floors beneath looked safe.

There was a picture of two young girls, playing on a swing under an old tree, sitting in the back of the china cabinet. We wondered which century it was from. Once the cabinet was empty, we slid an old blanket under one side to help us move it out onto the veranda, where Esmeralda used to sit. The old cane rocker was still there. So strange how she wasn't back with us yet, and no word.

"Coffee time!" Jake called out.

Jake and his father walked inside, seeing us struggling, trying to move the old sofa. They told us to go and make coffee and they would move it for us. We were happy to stop, as we hadn't even eaten breakfast this morning.

I got out some cake and biscuits for everyone that we had bought while out in the city with Jake. I made some space on the dining table and noticed a Christmas bauble. I don't remember seeing that there earlier. Surely, I would have noticed it before, when I was stacking the old china plates at the other end of the table.

I went to move it out of the way and the horrid feeling hit me again. I put it down and stepped backwards, just as Jake came in all dusty, with his father in tow,

"Did you have any other heavy stuff you wanted to move around today?" Jake asked.

"Just that nasty rug in the lounge room." I replied.

They laughed and said that it's going over the railing then.

We all talked over coffee and cake for a little, and I did notice that Shelly and Jake had a few hushed words between themselves too.

"Alright, no rest for the wicked!" Jakes dad said as he stood up from the table. "Or the beautiful ladies."

"Actually, I can think of something that we might need help with!" Shelly called out, just as Jake and his father were about to leave the room. "We could use a hand to bring some of those old mattresses down from upstairs.... Annnd maybe some of the beds too. If it wasn't too much trouble of course."

"Wellll, I'm your man! Yell out when you're ready." Jake said in a very flirtatious tone, I thought.

Then I saw Shelly gave him a little cute smirk. "Why thank you, Sir Galahad!"

I saw Jake's fathers' eyelids raise, very questioningly, when he heard that.

We were in the middle of washing the walls, when Jake came in and said to Shelly, to let him do the high parts with the ladder. I thought I might leave them and start upstairs. They never noticed me leave until one of the steps creaked. I called out letting them know it was just me.

When I looked down the hallway, I could have sworn I saw a door click closed. I instantly rushed down to the door, hoping to open it and find the woman. As I reached the door, I was thrown backwards, from an electric shock that had just hit me. The noise of me hitting the floor had Jake and Shelly running up the stairs to me. I was just stunned!

Jake said, "Don't touch it! I will get Dad's tool to check if there's a live wire somewhere." shaking his head when he realised, saying, "But it's a... doorknob?"

As Jake went out of sight, Shelly asked me if I had seen anyone. I told her that I only seen the door as it shut closed and heard the click of the doorknob. I stood up, trying to regain myself. My legs were a bit shaky.

"I've never heard in my entire career, the likes of a doorknob being charged." Jakes farther said, as he put his voltmeter to the doorknob. It read zero vaults. He then grabbed the doorknob and opened the door. "Just leave this door open, and I will check out the wiring in here shortly. Stay and help the girls, Jake. I'll be another half hour in the roof, with my fury mates."

I could see that Shelly knew what I was thinking.

We stripped down the beds and windows and rolled up the floor mats of all the upper rooms, then threw it all out the windows. The mattresses wouldn't fit, so over the balcony each one went.

"What the hell were those things made of!" Jake remarked, as we threw the last mattress over.

I stirred him a little and told him, "Old bones! And HAIR!"

He now had the heebie-jeebies! Shelly and I laughed.

The bases of the beds where still good, so we decided that we could just clean them up for now. I went to grab the scrubbing stuff from downstairs, while Jake and Shelly began emptying the cupboards, into big plastic bags.

When I returned, I was greeted by the ghosts of eras gone by! Shelly and Jake started laughing so loud, that I heard Jake's dad's voice echo through the roof asking us what we were up to. There's no way I would have tried on any of those dusty, musty old clothes.

Finally, we had this room clean. We checked the time and said to Jake that he better check that the hairy friends didn't get his dad. He went to find him, and as we walked out of the room, the door closed behind us! Shelly and I jumped. Thankfully we had remembered that the windows were still open! Neither of us wanted to go around and climb through, so we waited for Jake, who came back upstairs saying that is father was just over the top of this bedroom.

We casually mentioned to Jake that the wind had blown the door shut, and then came the request. 'Can you go and close the windows?'

Jake nonchalantly grabbed the doorknob, opened the door, and greeted his father with a cheerful, "Hi Dad, need anything?"

"No, I'm fine!" Jakes father replied. Then, with a creepy laugh, he added to the atmosphere.

Jake, unfazed, inquired, "Which one next?"

We initially thought he was kidding and rattled off a list of random things to do, but as the realisation dawned, we were left bewildered, as he casually declared, "You ladies rest! We men will carry fourth!"

This declaration reignited our girl power. Determinedly, we asserted that we were good to go, glancing at each other with a silent wish for a nice hot bath. The next room mirrored the previous one, and we efficiently completed the task. However, if my muscles had a say in this matter, we were on strike. Mr. Hays had kept pace with us, and now most of the upstairs rooms were complete. Both clean and rewired!

Shelly had a bright idea, "We have power up here, Hannah! We should heat the jug and have a bath!'

Jake, with a teasing laugh, remarked, "Is that all girls think about?"

He received a playful reprimand, in the form of a dusty, wet-smelling tea towel to the cheek.

Shelly went downstairs to fetch our towels and soap.

As Shelly reached the stairwell, Jake said, "So you girls are giving up!"

So, I chased him with the mop.

Jake yelled to his father "Don't go near the bathroom, or you will get a mop in your face!"

"Then I'm making a run!... To the burger shop. Who wants one?" His father replied.

The old house echoed with a uniform, 'Meeeee!'

The bath felt like luxury, and putting old dirty clothes on didn't feel right. The only solution was to go downstairs, and get some of the sheets we had brought, to wrap around us. Since Shelly was the first bathed, and dried, she had to go.

I laid back and closed my eyes, and suddenly the water went from warm, to freezing!! Then the window flew open! I nearly slipped over, jumping out to get my towel, just as Shelly came back in, saying that Jake and his father were not back yet. Then she saw the open window.

"What the hell, Hannah, why did you open the window?" Shelly asked, as she passed me a sheet to dress in.

Shelly saw that I was shaking, and quickly pulled the window shut. She helped me dress, then we walked outside, to sit in the sun on the veranda.

We burst out laughing, when the men drove in, open mouthed, seeing us sitting here in sheets. When they asked why we were wearing sheets, we told them that we were getting ready to haunt the house, tonight! Jake's dad mumbled as he walked inside. It sounded something like, '*those girls never cease to surprise me.*'

As Jake walked out onto the veranda, he said, "I like the toga look!"

Before we could hit him, his father walked out and passed out the burgers.

As we were finishing up, Jake asked if we had clothes for tomorrow, if we planned on staying here tonight. I was really liking this new Jake. When we told him we didn't have any clean ones, his father offered to swing past the hotel and pick some up for us. We told him that that would be amazing if he didn't mind, and we asked if he could let us know how Shellys mum was going. When he asked if we needed anything else while he was there, I asked if he could also grab some pillows too. I figured we could just roll our new blankets out on the floor and use those to sleep on tonight.

Jakes father laughed, and said, "Of course. You girls will need some pillows, to go with those sheets." Then he headed out.

We liked Mr Hays. I told Jake that we would have to have his family over sometime, when we have the house set up. That's when Jake told us that his mother said that she wanted to meet us. I have a feeling he's been talking about Shelly.

I was still putting off going home to get my things, because I was worried what my parents would say. I hate confrontation. Shelly had a great idea though, she told me that I should just tell them that her and I are only renting this place. They never drive past here, and I certainly wouldn't be inviting them over. Especially if they were drunk!

Jake said, "You know, maybe Shelly is right. Tell them you girls are renting the house. Clean break, no regrets."

Jakes father pulled back up, and walked in with bags and pillows, and a big smile. "Your mum is looking much better. She also told me to tell you girls, to enjoy your first night in your own home."

Jake then asked, "Are you girls going to be ok on your own?"

Laughing, we told him how much we loved ghosts, then Shelly and I said our goodbyes.

It was dark outside, but we had lights. A clean floor to sleep on, and hopefully soon, Esmeralda would be back!

We heard a noise coming from upstairs but decided not to go and check it out. We were happy to let whoever it was, do their own thing. Then hopefully, they would leave us in peace as well. We hung up our clothes for tomorrow, so that they wouldn't get creased, and changed into our nighties. Unfortunately, after getting into bed, it seemed that our unknown guest was not going to let us sleep.

First, I awoke to the sheet being pulled off. Then, lights began flickering. Shelly woke thinking that it was me and asked me what I was doing. I was frozen. I didn't want to move. I told Shelly that it wasn't me, but She was so tired she just put her pillow over her head.

Then something pulled the pillow from Shellys head. I felt the anger in its force. When Shelly realised what was going on she began yelling. Telling whatever it was, to stop, and get out, because this was OUR HOUSE!

It stopped flashing the lights. We held each other's hand until the moonlight reached the window and lit up the room. Now we could see.

Whatever it was, was now in the dining room, throwing around my books!! We both yelled and told it to GET OUT! A book then came flying at us! We held our bracelet hands up unknowingly together, and a spark flew across the room! Towards whatever that was, that we couldn't see. As it hit something, we heard a painful scream! Then a cold wind rushed right past us, and a door upstairs, made a loud bang!! Then silence...

We sank into our blankets. and held each other. We knew we must have won that battle, but we had no idea, who or what, or why, what went on, happened. This thing was so angry!

We called out Esmeraldas name, but neither of us felt her presence. It was half past midnight, when I looked at the time on my watch. We both knew enough, to know that around this time was called, the 'witching hour', from stories we had read.

Laying back on our pillows, hoping to sleep, but keeping our hands together, we slowly drifted off back to sleep.

As sunrise came, we woke early from the rays coming through the window. We had not moved from the positions we had fallen asleep in. We both needed the bathroom, so we slowly walked upstairs together. Whatever was in here last night must have left, as it was so quiet upstairs.

After breakfast, Shelly was going to head to the hotel to be with her mum, so that her father could go to work. Hopefully everything turns up for them today so that they can get into their house.

As we walked down the driveway, we looked up to that window, expecting to see that woman watching us. But she wasn't. I told Shelly I would be at the hotel before 12pm, so that she could make her interview, if her father could take over around 1pm, so that I can get back to work, and hopefully when I see her this afternoon, she will have great news! Then said goodbye and headed to work.

Walking to work, my thoughts replayed what had happened last night. Why was this ghost so angry at us? It had to be that woman from the window. She made me feel so uncomfortable. She made me freeze, when I was warm under my blanket. She took my cover off to make me even colder. Then took Shellys pillow, and what was with the throwing books at me! Did she think that I had maybe hurt her somehow? I wish Esmeralda was back! Walking into work seemed like a haven of sorts, after experiencing all of that.

My boss walked in behind me, "Good morning, Hannah. Did you get everything sorted in your time off?

"I have to let you know, I need to take my lunch break before twelve, as I have to sit with my second mum, while my friend goes in for a job interview, as she can't be left alone for a few days." I told him.

He said, in a caring tone, "Why, what happened?"

When I told him what had happened to Shellys mother, he told me not to rush back to work, and head in when Shelly is finished her interview. I thanked him and told him that I would make him proud when I finish my book. I caught up on as much as I could before leaving and told the receptionists to ring me at the hotel, if they needed to get a hold of me.

Walking to the hotel, I felt a presence overcome me. But I was not sure if it was Esmeralda. It seemed like more of a sad feeling that I was picking up on.

As I went past the street that Shellys childhood home was on, the house her parents were moving back into, I saw a big truck outside. It had to be their furniture! I hurried my steps, just in case Shellys mum was at the hotel on her own. She was and was in a state! Mr. Bryant wasn't answering my calls. Hopefully he was at the house now, as Shellys mum said she had gotten a call from the men that drive the truck, saying they had to leave if no-one was going to be there to let them in. That would have meant, that Shellys parents would have to wait even longer for their belongings. I settled her into the armchair and told her I would handle it.

I ran back down the road to talk with the men. Luckily, they had not left yet. I explained the situation, and they apologised if they might have upset anyone. I remembered where Shellys father use to hide a key out the back for Shelly, if ever she needed to get in. I went to check the hiding spot, and thankfully, her father must have put one back there in case we ever needed to get in.

I let the men in, and tried to explain where everything was to go, then drew them some diagrams on the back of the envelopes that were sitting on the counter. I told them that if they were unsure where to put anything, to just stack it in the front room. I asked if they could put the beds together while they were here, to help Shellys parents out a little, and the men were more than happy to. I looked for the linen boxes, and made Shellys parents' bed, so that they wouldn't have to do it themselves. That way Shellys dad could come straight in and do what he needed, while Shellys mum could rest on her old comfy bed.

I ran back to the hotel, and thankfully Shelly wasn't back there yet. I couldn't imagine how angry she would have been, if she had arrived and seen her mother alone. I apologised to Shellys mother for taking a little time to get back and told her that I had her bed all made and ready for her, so that she could relax in bed while Shellys father did the unpacking.

I tried calling Mr. Bryant again, so that he didn't stress about my earlier missed call. Thankfully I got through. He said he was in a meeting that went way over its allocated time. When I told him what had happened, he said that he would head back to the hotel first and grab everything, drop me back at work, and then head over to the house with Shellys mum. He thanked me, then told me he would be at the hotel directly.

When I turned around, I saw that Shellys mum had fallen asleep in the armchair, so I quietly packed all their personal belongings so that it was all ready for when Mr. Bryant arrived.

As Mr. Bryant was pulling in, Shelly walked through the door. She was Beaming!

She said, "I start at the beginning of next term!" Speaking so loudly, she startled her mother awake.

"Ooooh, congratulations my darling. I'm so thrilled for you." Shellys mum said, in a half-woken state.

"That's great news Shelly! But help me carry these bags to the car, because it's all going to the house, like right now!" I said to Shelly, shoving a bag into her arms.

We filled the car with all their belongings, and piled in. I told Shellys father not to drop me back to work just yet, as I wanted to help them carry everything in. As we pulled into the driveway of Shellys childhood home, it felt like old times. Even the looks on everyone's faces, the looks of joy, were just as I remembered back when Shelly and I were in school.

As we headed inside, Shellys parents let out a simultaneous, WOW!

"It's not even been an hour, and you men have already moved this much in, and have everything sitting in the exact same place they used to be!" Shellys father exclaimed.

The men laughed, saying, "Thanks to the help of that young lass." Pointing at me, as they walked out to bring the last of the boxes in.

Shellys parents walked down the hall, to get Shellys mum settled in the bedroom. Shelly was singing her favourite song and dancing all around the lounge room. I Couldn't stop laughing at her, but got up to join her, just so that I could ask her what grade she would be teaching. She said that Ms. Lee was leaving and that she was taking her place. I got a little excited that I was right, and we did an extra funny dance, for all the little new children that would never have to meet the horrid, Ms. Lee.

As Mr. Bryant came back out, I told Shelly that I had to get back to work and would celebrate with her tonight. As I headed to the car with Mr. Bryant, I gave the removal men my work details and asked them to send me the bill for the extra bit of work I had asked them to do. I was so happy they could finally settle into their house again.

I saw Jake getting off the bus near work, so I asked Shellys dad if he could drop me off at the corner. Jake waived as I was getting out of the car and waited for me.

He asked how last night went. When I told him, he thought that I was pulling his leg, because of all the ghost jokes that were made at the house yesterday. I laughed when he told me that he didn't believe in ghosts.

As we reached my workplace, Jake and I said our goodbyes, and when I walked through the office door, the receptionist girls looked as though they must have been eating chocolate and had just been caught out.

I walked through my office doorway, and sitting on my desk was a beautiful vase full of flowers, and a huge hamper of goodies. I pulled out the card that was sitting amongst the bouquet and opened it.

'Congratulations Homeowner!'
- Ray

"Ooooh. Myyyy. GOODNESS!" Came rushing out of my mouth, much louder than anticipated, and an explosion of laughter came rushing in from the front desk. Well now, I guess everyone does know.

My Boss came in to ask how Mrs. Bryant was. I explained to him what had happened, and he said that it seemed I had a lot going on around me at the moment.

"Yes, and everything seemed to escalate!" I told him.

He had a smirk on his face, and said, " Yes, even a homeowner, I hear?"

"YES! It's official now! We are moving in, but it will be quite the process renovating! The floor is quite uncomfortable..." I joked, "...and no curtains had given us an early start to the day, this morning!"

My boss laughed. "No wonder you were in here so early!" Then continued, "The sender of your 'new home gifts' wanted me to give you a message, that if you need a lift to carry them home, he's happy for you to call him at five, and give you a lift!"

I was unsure what to say to that, as yes, I did need a lift, but I was a little embarrassed at the thought of him seeing our semi decrepit house.

As my boss began to walk out of my office, he turned around at the door, then said. "He also knew that you would feel embarrassed if he might ever happen to see your renovators delight, and wanted me to assure that should you be curious, he would be happy to show you some photos of the homes he once lived in."

It suddenly occurred to me that I had been the subject matter of the office gossip today!

"Thank you for passing on the message. I will ring him from my office, at 5pm" I replied.

My boss shook his head and wandered back to his office. He must have thought he was out of sight, when I see him do a little jig as he walked off.

Nine

Mr. Ray Sallinger - Best Selling Author

The clock hit 5pm. I picked up my phone, and dialled Ray.

He answered, and said, "Doth thou fair maiden which to ride with me in thee chariot?"

I laughed, and said "Yes, Thy wishes it be so."

Ray laughed, and replied, "Tis the stroke of five, I shall mount my trusty steed, and collect you!" Then he hung up, before I could say anything more.

The fun Ray and I always have when we are in the office, came to the forefront of my mind. Then realised I started feeling ditsy thinking about him. I tried to gather myself, and he suddenly appeared my my office doorway.

"Doth thou need a man servant?" Ray asked.

I burst into uncontrollable laughter. "Yes, she doth!" I said, as my cheeks began to tingle from the overbearing blushing.

I shook myself into composure as we headed out into the foyer. All eyes were fixated on us!

"Good night." I said to the receptionists, as I was escorted out the office doors, towards a car that Jake would have absolutely drooled over!

Ray asked me if he may take my Chattels. I was under his charms. This man, he is something! His chariot smelled of beautiful new leather, that was very intoxicating to me indeed. But that smile, and that composure. That everything!

Ray suddenly disrupted my thoughts, and asked, "Where doth my fair maiden liveth?"

I said, "Thy fair maiden hails from Castle House, upon the hill. Number 270."

Ray replied, saying, "Ahhh, the witch's number as well! I doth think, I shall be turned into a frog!"

I was laughing so much that we drove right past the house. "I doth think, we passed thine castle house." I managed to get out, still laughing.

Ray kept driving and turned into a hotel. "Thee fair maiden doth deserves Champaign." He said, getting out of his car. "I Shan't be long, as I will make haste whilst the sun still shines!"

Ray came out with a bottle of champaign, and glasses as well. I wonder if he realises Shelly will be at the house too.

As Ray got back into the car, I thanked him and told him he didn't need to get anything. But he told me that I was speaking nonsense, as I must celebrate my accomplishments. He was a fun, easy going man.

As we turned into the driveway of Castle House, it was in darkness. Ray asked If we had the power on yet. I explained that we have most of it sorted but was surprised there wasn't any on. Ray told me to give him my keys, and he would open the house and turn on a light so that I could see where I was going.

"Where are the switches?" He called out, as he opened the front door.

"There's a string hanging on the right side, just as you walk in!" I hollered back.

It was making me laugh, seeing Ray being so protective, but at the same time I could see he was scared. He found the string, and then there were lights! I stepped out of the car with my vase of flowers, and he hurried to hold the door open for me.

"You weren't kidding!" Ray said.

I assumed he was talking about how big of a Reno job the house was.
He collected the hamper, champagne, and the champagne glasses from the car, and followed me in. I went into the dining room to put my flowers on the table. Having to make room for his basket, he asked if I was certain that it was safe for me to stay here. I explained to Ray that I had inherited it with a friend, and that Shelly should be here soon. Then told him we had slept on the floor last night, since our furniture hadn't yet been delivered. He sat on one of the old dining chairs, but I could tell he was unsettled. I walked into the kitchen and turned the light on, and he followed me. When Ray saw the state of the kitchen, he gasped.

"Don't worry, we are renovating that first!" I said to Ray. "You should have seen the things we threw out. The mattress felt like they had dead bodies in them!"

I thought my humour would make him relax, but I soon realised he was not seeing the funny side and was still quite concerned.

"Hannah, you are amazing. Any other girl I know, would not have even gotten out of the car for this house, let alone live in it." Ray said, looking at me as if he really did care about me being here.

"Oh, what fun they would be to be around." I said, to try and lighten the mood yet again.

He laughed. Finally! It was like a light bulb clicked on in his head.

"Dare I ask if you have any food?" Ray asked.

I told Ray that we had a toaster, and tins of baked beans or spaghetti, if those were enticing enough to his hunger.

"Champagne, and baked beans on toast! Let's do it!" Ray said, laughing at the entire situation.

"I'm sure that gift basket over there would have something more suitable for the evening." I said to Ray.

"No way! In for a penny in for a pound! Bring on the baked beans!" Ray exclaimed.

"Well then, shall we dine on a pillow on the floor, or the uncleared dining room table?" I asked.

Ray replied, holding out his arm as if he wished to court me, "I'd like to go with the pillow dining. It sounds quite exotic!"

I linked my arm with his, and as we walked to the lounge, arm in arm, Ray said, "You intrigue me, Hannah Adams!" Then he ushered me to my pillow, popped the cork and poured our drinks. "Here's to you and your friend!"

Ray asked me how many rooms there were in Castle House. I explained that from what we had found so far, we had only counted four. He nearly choked, saying that there must be places we hadn't seen yet. I told him how Shelly and I had walked around the outside and thought there was a lot more, but we didn't know how to enter them from inside.

"This just gets more mysterious with every word you speak!" Ray said.

"That's all I'm telling you, as this house and its mysteries, are mine. For my story yet to be written!" I told Ray.

Ray replied, "Well played, give nothing away to the opposition..." laughing, he continued, "...But I'm going to help you write it, because this is too good not to be involved in! All credits will be yours, but I have to say, it could be a bestseller!"

Ray shovelled some baked beans into to his mouth, telling me that my cooking skills were awesome. We bantered for ages, then he said that I should ring my friend to see if she is ok. I thought it was lovely that he was concerned for Shelly not being home yet. Then he passed me his mobile.

Shelly answered, saying "Hello, who is this?"

"It's me, Hannah! Are you ok?" I replied.

Shelly started crying and said that her mum was back in the hospital. She had collapsed at home. Then said that luckily her dad was home as they were able to race her to emergency. Shelly continued, saying that her mum was awake and seems normal, but she wanted to stay with her tonight. I asked if her mum would be ok, and Shelly told me that she was fine, and would call me tomorrow at work. I told Shelly to give her parents a hug from me, then we said our goodbyes, and I hung up.

Tears filled my eyes, and my happy place began crumbling. Ray asked if he could help in any way, but I told him there wasn't anything he could do. He moved over and hugged me, saying that it was ok to be sad, because it was family. I told him they are closer than family, he didn't pry, he just kept holding me. I felt safe and wasn't in a hurry to move.

I sat there in silence for some time. Then Ray kissed my cheek, and then gently moved my face around to kiss me on the lips. I felt no resistance within. It felt like I was being wrapped in soft fluffy clouds. He spoke softly, telling me that he was sorry, and that he would never take advantage of my sadness. My body wanted to say don't stop, but my mind was saying don't get into trouble! He kept holding me, saying that he couldn't leave me here alone like this.

"Please, would you let me take you to my home?" Ray asked.

I felt vulnerable for the first time, and it was not a good feeling for me. I told him that I could go, but I needed to get some things for work tomorrow. Ray said that he was sure Frank would cope without me for a day. I never actually knew my boss's first name. It sounded strange.

I went upstairs and as the stairs creaked Ray ran to get me. I told him not to worry, and that I should have warned him that the stairs creak loudly. I grabbed a few things from the bathroom and grabbed some clothes. I felt that same chill I felt the day before, but ignored it, and headed back downstairs to see a very worried look on Ray's face. He said that Shelly rang saying that they would be staying at the hospital tonight, and said that if I wanted, I could stay at Shellys parents' house for the night.

"Would you mind driving me there?" I asked Ray.

He said, "Not at all, if you prefer that."

He walked, with his arm around me, and as we reached the front door, he turned me around, and kissed me. Ever so gently. He said that he didn't want to leave me alone. I felt his sincerity, but I also felt his sadness. Sadness that he didn't deserve to be feeling as it was mine alone to deal with.

We arrived at Shellys parents' home, and Ray grabbed the spare key and opened the door, As he handed me my things, he said that he would ring Frank for me, and told me to just do what I needed to.

Ray kissed me once more, on the cheek, and said, "Good night my princess, your Castle House will wait for you!"

As he drove off, tears poured from me. I had never known this feeling of helplessness before.

Falling asleep was easy, I was drained emotionally, and physically, and I awoke late in the morning to the phone ringing. I answered and it was Shelly. She said that she was worried about me because I didn't go to work. So, I explained to her that Ray told me he was going to ring my boss, and that he would tell him I wouldn't be in.

Shelly said that her mum was staying in hospital this time, as the doctors wanted to monitor her. She said that her dad went to work, and that she would be staying there, until lunchtime. I was still a bit fuzzy, but asked if she needed anything brought up, but she said she was fine.

After we hung up, I crashed out again on the bed, and awoke to the sun setting. I felt a chill in the air and thought that there must have been a window open. But when I checked, they were both closed. I went to ring Shelly, and just before I picked up the phone, it rang!

"Hi Hannah!" Said the voice.

I laughed, and said, "I was just about to call you!"

Shelly giggled, then said that she, and her father, were heading home now. She said her mum was having dinner, then going to sleep. Shelly also said that the doctors think she has a blockage in a valve in her heart, but she is quite chirpy considering. She continued saying. that they told her father if that's what comes back from the test, she will be able to have some kind of bypass done. To me that sounded scary! Shelly said that she thought so too. I asked if she wanted me to cook something for dinner, but they were just going to grab some takeaway from the chicken place and said that they would bring me some back too. I thanked her for the gesture, and asked Shelly to give her mum a hug from me.

I thought I would have a hot shower to wake up. When I turned the shower on, I had that feeling again, of sadness. Or something wrong. I jumped into the shower while trying to ignore this feeling. The bathroom had steamed up, and in the mirror through the steam, I noticed some writing appearing on it. I turned the shower off and went over to the mirror to have a look. It read, HELP! This made my stomach lurch! Who was here? I called out Esmeraldas name, hoping that I would get a sign, but nothing. However, I so sure I had seen movement in the mirror!

If it was the bad ghost, why did she ask for help? But if it's Esmeralda, why can't she tell me. Or why can't I feel her presence?

I got dressed and went out to wait for Shelly. I thought about work, feeling guilty. The phone rang again, thinking it was Shelly, I asked her what she forgot.

"But madame, you speak of someone else, methinks. Do tell, who else holds your attention?" A very familiar voice spoke.

I laughed, and said, "Methought, it twas my lady friend, Shelly!" I was already overcome with a happy feeling, and the dread was no more.

Ray asked if I was feeling better, and if I got enough sleep. I told him that my day was spent in the mysteries of my dreams.

He said, "I hope I was the "white Knight, and not the evil black one!"

Once again, he made me laugh, and I said, "You are my heroic warrior!"

He asked if I needed to be taken back to my castle, or if he was needed in any way.

"My knight, your good deeds, you have fulfilled. You have made me laugh! Also, I must say, I miss you. But alas, I'm just about to devour spicy fried chicken!" I said, blushing behind the telephone.

Ray replied, "You eat well, baked beans, and now, unknown chicken from Spicy Fried! As long as you're cared for, that's all that matters. I will see you at our appointment. Sleep well, my princess" Then he hung up.

My heart was feeling strange, and it felt like it was racing. The car lights of Shelly and her father arriving, interrupted my thoughts.

Then, through the door, a big bag, and a very cute face walked in, saying, "Hello my soulmate. Are we doing better now?"

I laughed and ran over to hug Shelly. Her father walked in behind her, telling us not to squash his chicken, Spicy Fried. He loved his Spicy Fried. It seemed that my unrestrained laughter, was contagious!

After we finished dinner, Shelly said that she was going to go and jump in the shower, and then her and I could catch each other up on everything.

"Away you go! While I wash up all these dishes." Shellys father said, laughing as he threw everything into the bin.

I went with Shelly and waited in her room. I was so happy to finally have time to myself, without worries, to replay the events of Ray in my mind. Everything since the moment he stepped into my life. I wondered if he may have orchestrated my new position, and to be my first client. He has surely made me very fond of him, and his attention. I wonder if this is how Shelly has been feeling about Jake, too.

"Gee! The bathroom was cold!" Shelly said, as she walked back into her bedroom, drying her hair with a towel.

I told Shelly what had happened earlier, and she asked if I thought it might be Esmeralda, trying to get back somehow, but maybe she was stuck. I told Shelly it had to be her, as who else would ask for help?

"Yes, there has to be something wrong! but how do we find out?" Shelly said.

Shelley's dad said goodnight to us, as he walked past the bedroom door. I asked Shelly if she wanted to go to our house at all. She said no, and then brought up the fact that I hadn't told her what I was doing, using a very nice speaking man's phone. So, I told her Who Ray was.

"You're kidding! He's gorgeous! and rich!" Shelly blurted out.

I laughed and told Shelly that he was quite nice on the eyes. Then explained that I have been working with him on his latest book. Shelly was open-mouthed in shock and lost for words. I continued to tell her that I had done most of the editing, minus the last chapter I was still waiting on, and that he also asked me to be his publisher.

Shelly finally spoke, saying, "How can you not be swooning at his feet!"

"Honestly, up until a few weeks ago, he was not physically known to me. But now, I've had several meetings with him, and have had two bouquets of flowers, and a hamper that was so big I couldn't carry it home, show up on my office desk, from him!" I told Shelly, then continued. "He picked me up in the most luxurious car I've ever sat in, then pulled up to get champagne and glasses, and he was right by my side after I spoke to you last night, making sure I was ok. The funniest part is all I did was give him baked beans and toast!"

Shelly said, "Oh no! Did you take him home?"

"He asked to drive me there, but I think he was in shock when we pulled up. Before he even seen how bad it was inside. He was very sweet, and went along with sitting on pillows, and eating baked beans with Champagne. But when you told me about mum, I lost it. He was such a gentleman, and he may have even kissed me, ever so gently. He didn't take advantage of my loss of confidence either. I was feeling very lost, and he stepped up! He gave me the option, to take me somewhere safe. Originally he was going to take me to his house, out of genuine care, but your home seemed more comforting."

She said, "Do you know how many girls there are, throwing themselves at him!"

"You know, I don't care about the antics of the rich or famous. How he acted around me, with such respect, is beyond that." I told Shelly.

Shelly said, "I didn't mean that he was liking all the attention." Shelly exclaimed. "But there are some pictures of him that I've seen in the papers, with movie stars."

I felt a twinge in my stomach, then said, "Well he did say I was amazing. On another occasion, he said that he always leaves my office feeling exuberant."

Shelly then said, "Oooh, so he's crushing on you! You like him, don't you?"

I blushed and told Shelly that I liked his sense of humour, and that we do get on well. Then told her that he has offered to help me write my book.

"Annnd?" Shelly asked, waiting to find out more.

"When he kissed me, I felt all floaty. Like I was wrapped in fluffy clouds!" I told Shelly, as the butterflies in my stomach began to flutter.

Shelly hugged me, and said, "Omg! You are smitten with him!"

I Said, "He is very enchanting, and he loves speaking in Elizabethan. He laughs when I speak Elizabethan with him, too. Which makes me feel like I can be myself around him."

Then I realised Shelly was right. I am smitten on him! I had never thought I would be romantically interested in any man. I told Shelly that I have no idea what I was meant to do. I've never had these feelings for anyone before. Shelly assured me that I was doing it all perfectly right, especially if I had gained the interest of Mr. Ray. Sallinger, himself.

"We need get our license, and also a car! Who could we ask to help us?" I said to Shelly, thinking how great it would be to be able to head off on dates with Ray.

Shelly said, "Maybe we could ask Jake and Brad. I don't mind Jake, and I think he would be able to help."

Now it was my turn to question Shelly! I told her to tell me what's happening between them two. Her and Jake. But she said nothing yet. Then went on to tell me that she did fancy him. I giggled and told her that that was great, because I was sure Jake felt the same way about her. We giggled over how funny it was that we had both fallen for these men, around the same time, and how weird it would have felt if it was only one of us smitten this way.

"Do you mind if I hit the pillow?" Shelly asked, as she yawned and exhaled out the days tension.

I hugged her and headed out of the room, closing the door gently. I couldn't sleep with my mind in turmoil, so I headed to the kitchen to make a hot chocolate. As I walked in, I was overcome by that chill again.

"I wish you could tell me who you are. Or tell me how I could help." I softly spoke, hoping no-one else would hear me.

Strangely, the window above the sink, began to fog up, and the word Margaret, appeared. As if someone had just written in the fog with their finger. I quickly looked around behind me, and back to the window, and the window was no longer foggy. I was so confused. Did I just see that, and if so, how would Margaret know who I was? Or even find me here?

I felt very unsettled. Not scared, but concerned about what I was meant to do. I decided not to have a hot chocolate after all, and instead headed to bed.

As I turned out the light, I noticed a dim light fade to darkness, inside the cupboard. I wished this would stop! Everything was so mixed up! Why would that even happen here, in the spare room of Shellys parents' house of all places. My brain wouldn't switch off, thinking of every out of the norm event, that has happened since Esmeralda disappeared.

Over the last week or two, I had become deprived of much of my usual sleep. It was a challenge to get up to go to work this morning, but I managed to get myself out the door at a decent time.

When I reached work, I made a coffee, then headed into my office to check the diary. There were a few messages the receptionists had jotted in, including one from the delivery warehouse that mine and Shellys furniture was coming from. They were going to be delivering it all at the house, at noon. I thought I'd better give them a call prior, to let them know it was ok to unload everything on the front porch, if no-one happened to be there at the time.

A very gruff voice answered, "Express deliveries! How can we help?"

I told him who I was and asked if our delivery items could be left on the front porch if no one was able to be there.

"Yes, but we won't take any responsibility for the items if any go missing." He exclaimed.

I told him that I understood, and hoped that we would have someone there, however there was lots going on currently that I wasn't too sure. Then thanked him and said goodbye.

I called Shelly to let her know that everything would be delivered to at noon, regardless of if we were there or not, but also mentioned that if neither of us were, that they wouldn't cover any losses if anything happened to be missing by the time we could make it over there. Shelly offered to be there for their arrival to let them in at least but would then have to get back over to her mum.

"I'm hoping to get my work finished before then, and it wouldn't be an issue for me to head over after that. Gosh, I can't wait to get our beds!" I told Shelly, laughing.

Shelly teased me about my bed comment, then said she couldn't wait to have the kitchen sorted. Then said she would call around today to get the ball rolling on some quotes for it. I told her to ask them to quote on the bathroom as well.

This morning has worked out perfect, despite how tired I feel. Now to concentrate on my work. Tomorrow was my big appointment with Ray. It's funny, I've never had this before, but I found myself thinking if I should get a new outfit, and maybe a haircut. Then my reasoning came back saying why, he appreciates you as you are!

Lunch time came, and I thought maybe a quick walk home to see what was happening was in order. As I left, I asked the girls to take and messages, as I may be delayed, then headed out the office foyer doors.

As I got closer, I saw some trucks heading up my street. Wow! My heart started to thump. I had never been this excited. This was really happening! I saw that Shelly's dad's car was there, and I could see so many people unloading. Then I noticed Shelly, directing the men! We do make a great team, if I must say so myself. As I walked up the driveway, her eyes met mine, and we both jumped excitedly where we stood. I grabbed some pillows for our couch, that were sitting on the lawn, and headed up the front stairs.

Shelly hugged me and said that her dad was trying the keys to see if he could unlock that door. I had forgotten about that, but went in to see what had arrived, since the door was already open anyway.

The new rug was already down in the lounge room, and the sofas and armchairs were here. It feels so lovely seeing our home starting to come together, with our own stuff. I decided to see if anything had been taken upstairs. As I reached the upper hallway, the cold chill came over me again. I waited to see if anything would come flying at me. All clear. Maybe she knew we weren't scared of her and decided that she would happily share the house with us, I thought.

I went into the room we thought was Esmeraldas, and the cupboard doors were open. Then I looked around to see the drawers that had Esmeralda's pearl necklace open too. I looked over the top drawer, and it was. The pearl necklace was back again. Had Esmeralda been back while we were not here? Nothing else had changed though, that I had noticed.

I peered into the next bedroom, which was now empty except for the bed base. Nothing there. Hesitating to continue, I was feeling nervous, as I slowly made my way closer to the end bedroom. Did I want to look?

I heard Shelley's dad calling, "Shelly. Shelly!"

I raced downstairs to see that Shellys father had found which key worked the front door. Thankfully, we can now lock this place up! As I came up behind Shelly and her father, they both jumped. Then I saw that Shellys father had also worked out what key unlocked the room door that came off the lounge. The door we couldn't open. There was old furniture piled up inside, from what looked to be like generations of families. It was piled so high, with so much of everything! There was even an old children's trike, and books, everywhere! China cupboards lined one wall, full of antiques, and right at the back was another door. No one spoke, until one of the men walked in and asked which room we would like the mattresses to go into. We all jumped this time, startled by the man's voice. I told the man to pop one into each of the rooms upstairs, and to put any other furniture left to bring in, into the hallway.

I heard the delivery truck leaving and closed the door.

Shelly's father said that he needed to get back to work, and asked Shelly if she was ok to get back over to her mum. Shelly told her father that she would catch a taxi over, as she was exhausted from directing and rearranging furniture.

As Shellys father hugged us goodbye, as he walked out the door, he said, "Be safe. This place is so old, who knows what lives in these walls!"

As we giggled from the remark, two of the delivery men came back downstairs. We slightly jumped, forgetting that they were even here still.

"There must be snow on the roof of that end room! It's freezing down there!" One of the men said, as they headed out the door, towards the new delivery truck that had just pulled up in the driveway.

Shelly went to the kitchen to give her mother a quick call, while helped the men unload the rest of the delivery. It was all our electrical items.

As the last of our new things were brought in, the men carried in our new TV, and Shelly showed them where it was to go.

"Just pop it down on the floor against that wall for now. Thanks."

Shelly told the men, then she turned to me, and said, "Oh, Hannah. Mum said she is fine, and that I could stay a little longer to finish setting out everything."

As I went to tell Shelly that was great news, one of the men said, "Are you girls going to be ok organising connecting this TV? You're going to need to get someone to wire in a power point here, as you don't have one on this wall."

We giggled and Shelly told the man that that was fine as we knew someone that could help. I noticed that Shellys face was blushing a little as she spoke about it. She must have been thinking of Jake more than his father, who would be the one doing the work!

As the men walked out the front door to leave, Shelly and I fell into the couch. It felt soooo good, to sit in a soft, non-dusty sofa, in a clean fresh smelling lounge room. It was nearly impossible to get back up. We never realised how draining this would all be. Then a warm breeze surrounded us. It had to be Esmeralda!!

We both looked around for her, but we couldn't see her anywhere. We heard a noise in the kitchen, so we went to see if maybe one of the men were still here. Standing at the kitchen bench, using our new kettle, Esmeralda. Pouring cups of tea in a beautiful tea set, that we had never seen before!

Esmeralda smiled, and said, "Hello my darlings. I have been quite busy but tried to keep watch over you both. Have a seat so we can chat!"

I blurted out as I took a seat at the dining table, "I saw writing in a mirror, and a window, saying Margaret!"

"Yes, I felt her, but could not get to her. She is stuck between both worlds, and I've been trying to help her get back through. I have come back to ask you to read the book, maybe there is something written within it that will tell us how we can help her get back through. Then once I get my strength back. Then I will try again." Esmeralda explained.

Ten

Esmeralda Returns Just In Time

What an eventful day yesterday was! I was so happy that Esmeralda was back, but now I had to face the fact that today, I needed to go back to my parents' home and collect my things.

We didn't get to talk to Esmeralda much yesterday, as Shelly had to get back to her mother, and I had to go back to work. Last night Shelly and I were both so exhausted, that we had forgotten Esmeralda had even come back and fell asleep in our new beds quite early.

It was 5am, and I was already awake. So, I decided to head to my parents' home before work and get it over and done with. That way, at least I had work as an excuse to walk back out the door, regardless of what was being said.

As I arrived, I couldn't hear anyone awake, so I snuck in quietly and unlocked my bedroom door, but it was already unlocked. Everything had been turned upside down. I felt cold as I looked around to see the suitcase, and book, had been thrown against one of the bedroom walls. Thank goodness it was still here, and still in one piece.

I found some paper and a pencil and wrote a letter to mum. Telling her that I loved her and hoped that one day we could look back on these days and laugh together. Then mentioned that Shelly and I have rented our own house, and that I hoped that she was doing well. I placed it on my bed, piled anything else I wanted to take back to the house with me, into the suitcase, and tiptoed back to the front door.

I heard my mother call out. "Hannah. Is that you?"

My heartbeat begun rising even higher, and I quickly ran out the door, before she had a chance to get out of bed and see me. Tears streamed down my face as I felt both sadness, and the heavy weight leaving my shoulders. I was finally free from the chaos that was now, my old home. I could hear my mother screaming at me as I continued running down the street. I didn't stop running. Not until I got back to our Castle House.

As I ran inside, I closed the door and locked it behind me, just in case my mother had decided to run after me. Shelly had just walked down the stairs and into the lounge.

"Oh Hannah! Are you ok?!" She said, running over to me and giving me the biggest hug.

I told her what had happened as tears continued to roll down my face.

"Good morning, girls. We have lots to catch up on. I know some of the trials you have been dealing with." Said a voice coming from the direction of the dining room.

Just like that my tears stopped, and Shelly and I ran to the dining room to hug Esmeralda.

"I also noticed a very nice man in someone's company!" Esmeralda exclaimed.

We both giggled, as it was so exciting to have her back, knowing she was all right.

"Yes. he has taken my attention!" I told Esmeralda. "But I'm not the only one feeling that way."

Shelly blushed, and said, "Hey! You've certainly cleared a base I haven't yet, Hannah!"

We both burst out laughing, then pulled ourselves up as Esmeralda sat down.

"Alas, I saw by my leaving here, I have now awoken another evil spirit. She was banished from this home centuries ago. I was told of her when I was younger. Unfortunately, I wasn't told that to keep her at bay, one of our bloodlines always needed to be within these walls." Esmeralda continued. "When I left, in search of my friend Margaret, she gained entry. I have come back in the hope I that I can expel her, back to the world between.

She was evil back when she was living, hence my family had put a curse on her, to live forever in the underworld. That is, while this home had their blood running through it. By my leaving, and no children of my blood, she was able to come back through. I have felt her presence here. She had tried several times to block my path back!"

"That must have been when I had seen a dim light!" I blurted out.

Esmeralda said, "Yes it was. I had to regain my strength to override hers. When you girls joined together, and hit her with that bolt of lightning, you took her strength. I was able to make it back through, because of that."

Shelly and I were both mesmerised! Thinking back, this was all making sense. If only we had known!

Shelly asked, "Will there be any more ghosts from the old days coming into this house?"

Esmeralda said, "None that I know of."

I asked Esmeralda if we could somehow help her, to expel the evil ghost. However, she informed us that it was not for us to do. She did tell us though, that if she manages to beat this evil, we were to use our bracelets for our own protection. Then reminded us to be careful of our usage count that the bracelets had.

"Be careful to never use the last one!" Esmeralda exclaimed.

Shelly and I asked if Esmeralda would be staying now, or if she needed to go and keep looking for Margaret. She told us that she thought that once Shelly and I began using them, that she might have been able to make it back through.

"Now that you have the book, please read it, any moment you have free. There must be another way, besides the use of the bracelets, to get through." Esmeralda said.

Shelly then asked, "Why does this house have more rooms than we can get into?"

Esmeralda, for the first time, laughed! She explained, "When there was more than one family living in this home, people were more likely to argue. So, the newer families would make extensions of their own, with their own entrances. In those days, there was a lot more magic used than there is today, and a lot more secrets. Doors could look like walls, and windows might not be as they seemed. Margaret and I, used to love hiding and finding things. Once we found a whole farmyard of chickens, but when we went back the next day, it was all gone! We never really knew back then, if it was us making things appear, or us making them disappear, or something we just didn't even understand. We loved reading the magic book though and made a golden bike to ride once. But please be careful, magic can make friends leave as well, by accident."

Suddenly, we heard the front gate swing open. It must have been my mother! Someone at the pub must have told her where we were living!

I said to Shelly to go and hide. My mother was raging!

As my mother reached the front door, Shelly said, "I will ring..." but never finished her sentence, as she came smashing through it.

She came at me with an axe. I never even knew we owned one! Shelly screamed and ran to me! Then out of nowhere, Esmeralda appeared, sending a ball of electricity at my mother! It caught the metal of the axe, sending her flying into the wall. I was on the lounge room floor against the wall, with Shelly, unable to move.

My mother moaned and started to get up. Again, Esmeralda sent her through the door with another bolt, and the door closed behind her!

Esmeralda headed towards us, saying, "Evil begets evil!"

I looked at Esmeralda, as she held her hands out towards us, to help us back to our feet. She was a bit scary looking! It made me laugh, even though it was probably more shocking than it was funny.

I looked at Shelly. She was still stunned. I turned to her, saying "Shelly, it's all right."

Shelly looked at me, and then Esmeralda, and said "I just had the worst nightmare, and I was so scared! Why are we standing here?"

I remembered when I had nightmares, and my mother saying, 'It's ok, the bad people are gone now!' I guess the situation scared Shelly so much that she passed out somewhere in between Esmeralda hurling lightening balls at my mother.

Shelly then asked me what time it was. Answering her, I said "It's time for me to head to work!"

Esmeralda said, "I'll watch over Shelly." Then asked her, "Would you like a nice hot bath to settle you, darling?"

As I went to walk out the door to head to work, I turned to Esmeralda and thanked her, for stopping my mother so that we didn't get hurt, and for being there for Shelly in case she realises that what had happened, did indeed happen.

I then remembered that today was the big day with Ray, and my body begun to tingle with excitement.

Eleven

The Proposal

Walking through the foyer doors, I felt the exuberance hit me. This is my first official publication. I told the receptionists not to disturb me until my office door was back open, headed into my office, closing the door behind me. Then pulled up my sleeves, and got to it.

By 10am, I already felt as though I'd had the most productive day to date, even if I must say so myself. I opened my door to say good morning to everyone, just as Ray came walking through the front doors, hiding behind a very beautiful bunch of white roses.

There were a lot of oooh's, and Ahhh's, as I stepped back into my office, followed by this bunch of white roses, with legs. I started laughing at my thought as a head popped behind them, which made my laughing even worse.

"Good morning, my princess!" Echoed around my room.

"Good morning, my knight in white roses." I replied, still laughing.

"Care to share?" Ray asked.

I settled into my chair, and told him what followed me through the door. "...Then it grew a very attractive head!"

He looked at me for a moment, and started laughing, and said, "You truly see the world differently from anyone else I know."

"I shall take that as a compliment, as I do not want to be known as a sheep!" I exclaimed.

"You are correct again! Who would want to follow everyone else? This is what will make you a great writer, my beautiful princess." Ray said.

I asked Ray if he was ready to see his book cover, with all of his amazing work printed inside. He said that I was making him nervous. So I turned my computer around, and showed him what I had created.

He looked as though he was deep in thought, then said, "How on earth do you do that? It is the perfect cover to bring this story to life. It even makes me want to read what's inside!"

My heart started pumping a million pumps per second.

Ray stood up, and said, "Lets go grab a coffee."

I said, "Yes lets! My life is all about positivity now, and coffee is the perfect positivity potion for the busy morning iv'e had."

Ray said, "You seem like you have had an epiphany since we saw each other!"

Answering him, I said, "I believe I have!" Then I asked the reception girls to let my boss, Mr Winston know, that I was out with my client, celebrating.

"Oh, and ask him to have a look at the book cover on my computer." I called out, as we walked through the foyer doors to head outside.

It felt amazing, knowing all of my hard work has paid off, even with the days off I've had lately. And here I am. Being walked towards that luxurious car, once again. I'm not a movie star, nor do I ever want to be, but I am Very unique, and a whole lot more!

Ray opened my door and as I sat, he leaned in to kiss me, saying "You suit my style of car. You also suit the driver just as much!"

I giggled at the thought, that Ray has obviously had the same realisation as I had.

Travelling to his surprise destination, I sat back and breathed. Feeling on top of the world.

Ray looked over at me, with the most enchanting smile, and said, "I will never stop enjoying life, while you are by my side."

I was not used to this adulation, even though I loved it. My answer mimicked his words.

"No you don't. That's plagiarism!" Ray said, laughing at his joke.

I laughed. This man is the polar opposite to my father. This is now my turn to shine, with this man of my dreams, by my side.

Ray pulled into a very fancy looking restaurant, that had a beautiful garden gazebo, lit up with fairy lights. He came around to open my door and said that it would cost a kiss to exit the vehicle.
I said, "Wow! That's a very nice tariff. One that I would be delighted to pay."

We entered, arm in arm, and were escorted to the gazebo. I had the biggest smile on my face as we were seated. Ray told me that I was radiant, and that I was making him blush at the sight of my shining beauty! I simply told him back, that, when you accept the realisation, that someone else can make you even happier than you could ever imagine, and he is sitting opposite you. Well, how else could I feel?

He held my hands across the table, and told me that I have made his world complete. Then he put his hand in his pocket, and pulled out a tiny box.

"My princess..." He said. "...Would you do me the honour, of becoming my Queen?"

I almost couldn't get the word out. "YES!!!" I told him, with tears of pure happiness, running down my cheeks.

He placed the ring onto my finger, and said, "I have only one wish in this world. And that wish, is to forever make you happy!"

I teared up again, and he kissed them away.

When he finally let me go, he clapped his hands three times. A waiter carrying champagne and foods that I had never seen before, came out of nowhere, and placed them onto our table. What an amazing day, to publish my soon-to-be, husband's best seller.

We were both on cloud nine, and slightly tipsy at this point, so we had a chauffeur pick us up. Ray asked the owner, if one of his staff could take his car home, and we headed back to the office, to see Mr Winston, and inform him that Ray wished to proceed with the publishing.

When we arrived back to the office, Ray asked the driver to wait. As Ray opened the office door, we were met by my boss, Mr. Winston.

"Ray. Hannah. Please come into my office!" Mr. Winston said.

Before we sat down, Ray said to my boss, "I would like you to meet my fiancé!"

My boss turned to me, and said, "I couldn't think of a better match. Congratulations, to you both!"

We took a seat, and all sat down to sign the final paperwork. Then we shook hands with Mr. Winston, and wished him a good weekend as we walked out of his office.

"I will see you on Monday, Frank." Ray called out to my boss as we headed towards the foyer doors.

I couldn't help myself, so as we walked past the reception girls, I said, "My fiancé will be back Monday." Everyone just went bonkers!

We headed to Shellys mum's house, to see how everyone was, knowing that Shelly should also be there by now.

As we pulled into the driveway, Ray said, "I don't know their surname."

I proudly told him, "Mr and Mrs Bryant."

Ray again asked the chauffeur to wait.

Shelly had heard us drive in, and came running out to see who it was. She was so excited, asking us what was going on, telling me that she could feel so much happiness from me. She then looked at Ray, who was beaming from hearing Shelly's excited outburst.

"It's a pleasure to finally meet my fiancé's friend, and partner in the inherited, and possibly haunted, Castle House." Ray said, laughing, as he went to shake Shellys hand, but instead received the biggest welcome hug. "She never stops talking about you."

Shelly let him breathe again, and spied the shimmering, shining in-the-sunlight, diamond ring, and she squealed!

The noise she made brought her dad out, asking "Who, or what, was that noise?"

When Shellys father realised what was going on, he broke into the biggest smile, and stepped forward to shake Ray's hand, hugged him, and said, "Please, come in. Before all the neighbours come to hug you as well."

As we entered the house, Shelly mum was sitting in a brand new very comfy chair, with her feet up on a pouf. She put her arms out to hug me, and held my hand. When she saw my ring, her tears flowed.

"Congratulations! my darling. Now, introduce me to this very handsome, and very lucky young man." Shellys mum said.

Ray, who was chatting to Shellys father, turned around, and said, "Yes. I am the luckiest man on our planet. Not sure about the handsome part. May I too give you a gentle hug, as soon we'll be related."

Shellys mum blushed, and asked "Do you have a brother?"

Ray laughed, saying, "Unfortunately, no. But I do believe the days of your daughter, Shelly, being single, will be short lived. From what I have heard."

Everyone laughed at this comment, and Shellys mum said to Ray, "Oh, you are a charmer."

The afternoon was like a fairytale to me. Everyone I loved, all together.

Ray whispered to me that Shellys mother was beginning to sound tired, then he thanked everyone for welcoming him into their home.

"We will let you rest, and if Shelly would like a lift to Castle House, we would happily take her." Ray said, hugging Shellys mum goodbye.

Shellys dad was standing next to the front door. He shook hands with Ray, and hugged Shelly and I, and said to me, "I believe you are in safe hands."

Shelly and I grabbed our things, while Ray asked the chauffeur to help carry our luggage.
Ray was fascinated in Shelly. And at one point he asked her if she was enchanted at everything. I laughed and told him that she was.
The drive home was short, and when the chauffeur pulled up, he questioned us, asking if it was the correct address. We all laughed.

Ray said, "Yes. This is the Castle House of these fair maidens."

The three of us proudly walked through our door saying, "We're home."

Shelly looked at me, as did I look at her. We had both felt Esmeralda.

Ray commented, trying to control his laughter, "Wow! You have done a lot since our baked bean dinner."

Shelly and I heard Esmeralda giggle.

Ray asked if there was anything he could do to help.

"Yes! Can you paint, renovate bathrooms, renovate kitchens, and have a television power point put in?" Shelly said.

He took a seat, saying "No, though I do know people who can."

Shelly said, "A true knight in shining armour. You have won the heart of Hannah."

I kissed him, saying, "Yes, he has."

Ray ushered us off with his hand, saying, "Away with you, while I make some phone calls, to unburden you from this mammoth workload."

We both grabbed our things to fill our rooms with new life. Running up the squeaking stairs we heard him say, "...And remodel a stairway.

We laughed so hard as we reached our bedroom, then Esmeralda appeared, saying "Oh my, he is very pleasing to my eyes, plus you have made his heart very happy. I feel this home will now burst with joy again."

When we had finished unpacking, we could still hear Ray talking, his voice was sending waves of contentment over me, like a nice warm bath.

Shelly said, "I hope I will have that look on my face one day."

Esmeralda said, "That is in the hands of you, my precious."

This was true, fate had brought us together, but I chose to let go of my past, accepting I was worthy, to have a better life. Shelly was beautiful, inside and out, hopefully, she too will be noticed by the man of her dreams.

We went down to find our knight, looking at the pictures of the ancestors of Esmeralda.

He turned to us, and said, "I cannot see a resemblance to either of you."

I told Ray that they were that long ago, that we did't know who they were.

He accepted, saying, "Well, what should we do first?"

I said, "do you want to explore with us? The room that Shellys dad finally unlocked, has some amazing stuff in it! But it's all too heavy for us to move on our own."

Ray said, "Lead on, I will be your man slave."

Shelly giggled, and I told her to wait for the Elizabethan speech to start.

Ray turned to me, saying, "Doth thou maiden speak ill of thee?" then pretended to chase me, but I jumped over a couch.

I said, "Thou art beguiling thee with thou wit."

Shelly told us that we were absolutely insane together. Ray and I laughed as if we didn't care. Then we pretended to turn evil and chase her.

The time flew by. Ray was enthralled with the antique books. Shelly found a beautiful lamp candle holder for her bedroom, while I was wrapped up with admiring the hand carvings on the furniture. Some pieces looked as though they were carved by the same person. Some had initials as well. I thought we could spend forever here, just reaching the heritage of everything in this room.

Shelly said, "I'm hungry, we should go grab a burger?"

Ray said, "You know, I have never tried a burger before."

I told Ray, "Then let's go! But be prepared to get hooked!"

Ray laughed, saying, "I feel like I'm a fish."

We decided to walk down to the burger store to take in the setting sun, and its beautiful shades of pink, purple, and golden light. We ordered our meals, then headed upstairs to find a rooftop table. It was very busy tonight. We saw Jake and Brad, sitting with Jakes mum and dad.

As Shelly jumped up to go and say hello, Ray said, "Is that someone of importance to our Shelly?"

I explained the whole story to Ray, about Shellys parents house, and about Shellys little crush. As they were leaving they stopped at our table. Jake introduced his mum and dad, as Mr and Mrs Hays, and I introduced my fiancé, Ray. They all congratulated us, then started asking Ray questions.

Shelly got a sly kiss from Jake, as he asked her if us girls still wanted him and his father to head over and help out tomorrow. She told him that that would be great as we needed a power point put in for the TV too. Ray also told Jake and his father that he was struggling to get an electrician, as no one could spare any men, at the moment.

As they left we said goodnight, and had a little giggle about telling them that we would see them at sunrise, as that was also the name of Shellys bedroom. We had named all of the rooms in Castle House, as it seemed easier that way to know what we were talking about.

On our way back to Castle House, I had a feeling of being watched, but there was no one around. I snuggled in under Ray's arm, and the feeling went away.

Ray grimaced, and said, "Are you sending me home alone? Or do I get an invite to the sunset room?"

I laughed, saying, "We could put you in the 'moonlight room."

Again, he grimaced, and said, "Please don't! That sounds like something will happen to me at midnight."

Shelly, and I broke out in laughter, at his unknown correctness!

We had forgotten to turn any lights on before we left, but Ray remembered where the light string was and quickly pulled it. He seemed relieved everything was in its place. I felt Esmeraldas presence as we walked in.

"Silly question, but do you have hot water?" Ray asked.

My answer wasn't accepted very well, when I told him that there was no hot water system, even to fix.

He said, "Well, this will need to be sorted."

Shelly and I laughed. We loved our baths.

Ray said, "I will go back to reading that book, while you princesses have your bubble baths. Then he kissed me, and said, "I will stand guard!"

Shelly and I headed upstairs, and as they creaked, Ray shook his head. We enjoyed our time playing princesses. Shelly wanted to know more about Jake. I told her that he had always been a good friend, helping me with my studies at the library after school. I had never seen him show any interest in any girls though. He only ever spoke about wanting to get a good job, and work hard to achieve his dreams.

When Shelly said that he kissed her tonight, I told her that I had seen him do that. Shelly giggled telling me that she thinks that she likes him, but was worried it might just be a spot of puppy love. Then asked me how she could know the difference between puppy love and real love. To be honest, I didn't really know how to answer that, as I only knew what I knew, and that was how Ray made me feel. So I explained to Shelly, that if Ray was suddenly never around, I'd probably feel lost and like something was missing from my life. But yet, when he's around, I feel more whole than ever before.

Shelly thought that it all sounded so complicated, so I told her to go with her gut feelings, enjoy the company, and let what ever it is, unfold in its own time.

After we finished our baths and our lengthy chat about love, Shelly decided to call it a night for her. She hugged me and told me that I deserve all the happiness that I had once missed out on, then headed to bed as she called out to Ray, saying goodnight to him.

I went down to find my love, sound sleep in the armchair, with a book on his chest. I tried to quietly walk over to him, but bumped a lantern on the floor and he awoke.

"My dream is walking." Ray said, as he stood up and wrapped his arms around me.

His kisses were sending tingles down to my toes. Then, when he asked me if we could head up to the Sunset Room now, my bedroom, It felt like me feet had grown wings.

Waking at sunrise was easy, due to the lack of curtains letting the sun stream in. I looked at Ray who was lying on his arm, watching me.

He kissed me good morning, and said, "Did you know the first ray of sunshine landed right on your beautiful face?"

I said, "I think you have a great imagination." Then kissed him back.

We heard car doors close outside, followed by Shelly opening the front door very chirpily, saying good morning to Jake and his father.

Disappointment appeared on Ray's face, as I broke free of his embrace.

"Come on! The day awaits!" I said, as a pillow came flying at me.

As I headed downstairs, I felt Esmeralda again, and quietly whispered hello to her. Shelly had Jake bring in a ladder to help put up our new curtains, while his father was on the roof.

Ray asked, "Can we make coffee first?"

Laughing, I replied "Yes! Take a seat and I will even make you toast."

He laughed, saying, "You're spoiling me."

As Mr. Hays walked inside, Ray said to him, "Great to see you again. I hope you have magic powers, to get the girls power sorted in this house."

Mr Hays said, "I have a new switch box and will keep working in the roof with my furry friends."

I laughed as Ray replied with an astonished, "Really?"

Mr Hays said "Yeah, but they're too busy eating the wires, to worry about me."

Shelly came into the dining room, saying, "Guess who now has curtains?"

I said to Ray, "Shelly and I were thinking black curtains, with cute ghosts on them for the 'Moonlight room'."
He looked up to see if I was actually serious. When he realised I wasn't, he said "I need you every morning, you are way better than coffee."

Laughing, I walked out of the dining room to join the curtain team.

As I was walking out, Ray said, "I'm just going to ring my builder, while I finish this toast."

I entered the moonlight room, and I sensed Esmeralda's presence. I greeted her, saying, "I hope you've had a chance to rest and regain your strength."

She materialised and hugged me, exclaiming, "I have, and I can't wait to see what else is in the storage room!"

I informed her, that I'd plan to explore it today, but that I'd wait a little more, before I tell Ray about her.

She understood and replied, "That's fine. I'm just happy to witness the progress. Oh, and when you're ready to install a phone, there's a connection, but it's located behind where you have your lounge. I couldn't pay the bills because I was 'deceased', so everything was cut off."

I chuckled in the darkness, and Esmeralda disappeared.

Ray walked in, and asked, "What's so funny?"

"I was thinking of doing something with a little ghost on it, just for fun!" I told him.

He laughed and remarked, "As long as I never end up in here!"

I joined in the laughter and assured him, "You won't!"

I pushed away his concerns with a hug, just as the curtain team entered the room, announcing, "We're ready!" They were holding ladders and tools.

Ray exclaimed, "This princess wants to add some ghosts in here!"

Shelly couldn't help but burst out laughing.

Jake chimed in, "I'm with Ray. This house is creepy enough!"

Ray suggested, "You should bring everything you need for the next few days downstairs since the stairway is being fixed."

Shelly responded, "No problem. I can stay with my mum."

Ray looked at me, and I said, "I'd feel better staying with Ray. We can work on his book together!"

Ray asked, "Can I help with anything up here?"

We assured him that us girls had everything under control. Jake offered to take Ray home to get his car, and I noticed the twinkle in his eye. He would be thrilled to see the car.

Ray asked, "Do you mind?"

I replied, "Of course not. Do what you need to do. We'll be here."

He embraced me tightly, saying, "You're so easy to love!"

I replied, "Ditto!" Then shooed them out so Esmeralda could join Shelly and I for a chat.

While we worked on the curtains, Shelly asked Esmeralda, "Do you like the curtains we chose?"

Esmeralda replied, "I love everything! You girls have done a great job. It brings back good memories of when Margaret and I used to do this." She continued, "I'll try to remember where the key to the connecting room is. It's filled with things from my parents, so maybe you can use some of it!"

That was the exciting part of this house - figuring out where to put things! We discussed the floor lino and realised it needed to be painted first.

Shelly declared, "I'll take care of it. Mum has a phone book, I'll make some calls first thing in the morning."

I asked, "Should we go for colours, or just white curtains?"

We both agreed on colours, with Shelly choosing pink, and me opting for sky blue.

Esmeralda chimed in, "I always wanted duck egg color!"

We laughed and promised to find it for her.

With the curtains done, we proceeded to pack our bags when suddenly we heard the sound of a metal bell ringing.

Esmeralda warned, "Bad vibes! Be very careful. I'll keep watch!"

We opened the door and were surprised to see my father standing there.

I asked, "What do you want?"

He replied, "Your mum is still rambling about this haunted place you're living in!"

I chuckled and remarked, "Really?"

I have a feeling there's more to come. I wish Ray or Jake were here. Knowing my father, he was probably waiting to attack.

He asked, "So how can you afford this?" while peering over my shoulder.

I replied, "We've worked hard and saved, like most normal people do!"

This caught him off guard. I rarely spoke, let alone shared my thoughts.

Dad snapped, "Don't speak to me like that!"

I calmly stated, "You're on my property. Please leave. You're not welcome here, ever." I knew he hadn't had a drink yet, it being Sunday.

He claimed, "You owe me for keeping you for 20 years!"

I laughed and said, "Only you would think that way!"

He made a move to grab me, but Mr. Hays appeared behind us and warned, "I wouldn't do that if I were you. If you know what's good for you." In a stern voice, Mr. Hays continued, "You were asked to leave. Your daughter owes you nothing. Everyone knows where you drink. Lay a hand on these girls and you'll face the consequences."

I felt a sense of relief wash over me as that nagging feeling dissipated. With renewed strength and clarity, I pulled Shelly back with me and slammed the door in his face.

I heard him muttering as he left the verandah. I thought I was okay until I crumbled to the floor, shaking with tears that had been held in for so long. It was a release, and I felt numb. Shelly held me while Mr. Hays wrapped a blanket around me, stating that I was in shock. I was oblivious to everything after that.

When I regained consciousness, I was in a fog and found myself in Ray's arms.

He had tears in his eyes and said, "I will never leave you alone again! I should have been here!"

I noticed more faces watching me and reassured them, saying, "I'm okay!"

Shelly made me a cup of tea while Ray helped me to the sofa. I saw Jake, and Mr. Hays appeared deeply saddened.

I thanked Mr. Hays and he kindly replied, "I'm surprised you came out of that home as well as you have. Everyone knows them. Trust me when I say you're safe. They won't bother you again."

Ray was trying to catch up with everything and I admitted, "I know I should have told you, but I thought you might run away if I did."

He kissed me and said, "I love you. Nothing else matters."

Ray asked Shelly if she could go with Jake to get some burgers for everyone. He then handed Jake his car keys. Jake assured him, "I'll take care of her for you."

Ray smirked and replied, "I know you will."

I was feeling Esmeralda's presence around me, so I asked Ray if he could fetch a glass of water from the kitchen.

Shelly hugged me as Esmeralda appeared, saying, "What an evil man! You've chosen well. Your life will blossom from now on." Then she disappeared as Ray returned.

Ray asked me, "Why didn't your mother protect you?"

I answered, "She was lost in the world of alcohol, just like him. That is why Shelley's parents are so important to me."

He embraced me and said, "Our children will never need someone else's parents!"

I kissed him and replied, "Never!"

Our burgers were back, andMr. Hays was intrigued, mentioning, "There is a builder's ute coming in as well."

Ray jumped up and said, "Great! Say goodbye to those dangerous stairs!"

The man entered and said, "I used to wonder about this old girl. I'm glad someone is bringing her back to life! But I've always been curious about those add-ons. They seem to be everywhere!"

We all laughed and agreed.

Shelly said, "We couldn't even find our way into them!"

He shook hands with Ray, who introduced him as Shaz, saying, "This is the man who works miracles!"

Shaz then introduced himself to all of us, then raised an eyebrow and asked, "How did you get this stunning beauty?"

Ray defended himself by saying, "Miracles happen when you're an author!"

Everyone laughed, and Shaz congratulated Ray. He turned to me and said, "If he gives you any trouble, just call me. I'll take care of him," laughing at his own joke.

I could see why they were friends. It felt surreal last night to be introduced as a fiancée, but with Ray's friend, it seemed even more surreal. They walked off to inspect the stairway. I heard a few curse words and then some expressions of amazement. This was going to be fun for Shaz!

Shelly asked if I needed anything else from upstairs, to which I replied, "No, my bags are in the dining room."

Ray introduced Shelly to Shaz, and he cheekily remarked, "Another beautiful damsel from the tower, I see."

Shelly laughed and said, "You must be the gentleman who will be modernising our stairway."

Shaz looked at Ray and said, "Possibly a few more things to bring into the present century?"

We all laughed at that, and I added, "Please feel free to fix whatever you're happy to do."

Mr. Hays entered and thanked us for the lunch. He said hello to Shaz and introduced himself and Jake, as the electrician and his son. They would be here until dark, and Jake could help if needed. Mr. Hays mentioned that he would be on the roof with his furry friends.

Shaz jokingly said, "Sounds like you got the fun job!"

Ray remarked, "Who knows what Shaz will find under the stairwell?"

This got everyone laughing, though Shelly and I knew it was a possibility.

Ray asked Shaz, "Do you want to start now?"

Shaz replied, "Why not? I have no one waiting for my amazing presence."

Jake chimed in, "Cool, I get to smash stuff."

Ray said, "Then I'll take these damsels to their other castle. My phone will be on if you need anything."

As the lights flickered, a voice from the roof called out, "Just kidding!"

We all let out our held breath, and laughed off the fright. Ray and Jake took our bags to the car and then came to collect us.

We dropped Shelly off at her parents'. I could see she was worried about leaving Esmeralda. I smiled, hugged her, and reassured her that Esmeralda would be okay. Ray hugged her and said goodbye, then Shelly took her bags and went inside.

As we drove off slowly, Ray asked if I was okay. I told him that I had finally resolved all of my past issues and closed all of my doors. With him, I could now have a life I never thought possible.

As we pulled into his driveway, I understood why Ray wanted us out of that house. I also realised how much he must love me, as he was willing to sit on the floor to have dinner, despite where he was living. I asked him how he managed to overcome the barrier of economic inequality. Ray turned off the engine, leaned over, and kissed me.

He said, "Love crosses all barriers. I see you for who you are, someone who doesn't even realise how beautiful they are, inside and out. I'm the lucky one. Lucky that you love me!"

He came around and opened my door, saying, "Welcome to your new home, where you will never be treated as anything less than a princess."

He asked if I needed to be carried or if I would like to walk by his side. I chose to stand by his side as equals, knowing that together we would be unstoppable.

We laughed as we entered the house, and he scooped me up, playfully telling me, "You, my little princess, shall pay for your impudence!"

We ended up sleeping through dinner, waking up at sunrise to the sound of the ocean and the sun shining on his beautiful veranda. Ray was just watching me as I greeted him, saying good morning.

He said, "Not only do you look like a vision, but you also have the voice of an angel."

I laughed, understanding why his books were best sellers.

He asked if I was up for going to work, and I replied, "As long as you feed me, I'm starving." He joined me at the verandah door, opening it for me to venture out.

The view was truly breathtaking, but a cold feeling came over me. I asked Ray if he had any plans for the day. He said he did, but he could cancel if I wanted to stay home. I told him no, I wanted to go to work.

Ray asked if I would like a nice warm shower, to which I replied, "Now you're speaking my language! Where is it?"

He pointed to a door, and as I went inside and opened it, I was amazed to see the biggest bath and separate walk-in shower I had ever seen. Ray came up behind me and asked if I was sure I wanted to go to work. I replied that a bubble bath would be the ultimate luxury and that I could be a little late.

Ray then headed downstairs to the kitchen, while I ran a beautiful, luxurious bubble bath. As I stepped in, I had a feeling of being watched, but I ignored it, closed my eyes, and let all my worries float away.
Suddenly, I opened my eyes to see what the noise was, and through the door, I saw a cup of coffee being held by a man's hand! I laughed and said, "There has to be more than that to get me out of this amazing bath!"

A cheeky voice replied, "It awaits you on the patio."

I couldn't resist my hunger any longer, so I put on a fluffy bathrobe and made my way out into the beautiful sunshine, to table covered with a selection of delicious looking platters. A very handsome man pulled out a chair for me, and I stole a kiss as I settled down to this very impressive breakfast.

Ray informed me that he had called for me, saying that we would be working from home this morning. I thanked him, expressing how impressed I was with his abilities, while wondering how I would ever keep up with him. He mentioned that today he would begin preparing me to write my own story. After a moment of contemplation, I agreed, stating that I was in the happiest place I could ask for.

Ray then stated that he would meet me downstairs. He picked up the dishes, then kissed me, saying, "And so it begins!" Ray always knew how to make me laugh. I quickly dressed and tidied myself up before eagerly making my way down.

Twelve

Hannah And Shellys Story

As I entered the room, I found Ray organising a whole desk with a typewriter, Paper, notebooks, and a reading lamp. I looked around seeing beautiful polished wooden Shelves, with so many books, both old and newer. Some even leather bound. The room had a very calming effect on your mood. Ray turned to me and asked me if it was suitable. I hugged him and told him that it was perfect.

"Where do you write?" I asked Ray.

He took my hand and said, "You now get the guided tour of your second home."

We walked into the next room, it looked like mine, except it had a door that led out onto a veranda. There was a large, polished bar, with numerous bottles and glasses, and a few bar chairs, upholstered in deep rich leather. The small was so manly. But I quite liked it.

I asked, "What's outside of the glass doors at the back?"

Ray led me through the doors, out to a seated area with a beautiful pool, surrounded by hedges and garden settings. It took my breath away. We continued to walk past the pool area to another small but very classy house. I asked Ray who lived there. He told me that its usually used by guests that cannot drive home.

There was a stairway back inside Rays home, and I was very curious as to where it led. Ray walked me back inside and we headed up them. These stairs led to a set of bedrooms, bathrooms, and a hallway that had a small, separate spiral staircase. Which must lead to the attic.

"One day, this will be the children's area. Not to hide them, but for when they want to be away from the adults." Ray explained.

Back downstairs, we walked into a beautiful lounge room, attached to a dining room with seating for ten. I giggled and asked him if he was expecting to have eight children. But then Ray said that that will be up to me.

We went into the kitchen. It was so big.

"I wouldn't know how to fill all the cupboards!" I blurted out.

Ray teased me, and said, "There is plenty of room to store your baked beans!"

We both laughed. I told Ray that at least all his doors lead somewhere.

"Do you want to see the bedrooms next to ours?" Ray asked.

I told Ray that I saw them as we were standing at the stairway. There were both nurseries. One pink, and one blue.

"What can I say, I love children, and hope to fill those rooms one day." Ray said, laughing at the look on my face. Then he hugged me, and said, "I love you, but children will be your choice, as will the wedding date, the style, and where you want it to be held."

My heart was so full, it was bursting with warmth and love.

Ray said, "I think my princess has lost her voice."

I answered, saying, "If this is a dream, never wake me up." His kiss sealed our future. We decided that we would stop by Castle House to check on Jake before heading to work.

As we pulled up, I saw Shelly rushing out the door. She exclaimed, "I knew you were coming!"

I chuckled and remarked, "You look very happy."

Shelly blushed, then explained, "I've been helping Jake, probably just got hot. Come and see what we found!"

Ray greeted Shelly. She turned and apologised, saying, "So sorry, Ray, I'm overly excited!"

He laughed and glanced at me, commenting, "When is she not?"

We both laughed as we walked in, and then our laughter turned into astonishment when we discovered a room under the stairway.

Jake informed us, "We just removed the last of the floorboards."

Ray exclaimed, "That is so creepy, but wow, look at the antiques in there!"

Shelly turned to me and said, "Esmeralda is afraid of releasing other ghosts."

She was about to say something else when Ray approached and asked, "Now, what do you girls want to do?"

If Esmeralda was correct, it was too late now.

Jake suggested, "I can drop a ladder down if you want to go down."

We couldn't just cover it up again, but we needed a stairway.

Ray decided, "I will go down and see if there is a door to get out."

Shelly volunteered to join him. As for me, I was dressed in high heels for work.

I felt Esmeralda's presence, but there was a bad vibe with it.

Ray called up to say, "All safe, Shelly!" And expressed his amazement with a few wows as he wandered around.

Shelly exclaimed, "There is a door! But it's locked as well."

If only we could find that key, I pondered.

Jake suggested, "I can just knock it out."

We had to make a decision, and Shelly yelled, "Yes, let's do it!"

I agreed, and Jake went down with his sledgehammer. Now, I was alone, and I saw Esmeralda appear. She looked scared.

She said, "Bad vibes!"

I asked her, "Did you know this room was here?"

She replied, "No, I never was interested in all the horrid family history."

Just then, Ray called, saying, "The door is off."

Shelly called for me to take off my shoes and come down. I followed her instructions and saw what had her excited. There were more rooms in the hallway and another stairway. The stench was overpowering us. Jake and Ray were just watching us.

I said, "We need to see if there is a way out before we close it back up for the stairway!"

They replied, "After you, girls," laughing!

Shelly said, "Come on, Hannah, leave the babies here. We know our bracelets will keep us safe."

Stepping into the hallway, the smell of dust and musty stale air was even worse!

We stepped back into the room, saying, "We will wait until more fresh air gets in."

Jake suggested, "You can hire big air fans. I will get some and let you know when it's breathable."

We took it all in and knew that this was only the beginning! We all went back up. Shelly wanted to talk, but we couldn't. I told her that I would call her.

Ray asked Jake, "Are you okay with organising the fans? Let me know if you need anything. I just have to drop Hannah off at work."

Jake asked Shelly, "Are you okay here, or do you want to come with me?"

Shelly chose to go with Jake, and they left together.

On our way to my office, Ray asked if there was something wrong with Shelly.

I said, "No, she just hates waiting."

He laughed and said, "She is going to need a man who can do adventure!"

I said, "Yes, you're right! But once she starts teaching, she will put a lot of effort into the children."

As we pulled up at work, Ray asked, "Do you want me to come in?"

I laughed and said, "No, you will disrupt them even more!"

I kissed him and said, "Ring me if you miss me!"

He took out his phone to call me. My heart was so full. This man was my everything!

As I entered the office, everyone was still excited.

I said, "I'm still in the clouds, but I will try to come back down to catch up."

They laughed and said, "Good luck, your sticky notes are having babies!"

Settling into my office, I noticed the pile of sticky notes. I started at the bottom since they had been waiting the longest. Sometime after, I looked at the clock and realised why I felt so hungry. It was already three o'clock, but too late to grab a burger, so I settled for an office coffee.

I heard our front door open, and as I looked up, I saw an arm holding a bag of burgers. What followed next was a very handsome face peeking around the corner.

Ray walked in, and said, "Time out!" Then he sat on my table, and said, "It will cost you!"

I could hear the hushed giggles at reception, as I was enveloped by his arms. I stayed there until my stomach growled.

Ray said, "I have to feed the beast."

He allowed me to eat in peace while he told me what was happening at Castle House. Just as he was about to continue, my phone rang. He assured me that it was okay.

I answered the call, and Shelly was very hysterical. She blurted out that she was in her bedroom at her mother's house, when a sudden coldness enveloped her. When she turned, she saw a creature. She said that huge hands reached out at her from the mirror, and when she screamed her mum rushed in, and the creature disappeared. Shelly said that her mum said that she must have been daydreaming.

I asked Shelly, "Do you need me to come to you?"

She replied, "I think I'm okay, while my mum is here!"

I said, "I will check on you later." Then hung up.

Ray hadn't heard the conversation but said, "Your face tells me that Shelly isn't feeling well?"

I nodded and replied, "Yes, but her mum is with her."

Ray then continued to tell me what had happened. "When Jake returned to the house, vandals must have broken in and trashed the room we found."

I needed to go there immediately and make sure that Esmeralda was okay. However, I also needed Shelly. I asked Ray if he wasn't busy, would he mind taking me to see Shelly.

He responded, "Let's go. I wanted to check the house out anyway, just to make sure no one is still there!"

We left, saying, "See you all tomorrow."

Ray then asked, "Where's Frank?"

I replied, "Mr. Winton hasn't been in today."

He expressed his concern, saying, "I hope he's okay." It hadn't crossed my mind as he was often out of the office.

As we got to Shellys mums house, we walked in and greeted them.

Shelly immediately stood up and said, "Can you come to my room for a second?"

Ray sat and spoke with Shellys mum, while I walked off with Shelly. She was very disturbed by the creature that had appeared in her mirror. I assured her, that we would go and check on Esmeralda. and have a talk with her in the kitchen.

We put on a fake smile as we walked back out to the lounge room, and said, "Let's go and see what these vandals have done!"

Shelly's mum reminded us to be careful and told Shelly to be home for dinner, as she had a roast cooking. She also invited both Ray and I to join them, if we wanted. We thanked her but mentioned that tonight we might need to get some rest early. She hugged us goodbye as we headed out the door.

As we drove up to our Castle House, we saw Jake carrying some lumber. Ray said, "You girls go inside. I'll grab some of this for Jake."

We both entered the house and immediately felt a chill. Esmeralda was still here, so we greeted Jake then headed to the kitchen.

Esmeralda was waiting for us, but her aura was fading in and out. She explained that she had fought off the evil spirit, but it had been locked up for such a long time and was now after any ancestors of hers that it could find.

We told her that we weren't blood relatives, to which she replied, "That's why it is out searching!"

Shelly shared that it had come through her mirror. Esmeralda hoped that it would eventually leave and continue its hunt elsewhere. She informed us that she needed to rest in case the other evil spirit tried to return. We felt guilty for not being here with her, but Ray called out, and she left.

I asked, "Did he mention if anything else was missing or damaged?"

Ray answered, "No, but we could check the storage room."

Ray grabbed the key and opened the door, but everything seemed unchanged. Ray mentioned that Jake believed the air under the stairs would be fine tomorrow, and asked if I wanted to go downstairs to see if there was anything I wanted to secure, but there was nothing we were worried about.

We went to speak with Jake. He apologised and said, "I'm sure I locked the door. It seems like they might have come in through another entrance."

Ray suggested that Jake have another worker with him, and Jake asked if he had someone in mind.

Ray replied, "Yes, he helped me with your construction."

We waited while Ray made the call, and he returned to us saying, "All good. You will have help starting tomorrow."

Jake explained, "We can prepare the staircase in stages on the floor. This will give you time to work on the lower level." He added, "I'll continue working as I have a few more trips to the dump. Tomorrow, there will be a big delivery with all the necessary sizes cut." Then suggested, "I had a quick look around, and I think you should focus on the kitchen next. Do you have a budget for each room?"

Shelly and I told Jake that we were happy to pay whatever it would cost to finish, and that we would leave it up to him to design away.

Once again, Jake said to Ray, "You're one lucky man. Most women hover over my shoulder while I'm working!"

Shelly must have imagined this scenario and started laughing at the thought.

Jake said, "I'm serious, they would never carry dirty wood and rubbish like you did for me!"

Shelly blushed and said, "I like being helpful."

I chimed in, "Well, let us know if you need to be paid upfront so you're not out of pocket."

Jake replied, "By Friday, I should have a good idea of what you'll be paying."

We agreed to stop by tomorrow and see how things were progressing. We planned to wear appropriate clothing for exploring and bring flashlights in case there was no power.

Jake then asked Shelly, "Do you want to help me load up another dump run? I can drop you off at home after."

Shelly quickly agreed, and they walked off together.

Curious, I asked Ray to tell me more about his friend that was coming to help. He explained that when he worked for his father's company, a guy called Shaz was doing his apprenticeship with him. Ray praised Shaz's natural talent for visualising what something would require to make it more efficient. He mentioned that Shaz had a girlfriend in the past but wasn't sure what happened. He simply said that Shaz said he was too busy for drama.

We drove off, chatting about dinner plans, and I was jokingly suggesting that I could have a bubble bath while Ray worked his culinary magic.

Ray responded, "Challenge accepted!"

I teased, "Really? You also like cooking? My lucky star just keeps shining on me."

Ray playfully told me to enjoy my bubbles and then dress for dinner, as he would meet me in the dining room. It all felt like a dream, but one that I'd happily wish to continue.

I made my way down to the dining room and found a beautifully candle-lit table. Ray came up behind me, hugged me, and pulled out my chair. He poured wine and went to bring out the dinner. When he returned and placed my dinner in front of me. I was speechless.

Ray sat down and lifted his glass, saying, "To us!"

Dinner was absolutely incredible, and I couldn't help but ask, "Do you have a chef hiding in the kitchen?"

He laughed and said, "You always see the funny side of everything! I once took a chef course for a novel I was writing. I wanted to be knowledgeable about what I was writing about." He continued, "There was a time when I had to write about a sailing ship, so I decided to take a sailing course."

No wonder your books are bestsellers," I remarked. "You do more than just research."

He replied, "It makes it more interesting for me as well. For my next book, I'm thinking of going to France to experience and understand the lifestyle. Maybe we could have our honeymoon there. It would make it more genuine and memorable."

I agreed, saying, "That would be wonderful. I've always wanted to travel, and one of the few things my dad did, was give me a book with pictures from around the world."

Ray then said, "That's what we'll do, then."

My heart raced with excitement once again.

He asked, "Do you want dessert or an early night?"

I chose an early night. He pulled out my chair and said, "The leprechauns will take care of the kitchen. I will escort my beautiful fiancée to her bed."

The next morning, we woke up entwined in each other's arms, without a care in the world. We were both happy to stay there forever. However, the phone had other plans for us. Ray moaned as he left me to answer it, but it was Frank calling him.

I overheard Ray saying, "That's alright, Frank. I understand. I'll come in with Hannah."

I quickly showered and dressed and made my way downstairs to see if everything was alright. Ray emerged from his office just as I was about to enter.

He laughed and said, "I always knew life would be full of surprises with you."

Before I could ask, he explained, "Frank just wanted to apologise for not being able to come to my book launch on Friday."

I asked if Frank was okay, and Ray informed me that he had a minor surgery that was needed sooner rather than later. I didn't pry further, as I knew he would share if he wanted to. My initial thought was that's why Frank wasn't at work yesterday. I asked if he was coming in today, and Ray confirmed that he was just coming to pick up some things and inform the staff about the book release details for Friday. He also mentioned that he hoped I would be able to accompany him to the event.

I replied, "Always."

We had a quick breakfast and then headed to work. While Ray spoke with Frank, I called Shelly. She reassured me that she was fine but would avoid going near the mirror. I asked Shelly if Shaz was working today, and she confirmed that he was at our house with Jake, and that he had someone else coming to help them. She mentioned that he wanted her to stop by with lunch, then laughed. Curious, I asked Shelly what time she was heading there.

Shelly replied, "Around midday. Will you come down?"

I replied, "Hopefully. I'm getting caught up."

We said our goodbyes and hung up.

When Ray walked in, I was engrossed in my world on the computer. I had so many emails from authors, asking me to read their manuscripts. Ray came up behind me and gently held my hands to stop me from typing. I jumped and accidentally bumped his chin. Even though he said it wasn't that bad, Ray was looking for sympathy. Standing up, I kissed it better.

He mentioned that he needed to go and organise some things for Friday night and asked if I would like to come along. I was about to decline, but he insisted, saying that it would be a good experience for me, as he usually handles these things on his own. I agreed and closed my computer.

Mr. Winston appeared at my office door, and said, "If you want to take the day off, I'll stay here. It's part of your job now, Hannah."

He also mentioned that I needed to buy a phone, and that I could put it on the company account. He asked me to send him my number once I had sorted it out, then added that he wasn't sure how long it would take, but he would be able to call me anytime, which would be better than trying to get through on the office phones.

I agreed, as it had become a nightmare trying to communicate. I wished him well with his procedure, and Ray shook his hand, saying, "All the best, mate."

We headed off in Rays car. I was still getting used to being a passenger, when Ray mentioned that it was time for me to start learning how to drive, and eventually buy my own car.

I replied with a "yes" and mentioned that Shelly also wanted to be more self-reliant.

Ray was pleased and suggested that we check out some cars together. He asked if I had a particular style in mind. I mentioned that I liked the little mini's, and how awesome it was that they were painted in number of fun colours.

He laughed and asked, "No sports cars?"

I replied, "No, my hair would never survive the wind!"

We both laughed, and he said, "Very logical. And when you want to let your hair down, we'll take mine!"

We arrived outside a very ritzy hotel, and a doorman opened the door for us. We were escorted into a glitzy room.

A young lady greeted us and said, "Just get a feel for the room, then let me know where you would like things to be placed."

She excused herself while Ray carefully studied the room. He mentioned that there would usually be around one hundred guests, who would be expecting cocktails and hors d'oeuvres, and that they prefer scattered seating and a few tall tables. Ray thought it would be best to have his book signing table in the middle of the side wall, with the window behind him.

"In case we need a quick exit!" he looked at me and laughed, "just kidding!"

I replied, "This event is much bigger than any I have attended before."

Ray responded, "Well, you'll be attending a lot more now that you have your new position."

As I thought about it, I realised Ray was right. I needed to learn more about these events and be prepared for the next author's book signing. I never fully understood what Mr. Winston was doing when he was out of the office. But now I'm getting more of an understanding.

Ray had been given a menu and catering cost, which surprised me.

I jokingly remarked, "Their drinks will cost more than the price of a book!"

Ray laughed again, then said, "The guests invited are owners of bookstores, and members of ladies' reading clubs. Some attendees are also from schools, checking out books for educational literacy. Others are influential figures on the social scene. If they recommend a book, it'll be in every home by the next day! Men's groups are also part of the audience, and they'll recommend it if they enjoy it. The main goal is to gain recognition beyond just this state. Most of the bookstores are chain stores. I've also invited owners of large retailers worldwide. They buy in bulk, which greatly helps with distribution. The media plays a crucial role in these functions as well. They will interview the well-known guests."

I suddenly had a light bulb moment! Curious, I asked, "How many of these events do you attend, Ray?"

He answered, "It depends on how well the book takes off. I've done overseas tours and have been invited as a guest speaker on television and radio. Usually, they cover the organising and flights. The media is everything. Now that I'm an established author, readers eagerly await my next novel. I consider myself lucky to make a very good living from writing. It took a long time to get here, but now I can take it slower and enjoy my passion."

Finally, I expressed, "I've led a sheltered life up until now. Mr. Winston has placed a lot of faith in me."

Ray saw my apprehension and reassured me, "You're a learner, and each new endeavour will make you more confident. You have the ability, and I'll always support you. We'll make a great team."

I agreed, saying, "You're right. I love challenging my abilities, and even more, I love excelling at what I do!"

Taking the menu, I continued, "Show me what you think is best, and then you must teach me about wines, and familiarise me with the attendees. I'll need to engage in conversations with them, and knowledge is key."

Ray hugged me and said, "I knew you had all these hidden talents, just waiting to be challenged!"

Ray and I made the necessary arrangements with Kylie, the events coordinator. As we were about to leave, I mentioned to Ray that I wanted to buy a mobile for work but needed to stop by Castle House to see Shelly first.

Ray responded, "Great, I wanted to have a chat with Shaz. It feels like every day now is an opportunity for us to become scholars again."

Just as we pulled up, we saw them all on their lunch break. Shelly came out excitedly and said they had found another key. Apparently, it was hidden in the kitchen behind a curtain, and they had almost thrown away the entire kitchen!

I laughed and said, "I thought you were just bringing the men lunch!"

Shelly laughed, then remarked, "Well, you woke me up early, and I had nothing to do. I love helping!"

We all headed inside. Ray spoke with Shaz, while Shelly and I went to the kitchen to talk with Esmeralda.

I asked Esmeralda if she was okay, and she manifested, saying "Yes, but we have to stay vigilant because our powers are only effective together."

This was difficult since we weren't always together. So, I asked Esmeralda if she could send a vibration or something to let me know if Shelly needed me, anytime that we were apart. Esmeralda said she didn't know, but mentioned tha the book might have the answer.

We informed Esmeralda that we had found a key and wanted to try it in the door at the back. Esmeralda revealed that she had never known about, let alone opened that door.

Shelly asked Esmeralda if the evil creature had returned, and she replied, "No, but if it did, would it come through the same portal?"

Esmeralda confirmed that these portals were not visible to the human eye, but evil spirits could transport through them. Shelly asked if covering the mirror would stop them.

Esmeralda said "Yes." Then explained that we would always feel the cold before the spirits came through, and if there was no portal, they would move on.

Shelly then asked how we could identify a portal, but Esmeralda sadly replied that there was no way.

As the men approached the kitchen, Esmeralda left.

Ray said, "There you are, Shaz has some great ideas for the kitchen. Do you mind if he shows you?"

"Not at all, show away!" Shelly said, with what looked to be slightly blushed over cheeks.

Shaz's ideas for the kitchen were amazing, and far better than we had imagined. He suggested ordering everything and paying for them by the time of delivery. Another task successfully organised! It made me realise that Shaz excelled in his work. It made me think, to receive recognition, one had to be the best at what they did, and this was now my challenge.

Shelly shook me, asking if I was okay. I laughed and assured her that I was fine, suggesting we try the key. This time, Ray joined us. We expected the same foul air, so we held our arms over our noses, as the door creaked and opened. We moved some items out of the way, so that we could get a better look in. Shelly held my hand, as Ray pulled the door the rest of the way open.

The smell this time was even worse. We only had flashlights, but it seemed like an old bathroom with another door on the other side.

This time, Ray said, "NO!" Holding his arm in our way.

We decided to bring in professionals to check the floors and ceilings, as they might be rotted. We headed back out, then locked the storage room door again. Jake asked Shelly if she was staying, as they had another dump run ready. She declined and asked Ray if he could drop her home. Jake left, and we locked up the house.

Ray suggested that we had time to buy a phone, and Shelly asked if she could come along. We both agreed, and Ray took us to a shopping centre he knew. It had so many shops that we felt like we were in heaven. Ray jokingly asked if he could trust us not to get lost, and we laughed, assuring him that we would be fine, even if they locked us in. He instructed us to meet him back at the café when we were done.

We started at the first shop but soon realised that we needed a trolley. We found one from the grocery store in the walkway, which was perfect. Then continued our shopping adventure. We checked out a few dress shops, and I spotted a stunning dress on a mannequin. Shelly encouraged me to try it on, and the assistant happily took it off for me. I felt like a princess as I went out to show Shelly. She contained her excitement, only barely, giving her approval, and as I paid for the dress at the counter, I choked at the price!

Realising that there was only half an hour until closing time. I suggested that we head back to the cafe.

Ray spotted us approaching with our trolley, laughed, and said, "Well done, ladies, only one trolley full!" He loaded our purchases into the car, as he asked, "Where to next?"

I replied, "Can we drop most of this off at Castle House?"

Ray was more than happy to swing by.

As we drove in, a feeling of unease washed over me, but it was probably just because it was getting dark. We all grabbed our bags, and Ray unlocked the door, then flicked on the light switch. Everything seemed the same, so we decided to unload in the dining room. However, we quickly changed our minds when the lights started flickering.

We stood still, waiting for them to come back on, but nothing happened.

Ray said, "Wait here, I will go and get the flashlight from the lounge room."

As he left, we felt a chill in the air, but nothing appeared. We wondered where Esmeralda was. Soon, Ray returned and safely led us out.

I asked Shelly if her mum was expecting her home, and she replied, "No, but I could give her a call."

I turned to Ray and asked what he was thinking. He suggested we get some dinner, and all go back to his house, that way Shelly and I could catch up and he could make some calls. Ray then asked us what our favourite takeout was. We both answered in sync, telling him that we loved Chinese.

Ray chuckled and commented, "You two really love Chinese, don't you?"

We grabbed our dinner then jumped back into the car, and as we headed back to Rays house, the aroma of the food made my mouth water.

Shelly saw the driveway, she couldn't help but gasp. Ray laughed at her reaction, as he was prepared this time for the excitement. He opened the doors and told us to go inside while he brought in our bags. It still felt a bit strange, but I knew the way, so I led Shelly into the house.

She couldn't contain herself when we walked in, and started tearing up, expressing how happy she was for me, and how deserving I was of this.

Ray came up behind us and remarked, "You are a beautiful friend, Shelly. Most girls would be jealous."

I held back my tears, feeling so grateful to have such a wonderful friend, and now a wonderful man. Ray gave us a hug and encouraged us to go to the dining room. He went to the kitchen while we sat at the table, and he brought in our dinners along with placemats and cutlery.
Shelly jokingly commented, "This isn't takeout anymore!"

Ray laughed and asked, "Would madame like a glass of wine with her dinner?"

Shelly replied, "Yes, madame would," and we all giggled.

Dinner was lively and full of conversation. Eventually, Ray excused himself to make his calls, and I told him that we would be in the bubble room.

Shelly followed me, providing a colourful description of the house as we walked. When she saw the bath, she exclaimed, "You must be joking!"

I ran the bath for her, saying, "Your bubbles await you!" I gave her some of my clothes and knew that I wouldn't see her for a while. Ray was still on the phone, so I went downstairs to clean up the kitchen.
Ray must have heard me, as he snuck up behind me and wrapped his arms around my waist. His kisses were making me dizzy, so I wiggled out of his embrace and said, "Sir, I am spoken for!"

He replied, "I demand full payment for the use of my cutlery!"

I giggled and ran back up the stairs.

He warned, "You have escaped this time, but rest assured, my memory is long!"

I laughed, and Shelly exclaimed, "Oh, to be a princess! Where is my knight?"

I answered, "He is fighting off your suitors, and once he has defeated them, he will sweep you away on his white stallion to his castle on the hill!" I heard her laughter, and my heart was filled with joy. Who would have thought that this would be my life? Shelly has this to look forward to as well. I wonder who her knight will be.

Shelly emerged from the bathroom and asked, "If that was the bubble room, then can you please show me where I'm sleeping?"

We walked down the hallway, and Shelly saw the nurseries. She exclaimed, "She hasn't made a peep!"

I took her to the visitors' side, where she fell in love with the palm trees on the walls. I told her she could name her room, and she chose to call it the Bahamas.

We spoke for a while, and then I heard a voice saying, "Wherefore art thou?"

I laughed and replied, "In the Bahamas room!"

Ray asked, "Do you need me to escort you to your bubble room?"

Shelly giggled and said, "Go to your man. I will sleep in the Bahamas tonight."

We both wished each other sweet dreams, and I closed her door, feeling like I was floating down the stairway into the waiting arms of my love. He asked if Shelly had settled in her tower, and I replied, "She is sleeping in the Bahamas room."

He chuckled and said, "Of course she is." Then he asked where I would be heading.

I said, "To the bubbles room."

He smiled and said, "I like that. Shall we retire to our bubbles?"

I replied, "I feel like I'm already floating in bubbles."

Thirteen

The Event!

Days flew by with my work. Shaz needed assistance with me answering some questions, and then Ray had another request to do a book signing in London. He was overjoyed with this opportunity, expecting a very big formal evening hosted in the grand library. Shelly was great at helping Shaz, to the extent that I felt she enjoyed his company. My new phone was both a blessing and a hindrance. I would hang up from my work calls expecting to continue with finishing a manuscript, only to have my phone ring asking if I could contact someone for payment related to the event. They claimed they couldn't get through on my work line.

Finally, Friday came, and I hoped I had planned it perfectly. Ray called asking if I could leave early as he had a private meeting beforehand. I agreed.

I called Shelly to let her know I was turning off my phone for a while to finish work and asked if she needed anything.

"Something is wrong with Esmeralda!" Shelly said. She sounded unsettled, saying Esmeralda hadn't been at the house all day, and that the cold was getting worse.

I knew what this meant. I asked if the kitchen floor had been re-laid, and Shelly told me that it had. She also said that the walls were back up too. I asked her if anyone had gone back into the storage room. Shelly said she hadn't, but it was possible that Shaz or his apprentice might have.

I asked, "Does Shaz need you there? I can't come to be with you."

She answered uncertainly, saying, "But what if it's another evil spirit? Should we leave Shaz here alone?"

I felt helpless. I couldn't think of a reason to tell Shaz to go home, but I didn't want Shelly there either.

Shelly said, "I can't get upstairs to see if Esmeralda is up there."

It was strange that Esmeralda wasn't with Shelly. I told Shelly she needed to leave and that we would both be there tomorrow, along with Jake and his dad.

Shelly said, "I'm not sure if Shaz is safe or not."

I replied, "All you can do is tell him you have to go, and it's okay if he wants the afternoon off."

Shelly said, "Okay, I will try."

Hanging up was unsettling for me, as I had felt for days that something was wrong. Tonight was too important for Ray, for me not to be with him. I closed my computer just as Ray walked into my office, and he immediately asked what was wrong. I told him that it was nothing, and that it had just been a hectic day. He hugged me and said that the bubbles were waiting for me back at home.

I turned to my sticky notes and told them, *'Until Monday'*. Ray and I said our goodbyes to everyone at the office and left.

My mind was churning as I turned on my phone, and saw a message from Shelly, that read:

'Shaz wouldn't leave, but I did.'

Ray began talking, and said that tonight would be a great night, and that I would meet many special people, and make great contacts for my next event. Annnd, be introduced as his fiancée. I looked at him, beaming, and thought, I had to focus on Ray and do my best to make him proud.

Ray held my hand and said, "You're going to be the talk of the room tonight. I'll be lucky to get a look in."

I said, "Well, I am your publisher!"

My mood shifted back to the evening events, making my mark in this new world with my soon-to-be husband.

Back at Rays house, I had my bath and began to get ready for the event. I put on my beautiful new gown and started doing my hair and makeup.

Ray walked in with a velvet box and said, "This is the first of many surprises you will receive for the rest of your life."

I opened it, and within was an emerald necklace. He asked if he could put it on for me, and when I looked in the mirror, it was stunning! It even went so well with my new dress.

Ray pulled out another small box, saying it was for his bride-to-be as well. This time, I couldn't stop the tears.

Ray kissed my tears away, and said, "Put them on, so my eyes can see how they frame your natural radiance."

Now I felt like Cinderella with her prince.

Ray said, "How could you possibly be more beautiful?" Then guided me down the staircase, out the door, and into his chariot.

As we entered the event, the room was set up perfectly.

I had a proud moment, as a man in a tuxedo, stepped forward to shake Ray's hand, and said, "Thank you for meeting me early."

Then this man looked at me, and said, "Ray, who is the vision holding your arm?"

Ray's face shone as he said, "This is my fiancé, Hannah."

I smiled and said, "Very pleased to meet you."

The man replied, "The pleasure is all mine. Would you like me to introduce you to my wife and daughter? They will be very excited to meet the lady who stole this one's heart."

Ray said, "She certainly has done that. But this vision is also my publisher."

I was escorted to a table where two very elegant ladies were sitting.

As I was introduced, their smiles turned into an invitation to sit with them.

I looked at Ray, who said, "We have business to discuss. I'll leave you with these beautiful ladies until I can join you." He leaned over and kissed me in front of them, and I blushed as I sat down.

I found myself enjoying the night more than I had imagined I would. I had so many conversations and received lots of envious looks from certain young ladies. This was a new world, and for a minute, I watched from the doorway thinking, Hannah, who would've ever thought this would be your path in life?

I snuck out into the hallway to make a call and check on Shelly. She said that everything was okay, and that her mum and dad were home with her. I told her to wear some old clothes tomorrow, so that we could search the house until we find Esmeralda, or the evil demon, and expel it to the depths it came from.

Shelly brightened up, and said, "Yes, it's time we took ownership of our house!"

Hanging up, I felt good. That thing was not going to spoil my life, or hurt Esmeralda.

Ray came out and said that I was being asked to join him, for photographs.

I said, "Let's do this!"

As everyone left, they spoke about what a wonderful night it was and how lovely it was to meet Ray's fiancée, and the new editor.

Ray finally signed his last book and came over to help me say goodnight to everyone.

He whispered to me, "You have made a very good impression on a lot of people tonight."

I looked at him and said, "We do make a great team!" He kissed me, and a flash went off in our direction.

Morning came too early, and Ray and I pulled the covers over our heads. Eventually, guilt got the better of us.

I said, "I have promised to spend the day with Shelly at the house. Could you drop me there?"

Ray said, "It will cost you!"

I jumped out of bed, and said, "You can collect your price tonight."

His answer was, "Now it's doubled!"

I laughed because he was so easy going, and nothing was too much trouble.

We decided to take coffee and donuts around to the house, for everyone.

Ray said, "You are such a caring soul. You make me want to hug you all day, and night!"

I replied, "That might be hard to do when I have clients," and we both laughed.

He said, "From the gossip I overheard last night, you will be getting a lot of major writers coming your way!"

As we pulled into the driveway, we saw so many cars parked on the lawn. This was going to be a very hectic day! Ray said that he had a phone call to make but would get back to me as soon as possible.

I kissed him and said, "We have this! Girl power!"

He jokingly said, "If anyone else said that to me, I would be worried!"

I told him to say hi to everyone. Then I kissed him goodbye.

I headed into the demolition zone of Castle House, where I found Jake and Shelly putting up a sheet of plasterboard.

Shelly said, "I thought you were here, but couldn't move as I was holding this up!"

Jake asked me what my thoughts were on everything that they had done to the kitchen so far.

I took it all in, then answered, "This is incredible! How did you make the kitchen bigger?"

Shelly was excited to tell me, that when they knocked down the walls, they discovered an old veranda, so they extended the side wall. She also mentioned that when Jake went outside, he found a door, but she told him to wait and see if I wanted him to open it, or just wall it in.

I asked Shelly if Esmeralda was here, because I couldn't feel her presence, and Shelly said no. We knew we could fight off a demon ghost, but we didn't want to let them into our world. Shelly suggested we check the storage room that we have a key to, as it might lead to the one we're looking for.

I said, "I'm ready to go. We have lots of flashlights, and we need to be able to feel safe in our own home."

I could tell Shelly was scared, but we assured Jake that we were going into the storage room to check what was there.

He said, "Holler if you need help lifting anything," and also asked what we wanted to do about the stairway.

It had been assembled, but we still needed to put a floor down.

I looked at Shelly and asked, "Should we do that first?"

She nodded and said, "Okay."

Jake mentioned that the ladder was still in there and asked if we wanted him to come.

I replied, "No, we'll holler if we find a dead body!"

He laughed and said, "You girls are tougher than most girls!"
We chuckled, thinking if only he knew.

We put on our masks and loaded our pockets with torches, then descended into the smashed-up room. The moment our feet touched the ground, we felt the cold. Turning on all our lights, we opened the inner door. It was still very musty, but the machine was still pumping fresh air in. As we walked, we tripped and both grabbed each other, only to see a huge tree root coming through the floor.
We had reached the first door, which was locked, but the key worked in this one as well. It felt heavy, and we had to push hard to open it. When our eyes adjusted to the light, we saw old furniture, and what looked like a boarded-up window.
As we walked towards the window, we stumbled over something. It moved and made weird sounds. We quickly got to our feet and turned the lights towards the ground, to see what had tripped us over.

We both screamed! Jake called from above, asking if we were okay. We had tripped over a human skeleton!

We both yelled out, "NO!"

He called out to the other workers, saying he needed help. We hadn't moved, but they made their way to us, and obviously also tripping on the tree root, based on the words we heard. Then they saw what had scared us. They all said the same expletive.

Jake said, "I think we need the police."

Shelly and I agreed, and realised, that we now knew where the other evil spirit had come from.

We showed Jake the window and he asked, "Do you want us to knock it open?"

I replied, "Yes, we need to know what else is down here."

The men had tools with them, and while the apprentice, still in shock, went up to call the police, we used our flashlights to explore another room with a door on the far side.

Jake commented, "This place is like a maze. Pity there are no building plans."

We asked Jake if the ceilings were safe to continue.

One of the other men, who was tall, stood on the old rickety chair and pushed on some of the wood. He said, "It's wood, not plaster, so it should be safe!"

Jake told us to wait while they knocked a bigger hole to get through. As we waited, we felt a cold breeze pass us.

Then the man who was still standing at the door said, "Wow, there's a cold breeze coming from somewhere!"

We both knew there was only one thing that could cause that, and we had just let it out.

Jake had gotten through the window, and said, "It's an old bathroom, so maybe there's another bedroom through the next door!"

Shelly and I went through the hole, now expecting the worst. The space was very tiny and smelled terrible.

Jake asked, "Are we doing this?"

We couldn't help but wonder if we would let out another demon, and if we could even handle more than one. Had they hurt Esmeralda?
The tall man suggested that they check if the floor was safe to be built on.

Shelly agreed, saying, "That's true. We don't want this to affect our house. If these are what's holding our house up."

I walked over with the key and, once again, the same key worked. My heart was racing, but Shelly seemed to be handling it well. As they pushed the door open, we saw a stairway going up.

The tall man exclaimed, "Wow, we need to see if this is safe before you girls go up there!"

Jake wasn't saying no. I think all of this fascinated him more than any of us. He started to climb, and the boards scattered dust everywhere.

Luckily, we had masks on. Jake kept going. When he reached the top, he called down to say that it was a door but not locked.

He asked, "Do you want me to keep going?" And suggested that it could be the entrance to the other hallway behind the storage room.

We both followed Jake up the stairway. He was right. It opened into the hallway where the other rooms were. the ones we had seen from the storage room. Now, we felt safer being back on the normal level of this weird house.

The men all seemed to be enjoying this horror show, while Shelly and I were hoping there wouldn't be any more cold breezes. We entered the hall.

"I can't wait to draw up the plan of this place. The cellar turned into a bedroom and bathroom for visitors, even though there are already so many rooms! It's so weird," Jake commented.

The plumber tested the floor and confirmed that it was safe. But when he tried to open the first door, it was locked.

Jake questioned, "Why lock doors?"

I gave them the key. Shelly and I were happy to just follow along, even though the smell of stale mouldy air hit us again. I asked Jake to open the door at the end of the hall, and then go through the storage room to open that door as well. I thought at least some fresh air might make it's way through.

Jake said, "I will move the air machine into the storage room."

Shelly and I agreed that it was a great idea. We were starting to feel light-headed from the lack of air.

I suggested, "We should go to the storage room and take a break." The plumber agreed and went with us.

He asked if we had owned the house for very long.

We replied, "No, but it's certainly a money pit!"

He laughed and said, "It's much more than that!"

He went through the storage room to help Jake bring in the air machine, while we went and sat on the chair that Ray had cleared, to read his book in. It was a chance for us to regroup.

Shelly said, "I think that sounds like the police are here!"

We went out and saw them talking with Jake. Ray came through the door, followed by Jake and his dad.

I quickly said, "We're all okay, but there's a skeleton underneath the floor in those rooms!"

Ray, who had already grabbed me, exclaimed, "What the f-word?"

The police turned to Jake and asked, "Can you show us where this is?"

I went to go with them, but Ray held us both back, saying, "This is their job now. I think you girls can come with me for a coffee."

We both took it as a wake-up call and agreed.

I said to Ray, "Yes, you're right. Jake knows as much as we do."

We walked past the kitchen, and Ray commented, "Now that's a kitchen!"

Shelly proudly said, "I've been helping them."

Ray laughed and said, "Of course you have. There's nothing you girls can't do!"

Again, I thought, if only you knew! The fresh air outside was wonderful, and our heads cleared. We went to a place by the river, enjoying the quiet. Ray came back with coffee and sandwiches.

We found a grassy spot under a tree, and I said, "What a beautiful place to write."

I saw his eyes light up and he asked, "Are you feeling ready to start?"

Shelly looked at me and said, "Really, are you going to?"

I thought about it for a moment and then replied, "Yes, I am ready."

The conversation shifted from one topic to another, as we caught up on everything we had been doing.

Then Ray said, "I forgot, with all the excitement, why I came."

He went back to the car and retrieved something from the trunk. He seemed very pleased with whatever it was. First, he gave Shelly a signed book.

She squealed and said, "Thank you!"

She continued, "I saw the event on the news. There were so many well-to-do people in the room that I couldn't spot you guys!"

I exclaimed, "Wow, I never even saw the camera people there!"

Ray let Shelly settle down, then handed me the newspaper. We were on the front page with a huge write-up, and more pictures below it, from the event. Shelly couldn't contain her excitement as I read it out loud.

Ray sat with his arm around me and said, "This is the most exposure I have had for any of my books!"

When I saw my name as the publisher, I got goosebumps. And then it mentioned "the soon-to-be Mrs. Hannah Sallinger."

Ray hugged me and said, "We need to set a date."

I hadn't thought about it, but I agreed, "Yes, we need to work with our schedules now!"

Shelly had taken the paper to read it again, while I asked Ray if he had heard any more about his trip to England.

He chuckled and said, "You're also a mind reader!" He continued, "Yes, I had a call today and it has been booked for November 10th. They will send tickets, hotel arrangements, and event details this week."

He was beaming with excitement, and I knew that this was his life, and his passion. I was marrying the right man. We were already in sync with each other, and best of all, he loved Shelly and her parents, just as much as I do.

While thinking about this, I realised that we had never spoken about his family. Just then, his phone rang, and Shelly started speaking again. Ray wandered off to take his call.

He was laughing and enjoying his phone conversation.

Shelly finished reading and hugged me, saying, "My sister is a celebrity!"

I laughed and replied, "It was a lot of fun meeting so many lovely people, but most of them were wealthy owners of big companies like Myers, David Jones, and big book distributors. Some of the young ladies weren't that interested in me though!"

Shelly chuckled and said, "I bet they weren't!"

Ray came back and asked, "What are you two giggling about?" We both looked guilty, and he said, "Oh, one of those discussions, women only!"

He mentioned that Frank had seen the news, and the newspaper, and wanted to congratulate us on such a great event. He continued to tell me that he told him about the offer to go to London, and that Frank was ecstatic. He said that Frank suggested, that because I have so much holiday time, we should extend the stay.

I exclaimed, "Wow, that's true. I never bothered with holidays."

Shelly said, "I can't take this all in. My mind is overloaded with happiness!"

Ray suggested that we should go back to the house and see what's happening. Shelly and I agreed.

"Yes, we need to continue our quest. So that Shaz could give us some stairs back." Shelly said.

While driving back, Ray asked Shelly, "Do you want to get your driver's license as well?"

Shelly looked at me, and then said, "Yes."

Ray replied, "Good, I will book you in for lessons as well. What time of day suits you?"

Shelly answered, "In the morning."

I added, "I might have to do it after five."

Ray assured us, "I will arrange for both of you at the same time." Then said, "We need to find Hannah a car. Would you like to look as well, Shelly?"

This was something we had been putting off, but we knew we needed to be mobile.

Shelly responded, "Yes, that would be great!"

As we pulled into the driveway, the undertaker's car was just leaving. This quickly brought our mood down. I asked Ray if they would be able to do tests to identify who it was.

He replied, "More than likely, as they know it has to be someone from this household." He continued, trying to scare us, "Unless they were evil and kept people captive."

We pondered who could have lived in this, Castle House of mysteries. It could even date back to when servants were residing in these types of homes. Servants usually lived underneath the main areas, that would make more sense of the locked doors and hallways. I wish we could talk with Esmeralda about it.

We walked in to see Shaz back at work in the kitchen, and the plumber was under the new sink that had been installed. There was noise in the ceiling, so we greeted Mr. Hays, who responded with a ghostly noise!

Jake emerged from the hole, and said, "No Dad, there are no power points or lights down there. Whoever that was had no lights."

The plumber added, "There is no plumbing down there either, ladies."

Shaz asked if it was okay to board over it.

He mentioned, "If you need to, you can use the other entrance with the stairs."

Shelly and I agreed to board it up.

Shaz asked Shelly if she was ready to help, and she replied, "I sure am!"

Ray asked me, "What do you want to do?"

I asked if he would come with me to check out the other rooms, behind the storage room.

Shaz mentioned, "The air is much better, just keep the doors open!"

Ray agreed, and said, "Sure, let's see what this place is made of!"

He seemed very carefree today, which must be how he comes down from his books. As we walked in, he took a call, so I wandered through all the furniture, and opened a drawer. I found the most beautiful necklace and earrings, that had rubies embedded. I thought they looked real, but I wasn't qualified to say. I kept them out to show Shelly.

Ray finished his call and mentioned that it was one of the bookstores. Their copies had arrived this morning, and they now have a waiting list for the next shipment.

He was beaming, and said, "Thank you, for your magical touch on this title!"

I replied, "You wrote the story, I just critiqued it!"

Then he saw what was in my hands, and exclaimed, "Geez, they are stunning. They would be worth a pretty penny!"

Now I knew they were real. Ray handed me torches and asked, "Ready to explore?"

I was happy that he was excited, but my fear was still with me. The same key opened the first door, and the stench hit us first. Thank goodness for masks. We quickly looked in - very mouldy ceiling and walls, a filthy mattress on the floor, and what looked like a bucket. There were no windows or doors. I closed the door and locked it back up.

Ray asked, "Do you need to know what's in the others?" With a seemly disgusted look on his face, at what he had just seen.

I replied, "Yes, then our minds will rest."

We opened the next one, and it was worse. We crossed over to the other side where there was only one door. Opening it, the smell and the cold engulfed us.

This time, it was Ray who said, "Something just went through me like a cold wind." He looked around, and said, "This must have been their kitchen."

There was a picture on the wall, so I walked over to it. It depicted a couple with a baby. It appeared to be from the 18th century.

Ray said, "Surely they didn't have a baby in here."

I replied, "What troubles me is that they must have had money to be able to afford a photo in those days. Why would they be living down here?"

Ray suggested, "Let's take the picture and I can get my friend to analyse the paper and ink used. He loves antique stuff."

He picked up the picture and as he walked out, he noticed a wooden doll on the floor. "This could be dated by a specialist, or the library might have some kind of pictures we can look at to work out its age."

I went out to Shelly to show her the jewellery and tell her about what we found in the disgusting rooms. I also warned her to be careful, as I had felt the cold twice.

Shelly was mesmerised by the jewels, and asked, "How much would they be worth!"

Ray suggested, "We can find out, if you want to sell them."

Shelly and I looked at each other, and she said, "Let's find out!"

Shelly and I left Ray chatting with Shaz, about the kitchen. We returned to the storage room together and closed the door behind us to have a private conversation. I locked the other door, placing a sign on it, that read, 'Never Open!'

Shelly and I agreed that the room couldn't be cleaned out. No wonder the new owners just added to the house. Without thinking, we began opening all the doors and drawers of the furniture, to see what else was in here.

As Shelly opened a wardrobe door, a screeching noise startled her. She froze her in place, and the noise flew around, trying to escape.

I tried to reach Shelly, but the noise flew at me! I grabbed a chair and held it over my head, hitting the noise, and causing it to retreat to a corner. I hurried to Shelly as the noise flew at me again. This time, it was clearly angry and began materialising.

I fell to the floor, just within reach of Shelly's hand, but our bracelets didn't work. I desperately tried to snap Shelly out of her fear trance, as the noise dived at us. It scratched my arm as I pulled Shelly under a table with me.

The noise continued screeching and swooped again. I pulled Shelly further under the table, and she began coming to. I pleaded for her to hurry up and snap out of it, as she opened her eyes. The noise had now almost taken on a complete physical form, and was lifting the table from its strength, as it swooped.

I screamed at Shelly, and she finally grabbed my hand. With that, a charge shot out of our bracelets. I held her hand up with mine, and the electricity sped through the air, hitting the noise, right between its evil red eyes! It screamed and withered, fading as it hit the floor.

I looked at Shelly, and she had lost consciousness again. Her body was cold. I jumped up and raced to the door, screaming for help, but the tools the men were using, were so noisy that no one could hear me. I rushed back to Shelly and checked her pulse. She didn't have one.

I remembered that I had my phone in my pocket. I called 000 and requested an ambulance urgently, then started performing CPR, relying on what I had seen on television.

Shelly coughed, and I could see her eyes twitching. I kept going until she opened her eyes. My tears had washed over her face, but I felt her heart pumping again. I sat behind her and hugged her to keep her warm.

I heard sirens approaching, and Ray and Shaz appeared. Their faces turned white when they saw us. The ambulance personnel pushed past them, checked Shelly's vitals, and put a blanket around her. They informed me that she had been electrocuted and asked if I was okay.

I said, "Yes, it's just Shelly."

They replied, "You did a good job, but we need to get her to the hospital to assess the damage."

Another man entered with the ambulance bed, and the men swiftly lifted Shelly onto it, and immediately administered oxygen, and attached an IV.

They informed me, "You need to be checked as well."

Ray helped me up off the floor. I hadn't realised I couldn't stand. My body had gone into shock, and I suddenly fainted.

I woke up in a hospital bed next to Shelly, with machines hooked up to both of us, it was terrifying.

Ray exclaimed, "Thank God you're awake!" Then he called the nurse.

I noticed Shelly's mum and dad were also in our room, and Ray had tears in his eyes. I tried to speak, but I had no voice.

The nurse entered, and advised, "Don't try to talk. You've strained your vocal cords, but there's no permanent damage."

I tried to ask if Shelly was ok, and Ray squeezed my hand. I smiled at him to reassure him that I was okay.

The nurse assured me, "Don't worry, she is in good hands."

However, I could see tears streaming down her parents' faces. They looked up at me, then walked over to hug me, saying, "Thank goodness you're awake!"

With my eyes, I asked them how Shelly was doing. They explained that they were concerned about her heart, and were waiting for the doctor's results. When I went to lift my arm out towards Shelly, I noticed it was bandaged. Then I remembered that the creature had scratched my arm with its nails. Shellys mum said that they didn't know what had caused the cuts on my arms, but they had stitched them up, and the IV was antibiotics to prevent any infection.

Ray was still standing there, holding my hand tightly, tears flowing down his face. Shelly mum mentioned that he had been beside himself, sitting next to me for hours. She kissed my forehead and went back to Shelly. Ray then sat on the edge of the bed. I raised my other arm so he could rest his head on it, and finally, his shoulders relaxed.

Ray said, "I couldn't figure out what had happened, but I've never been so frightened!" He kissed me, and continued, "I'm tying a rope around you, and you're never leaving my side!"

I kissed away his tears and with my eyes, I told him, "I love you so much."

As he kissed me again, Shelly made a noise. Her mum jumped up and called for the nurse.

I could hear Shelly asking, "Mum, what's wrong?"

My heart skipped a beat as I felt Shellys weakness.

Shelly asked her mum, "Where is Hannah?"

I couldn't speak, so I sat up so that Shelly could see me. Tears rolled down her face, and at that point, I knew she was going to be ok.

Her parents urged Shelly to stay still, explaining that she had been electrocuted.

Shelly joked, "I feel like a bus hit me!"

Hearing her make a joke, was music to my ears.

An elderly man in a white coat, entered the room. He checked Shelly's vitals, and then said, "You are one lucky girl. The voltage that must have gone through your body would normally be fatal for any person." He then informed Shelly, "You'll need to take it very easy for a while. Your blood cells need intensive treatment to repair the damage and regenerate the cells. We'll be giving you high doses of zinc and vitamin C. You were extremely fortunate to have avoided any skin burns. However, your skin will feel very tender, and you must be cautious, as a cut may result in excessive bleeding." He continued. "We will keep you in the hospital until you have regained enough strength to move around. Additionally, we would like to conduct some brain activity tests, to ensure there is no long-term memory loss."

"Do you remember anything?" The doctor asked.

Shelly replied, "Not really."

The doctor reassured her, "It's possible that memories may come back as your body gets stronger."

Shelly's parents expressed their gratitude.

The doctor then turned to me, and asked, "How do you feel?"

He handed me a notepad to write on. I wrote:

'I can't recall much, but I remember performing CPR and holding onto Shelly until help arrived.'

He mentioned that I too, had experienced an electrical shock, though with less intensity.

"Do you know what you touched?" he inquired.

I wrote down my reply:

'No, I just heard Shelly fall and tried to stop her, accidentally hitting her head. Then she stopped breathing. I called out for help, but no one could hear us. I called ooo and performed CPR. The details after that are a bit hazy.'

The doctor suggested that the shock I experienced was more likely due to when I touched Shelly. Although I knew this wasn't the case, I appreciated the opportunity to avoid explaining further.

He then asked, "Do you know how you cut your arm?"

I pondered for a moment and wrote:

'I was looking at the crystal chandelier, and perhaps I dropped it while rushing to help Shelly.'

He remarked, "If the glass shards were sharp enough, that could explain your injuries. It's quite an unusual case. You have the option to go home if you feel strong enough, or you can stay here with Shelly."

Considering the state of my body, which felt as if it had been hit by a truck, I requested to stay.

Fourteen

Finding Esmeralda

Everyone stayed at the hospital, which felt like a safe circle of love. Dinner was brought to the room. However, neither Shelly nor I could eat. The nurse gave us special drinks and said that tomorrow they would assess how we were feeling. The drink was painful going down, but both Shelly and I managed to finish it.

Ray suggested getting hotel rooms across the road, so that he would be close if we were needing anything and offered to book a room for Shellys parents also. Her mum and dad expressed their gratitude for the idea.

Shelly, feeling tired, kissed her mum goodnight and Shellys mum reassured her that they would be back in the morning.

Ray said, "I don't want to leave you, but you also need to sleep." He kissed me gently, squeezed my hand, and then took Shellys mum and dad with him.

I overheard Ray telling the nurse, "If there's anything at all, you ring this number. I'll have it on all night!"

In a tired voice, Shelly said, "Thank you, Hannah. I know you lied to the doctor, but you can tell me the truth when you're able to talk."

Sleep enveloped us, and I vaguely remember a nurse checking our machines, and my arm, throughout the night.

I was awakened by the sound of rattling trolleys. Shelly remained asleep. I lay there, pondering what that creature was. It wasn't a human, it was ghost-like. Was it trying to kill us?

My heart ached, not from what had happened, but for Shelly, who never hurts a fly. Why did this have to happen to us? I desperately wanted to talk to Esmeralda, but hesitated and thought to myself, did I want to leave Shelly unprotected?

I decided to tell the nurses and doctor, that I still felt weak and unstable. That would give me another night in hospital with Shelly. I then drifted back to sleep, only to wake up to Shelly talking with her mum.

Shellys mum mentioned to me that Ray was here but had to pop out and would be back soon. I smiled at her and closed my eyes again.

When I woke up, there were flowers on mine and Shelly's side tables. I was kissed and hugged, by Ray, and he asked me how I was doing. He had brought a notepad and pen in for me so that I could write to him more privately.

I wrote a note to Ray:

'I still feel weak and am in need of assistance getting out of bed.'

He asked if I could stay another night, just in case there were any effects. I nodded in agreement. I think Shellys mum was happy with that decision as well, from the look of her face.

Ray mentioned that everything was going fine at the house, but Mr. Hays still couldn't figure out where the charge had come from. He then said, "He told me about the door handle incident, where it went through you and sent you backwards.

I wrote a note back saying that it was strange. Ray let it go, but I knew he would persist.

Breakfast arrived, but I was still only allowed fluids. Shelly managed to eat most of her meal, which was good. She needed it. Ray asked if it was alright if he checked on Frank while Shellys mum was with me. I encouraged him to do so and wrote a note asking Ray to explain to Frank that although I couldn't talk, I could still type.

The nurse came in to remove my drip and asked if I needed any pain medication.

I wrote down a firm no, the wrote her a note asking when I would be able to use my voice. She informed me that my doctor was on the ward already, making his rounds, and that he would explain my on-going care.

Shelly asked me if I would go to the house. I nodded and wrote her a note saying that it would depend on work, and if the stairs were now installed, I would use that as an excuse to go and check for Esmeralda.

Shelly then told me that she was still scared of the creature that had come through her mirror. It was different from the one in the cupboard.

I wrote Shelly a note saying that I thought she would be in the hospital for a few more days, but would visit as much as I could if they do keep her in. Then asked if she was feeling any stronger.

Shelly said, "Kinda, but my dreams are still scary. However, Mum needs to rest. Would you convince her and Dad to go home? I'm safe here. I'm not feeling any bad vibes."

I wrote a note telling her that I would do my best to convince them. Shelly expressed that she would like me to grab her book, so that she could read it while stuck in bed.

I gave her a thumbs up just as Ray walked in with flowers, and Shelly's book, saying, "For my sweet Shelly."

Shelly brightened up and said, "You have ESP."

Ray replied, "Now that's a talent that would help all men!"

Shelly laughed and said, "You take good care of my Hannah."

Ray bowed and said, "At your service, my princess."

Shelly gave me one of her "I love you" smiles, while Ray came and sat with me.

I wrote a note to Ray, saying that the doctor was doing his rounds and should be here soon.

Ray's face lit up and he said, "That's wonderful news! Frank also said that if you could do the writing and typing, he could take the calls."

I smiled at Ray as the doctor walked in. He went to check out Shelly first, just as her mum arrived.

I wrote a note to Ray, saying that Shelly wanted her mum and dad to go home, so that her mum could rest, and dad could go to work.

Ray said, "Okay."

Shelly didn't receive great news from her doctor. He said she needed another infusion for her blood. When he came to see me, he asked how

I was feeling. I wrote a note saying that I was feeling good, and if I could go home, and when I would be allowed to talk again.

He chuckled and replied, "Today you may go home, and in two to three weeks you need to refrain from speaking. You will need to see a voice specialist who will assess you further. The rest of your stats are good. Keep changing the wound dressing, and if any redness starts, come straight back here. The stitches will need to be taken out in a week. Maybe check in with your GP, so that they are aware of everything also, I'll send them our reports."

I wrote a note thanking the doctor for all his help.

The doctor told Ray, not to overexert me, as he thought I seemed like I was ready to run, but I wasn't.

Ray chuckled and said, "You already know her too well!"

I gave Shelly a very gentle hug, whispering softly, "Get better. We have more to conquer!"

Shellys mum said, "Take care, sweety."

Ray asked Shellys parents if they would be heading back home today, as he would take care of the hotel bill for everyone.

Shelly said, "Yes, they are!"

Ray and I left before her mum could argue.

On the way home, I softly asked Ray if we could stop by Castle House.

Ray asked, "You still love that place?"

I wrote a note on my phone and had an app read the words out, to reply to Ray, "Shelly and I both do, and that house will be beautiful again soon!"

He smiled and said, "I hope you love me that much when I'm old and wrinkled."

I almost laughed but stopped myself, giving him a loving twinkly smile.

Ray said, "You beguile me into anything."

Shaz and his apprentice were in the house working. As we walked in, I looked at the stairway.

Shaz commented, "She knows it's a thing of beauty! How are you feeling? How is Shelly?"

I smiled, and Ray answered for me. Shaz asked if it would be alright to visit Shelly. I smiled, touched my heart, and nodded. I thought this guy was nice, and I had a feeling overcome me, that he is feeling for Shelly, the way Ray feels for me. Oh, I hope that's what it is. I could see Shaz and Shelly together. Not that there was anything wrong with Jake, but Shaz is such the gentleman, just like Ray.

Ray invited me to come and have a look at the new kitchen.

Shaz added, "It's pretty good, if I do say so myself!"

When I walked in, I was speechless. I couldn't believe all the space. Then, I noticed a door and looked at it strangely. Ray opened it and revealed a small verandah with stairs leading into the garden.

Ray said, "I had to make some decisions for you. Hope you like it!"

I replied to Ray with my hands on my heart. We walked back inside, and with my hands on my heart once again, I tried to express to Shaz how much I loved it.

Shaz mentioned that Shelly wanted to surprise me with this. Then he pointed. There was a special tile on the backsplash with two sunflowers. Shaz mentioned that Shelly is a natural, and that he only showed her how to do tiling once, and she was able to do the entire backsplash on her own.

Ray asked if all the bills were paid up to date. Shaz confirmed, "Totally! Shelly did them straight away."

I looked at Ray, an indicated that I was going up to the bathroom. He asked if I needed help, and shook my head and hand to say no. As I walked up the now beautiful stairs, I felt something. Not sure what it was, I continued heading to Esmeralda's room. The feeling grew stronger. It was Esmeralda!

As I walked into her room, as she tried to materialise. She flickered into physical form, and I ran over to hug her.

Esmeralda whispered, "I found Margaret, but it drained me getting to her. I need to rest, but I will tell you what we think will..." She faded before I could ask her what she meant.

I left the room and went to walk down the stairs. Ray stood at the bottom, and asked if I needed anything brought down. I shook my head and hand again, saying no.

As I walked downstairs, I really wanted to go back into the locked room, the one where Shelly and I had hidden the magic book. I wondered if it was wise to go in without Shelly. I wished I could help Esmeralda.

Shaz came out of the downstairs back bedroom, which I had forgotten was there. Ray joined us and asked if I wanted that room to stay as a bedroom. Shaz suggested that it was under the bathroom, and when we redo it, we could run water into it and make it a laundry room. I didn't have to think hard, as that was a great idea.

Shaz then added, "If you want, we can also add a small powder room for this level."

I wanted to squeal, as that would be amazing! Ray saw my excitement and expressed my approval. Shaz informed us that the plumber was ready to start, so they would begin knocking down the old bathroom.

"Have you picked out your bath, shower, vanity, and rails for it yet?" Shaz asked.

I shook my head to reply with a no.

Ray asked Shaz, "When do you need them?"

Shaz answered, "About three days."

Ray then asked, "Are you up for a drive to look, or do you prefer to rest?"

I felt sad, but not unwell. My arm was still sore, but the sling was helping. I nodded to indicate that I was up for a drive.

Ray told Shaz, "We will get it ordered and hopefully here in time!"

As we were about to leave, Shaz said to me, "I will say hello to Shelly for you. I am going to head up there tonight."

Ray responded, "She would like that."

The drive was quiet, as not speaking was very unusual. Ray put on some music to brighten me up. He was so sweet. I wished I could share the real reason for my sadness. We drove past a car yard where I saw a bright red mini, sitting in the showroom window. I jumped to look back, and Ray noticed what had caught my attention.

He asked, "Do you want to go back?"

I nodded yes, and he laughed, saying, "Of course you do!"

I blew him a kiss, smiled, and he jokingly told me to stop that because it was unfair.

As we walked into the car yard, he held my hand. I was very excited. Luckily, Ray was level-headed and was able to negotiate a lower price with the salesman. I climbed in and out of the car, pressing buttons and smelling the new leather.

Ray asked, "Are you sure you want this one?"

I hugged him and replied with my hands on my heart and made puppy eyes.

He pulled me aside and asked if I wanted to take this exact one, or if I preferred to have him order a new one. I pointed at this one.

Ray turned to the salesman, and said, "We will take the stock one, but you will have to deliver it to my address because my fiancé hasn't taken her license test yet."

The salesman agreed, and we completed all the paperwork. As I walked out, It dawned on me that now I really do have to learn to drive! Ray told me that that car would be perfect for me to run around in. I hugged him, and he asked if I was still up for the bathroom shop. I checked the time and nodded yes.

He chuckled and said, "You are a tough little cookie, aren't you?"

The bathroom shop turned out to be bigger than I thought, with so many options to choose from. I spotted a very pink bath, toilet, vanity set.

Ray laughed when he saw what I was looking at, and said, "Of course!" He asked the assistant if this set was in stock, and the assistant went to check. He then turned to me, and said, "Your new bubble room."

I nodded with a huge smile.

Ray then asked, "Do you want a walk-in shower like mine?"

My eyes said it all. I was worried about space and gestured to ask if we had enough room. Ray assured me that they could knock through the wall again and see what was behind it.

My mind went into panic mode as I thought about Esmeralda being there on her own. I had to be with her, but I also had to work from Ray's house.

I saw Ray coming back with the sales assistant, who informed us that the set has to be brought up from another warehouse and would take at least a week. This was good news to me. I nodded to indicate my approval.

We walked down to the desk and placed the order, which included the shower and accessories that Ray had picked out for me.

I must have fell asleep on the way home, as I woke up in bed. Looking around, I noticed that the sun had set. I stood up slowly, feeling a bit shaky, and headed downstairs. Ray came out of his office and told me to stop.

He said, "Back to bed. I will bring your dinner up, and some meds that the doctor prescribed for you."

I didn't argue, as I was feeling very weak.

Ray entered the room with a worried look on his face. He helped me sit up and placed the tray on my lap. With one hand, I felt useless.

Ray said, "Just use your fingers, I won't tell anyone." Trying to make me smile.

He said he had called the hospital doctor, and that he has given me a new prescription to pick up, but he didn't want to leave me alone.

"I called Shaz to ask him to bring it back after he visits Shelly, as the doctor was happy to leave it with her." Ray said.

I asked how Shelly was doing. He said that she was recovering well. Her body will be weak for another week, but she might be able to have her drips taken out tomorrow. Then they will do her tests and assess her condition.

Tears filled my eyes as that horrible moment visualised in my mind. I knew I had to get stronger for everyone.

I ate everything on my plate, and asked, "Could you run me a bubble bath?"

Ray lit up and said, "Yes, if you're up to it!"

I replied, "You will have to help me."

He laughed and said, "Your wish is my command, my princess."

He went to the bathroom so sort the bath, then came back to assist me.

While I relaxed my muscles in the water, Ray went down to answer a knock at the door. It was a man's voice. I think it was Shaz. I then wondered if I should give Shelly a call. Just as I had that thought, the phone rang, and I heard Ray answer as the front door closed.

Ray came up and said, "Your meds are here, and Shelly called."

I smiled, thinking that I should have known she would know I was wanting to call her. It was so hard not talking, but Ray was doing such a great job. I felt better after the bath and food. I took my new meds, hoping that they would also kick in quickly.

When I finished dressing, Ray asked if I wanted to come downstairs. I nodded yes, smiling. He helped me down the stairs, and there I see a big bunch of white roses. I gave him a one-armed hug and a big kiss!

I went to walk into my office, but Ray stopped me as I was walking in, and said, "I will come and help you."

He opened my computer to my emails. We both went quiet. There were so many!

He asked, "Are you really up to this?"

I nodded, so he kissed my head and left me to it.

I immersed myself in my emails. Time flew while I answered as many as I could. The phone rang here and there and took me out of my focused flow.

I heard Rays footsteps, then he popped his head around the door and asked, "Are you doing okay?"

I nodded and signalled for a drink. He disappeared, coming back with a cup of hot chocolate and some yummy-looking cake. I happily stopped working while he caught me up with the renovation details, the book sales, and more information on the London trip.

He was very excited, saying, "This is heading for the bestseller list!"

I hugged him with pride. Ray has been so amazing, and nothing but helpful to me throughout all of this.

Ray told me that Shaz had called in and said he would start on the veranda outside, and if he was over early, he would work on the bathroom too. Apparently, Shaz said that we needed to pick out tiles, as he was expecting the area to be waterproof by the end of the week.

I had been letting Shelly handle all the flooring and paint colours. Ray said that we could just go with white, since the colour is in the fittings. I smiled and nodded in agreement. Ray then bowed, as he walked out to call Shaz.

I went back into my zone and continued answering more emails. Finally, I saw the end of them approaching. A big sigh escaped from me, and I realised I had made a noise without feeling any pain. This gave me the boost I needed to finish.

The clock had already passed midnight. I stood up and walked into Ray's office to see him deeply engrossed in his writing. I quietly left and headed to bed.

Sleep came easily, but the sun came too early. I tried to move, but my arm reminded me that it was still healing. I gently got out of bed, leaving Ray in his dream world. I knew he would have set an alarm. I made my way to the kitchen, feeling a bit lost among all the cupboards, drawers, and appliances. I found the kettle and a toaster, which would have to do.

After making some toast and a coffee, I then went to my office and checked on my emails. Surprisingly, there were only a few. So, I dealt with them before closing the computer down, then took a walk out onto the veranda.

It was so beautiful and fresh after the light rain. I could feel my arm hurting again, so I unwrapped it. Some of the stitches were a bit red, and I hoped the fresh air would help.

I heard footsteps behind me, and turned to see a very happy face that asked, "Are you feeling better?"

He couldn't contain his happiness as I quietly replied, "Yes."

He noticed my stitches and asked if I wanted my medication. I nodded yes, and he pulled them out of his pocket.

He seemed so prepared, all the time. Which reminded me to ask him about his parents. So, I asked, "At what age did you leave home?"

Ray looked at me somewhat sympathetically, then said, "I lost my parents when I was at boarding school. They were hit by a drunk driver. I was then taken care of by my grandparents, who are now happily living in a retirement home that is run by their church. It's on my list to take you to meet them, but there just hasn't been time."

I expressed my condolences for the tragedy he experienced, and said, "I would love to meet your grandparents. I never had a chance to meet mine."

Ray said, "It was hard for me to cope." Then continued, "My grandfather told me I needed to keep my mind occupied, so I took another course after school. He was right. That was the hardest time of my life. I went through all the evening classes, and eventually chose writing. Once I started, I found myself getting caught up in the stories, and it brought me a more peaceful place in my mind. I inherited my parents' estate and lived there on my own for years. My writing became my life. Then I decided to move closer to my publisher. The rest, you know."

I felt like a light came on. Everything he had done and said made sense, considering the great loss he experienced. His protection of me, his desire for a big family, even his immediate attachment to Shelley's parents, and Frank. His writing is truly amazing!

He got up, and asked, "Can I get you anything? I need to do some rewrites. They came to me while I was asleep."

I asked, "Do you need help?"

He looked at me and replied, "No, I don't want you to read it. Not until it's complete."

I said, "I understand."

Ray then asked what I wanted to do. I told him I had already caught up on work emails for now and asked if he could drop me off at Castle House.

Ray had a concerned look but agreed, and said, "Sure."

I loved that he didn't question me.

Then Ray added, "As long as you don't talk, and take your pen and paper."

I wanted to laugh, but I knew he was serious, so I nodded. He helped me stand, then hugged me ever so gently, saying, "I love you," kissing away my sadness.

We arrived at Castle House. Ray slid my phone into my sling, and instructed, "Call me, but don't talk. I will come."

Shaz was already working, along with the plumber, and the tiler.

Ray asked, "Are you sure that you want to be here?"

I replied, "Yes, I'm going into the storage room to get some things out."

Ray said, "Make sure one of the men carries them for you!"

I kissed Ray and told him I loved him.

As I watched Ray drive away, I turned around and went to head straight up to Esmeraldas room. The men greeted me, so I waved and pointed upstairs. There was nothing left of the bathroom, but I noticed that the wall had panelling removed. I hoped there were no new surprises.

I felt Esmeralda's presence as I approached her room, and as I walked in, I closed the door behind me. Esmeralda then appeared. I hugged her gently and asked with my hands, and my expression, if she was ok. She spoke much stronger, and I breathed a big sigh of relief as I gave her a big smile.

She said, "A very happy soul floated through this morning."

It took me a moment to understand. She continued, "I opened the window, and a warm breeze came through. I felt like she was a young girl. I hope she finds her parents."

This was a lot to take in, knowing that a child had been locked in. Esmeralda explained that in the old days, girls who got pregnant out of wedlock, would have their babies taken away, and some mothers hid their children to protect them. Maybe something happened to her mother, and she couldn't return. Many servants were traded or sold during that time. This made me wonder about the toy we found.

I wrote a note, asking Esmeralda if she was strong enough to come with me, to retrieve the magic book.

Esmeralda said, "Yes, but you will need help to carry them."

She faded away so that she couldn't be seen by anyone else. I went to the bathroom to ask Shaz for assistance in carrying.

He agreed, saying, "Sure, I need a break!" Then asked, "Do you want to go into, that room?"

I assured him that I had rubber soles on and had brought gloves with me.

He chuckled and remarked, "Gloves? You and Shelly are very de-termined girls."

I asked, "Why?"

He replied, "She wants to come home so she can stay here and help!"

We entered the room, which was still cold, but it felt safe. I could feel Esmeralda standing right beside me, as I went straight to the drawer where we had hidden the book.

Shaz exclaimed, "Wow!" As he saw me pull the book from the drawer.

I whispered, "Shhh, It's a secret!"

He chuckled and said, "Scout's honour," thinking it was just kids' stuff.

Shaz carried the book to Esmeralda's room for me, then went back working.

Esmeralda spoke, "That was a very nasty demon you took on. Its anger is still in that room."

We sat on her bed and started flipping through the pages. She found the spell that had been used. I felt her hesitation to touch the page. I read out as many words as I could, but there were many symbols unknown to me. However, Esmeralda understood some of them, and explained their meanings. I wrote down the ones she didn't know, and Esmeralda said that she had always thought they were in Hebrew. I expressed my desire to take the book to the library and study it. Esmeralda expressed her concern, that it might cause me much grief if I was seen with it.

I reassured Esmeralda quietly, saying, "I'm okay." Hugged her, then wrapped the book in a pillowcase. Leaving Esmeralda to rest, I picked up the book with my uninjured arm, and headed out of the room to find Shaz.

Shaz offered to carry the book for me, as my jaw dropped at the size of the newly expanded bathroom. Shaz explained to me where everything was going. It was amazing, and the new bay window made the room much brighter.

I overheard the plumber downstairs greeting Ray. Shaz said that he would walk downstairs with me and would carry the book.

He jokingly asked me, "Is Shelly into this stuff too?"

I hushed Shaz as Ray came up to help me.

Ray asked me, "Did you find what you wanted?"

I replied, "Yes, can we go and see Shelly?"

Ray said, "Your car awaits you." Then took the book from Shaz, remarking, "Wow, is this thing made of metal?"

Shaz replied, "Back to my walls!"

As I walked out the front door, I saw my little mini! I felt excited, but I could only pretend to drive it. Ray informed me that he had booked me for driving lessons, starting on Saturday.

I let Ray assist me into the seat, and whispered, "Thank you." As I kissed his lips and floated away in ecstasy. Ray said he would show me some basic things as we drove, so that I knew them before my first lesson.

When we arrived at Shellys room at the hospital, she was drip-free, and sitting down for lunch. Her mum was here too, and she excitedly announced that Shelly was well enough to recover at home.

I looked at Shelly, who was beaming, as she said, "We need to recover together!"

I understood what she was really saying, but I also knew her mum wanted her back home with them for a while.

Ray had started talking with Shellys mom, so I took the opportunity to whisper to Shelly, telling her that I had the book, and that Esmeralda was getting stronger. Shellys smile illuminated her entire face!

Shellys mum then said, "You are the medicine she needs, Hannah."

Ray chimed in, saying, "I would love to have you both together, to take care of you. Knowing you both as I do, I'm happy for you to be together."

I looked at Ray and he winked, asking, "Would you both like a ride home?"

Shelly gathered her clothes, eager to see my new car, as I told her about it earlier.

While Shellys Mum helped Shelly get dressed, Ray and I went to see the doctor. He was pleased to sign Shelly out with her medication, then asked to see my arm.

The doctor gave me some cream, saying, "It's a bit infected, but this should help. We'll see you next week to hopefully remove the stitches."

Ray and I thanked the doctor and said goodbye. Shellys mum came down the hall with Shelly, who was still unsteady. We all walked out of the hospital together, and excitement hit me again when they saw my red Mini.

On the way home, I sat with Shelly, and she asked, "Should we check if the demon is still in the mirror? Just in case it goes after Esmeralda."

I agreed.

When we arrived, Shellys mum unlocked her front door, while Ray helped me out. Shelly took Rays arm, and we walked inside. Shellys mum offered to make Ray a coffee and a sandwich while us girls packed a few things for Shelly.

I took Shelly's arm, and we headed to the bathroom, closing the door to ensure the demon couldn't escape. If it was still here. Although our strength had returned, our bodies were still weak. We held each other's arms, ready to defend ourselves if it came at us again.

Slowly, we removed the towel, and as soon as it appeared, we sent a bolt straight at its head. The demon fell backward. It resembled the one from the wardrobe.

We waited to see if it would attack us again. Both of us were shaking, but we knew it was up to us to prevent it from escaping into the world.

It screeched and flew at us once more, but this time we hit it harder, and longer, until it crashed and disappeared in a puff of green smoke.

Shellys mum and Ray came running, asking what had happened.

I whispered, "I gave Shelly the wrong arm to hold."

Shellys mum remarked that it must be infected to be so sore, and Ray agreed, suggesting that I use some cream, and rest for the remainder of the day.

I suggested having a movie afternoon, and Shellys smiled, saying, "Good luck keeping these two still."

We packed Shelly's toiletries and closed the suitcase.

Ray joked, "Do you need the kitchen sink?"

We all giggled as Shelly defended herself.

We kissed Shellys mum goodbye, telling her to rest and that we all had phones if she needed anything.

Shelly exclaimed, "I can't wait to learn to drive now!"

It seemed that getting rid of her demons had lightened her mind. I hoped her health would improve more easily now.

When we arrived at Rays, he settled us on the lounge sofas, and put Shelly's things in the 'Bahamas room'. It was a perfect time for us to read the book.
We enjoyed juice and toasted sandwiches, accompanied by mountainous pillows. Ray mentioned that he had a beeper on the lounge

room door, so he would know if we moved, and before I could ask, he assured me that he would check my emails.

As I blew Ray a kiss. Shelly commented, "He is such a beautiful man, your Ray." Then, in her next breath, "Did you know Shaz came to see me?"

I replied, "Yes. What do you think of Shaz?"

Shelly said, "I love working with him. He's very funny, and excellent at his job!"

I agreed, saying, "Yes, he is. Did you know that he's single?"

Shelly responded, "I thought so. Since he never talks about anyone."

The movie started, and Ray returned, saying, "About 10 new emails from Authors, wanting you to accept their manuscripts."

I jokingly replied, "I would have to clone myself one hundred times if this keeps up." Trying not laugh.

Ray hushed me and left. Shelly and I both fell asleep during the movie, and were awakened for medication, and dinner on trays.

Shelly exclaimed, "Who are you, and where is your brother?"

I tried not to laugh. Our dinner was lovely.

Shelly complimented, "You cook well."

Ray blushed this time. He mentioned that Shaz had called to check on Shelly, and asked if he could visit.

With that, Shelly blushed, and said, "Okay."

Ray took our trays and mentioned a powder room, behind the door near the television. I hadn't even noticed it. Shelly asked if he could help her up, and he returned gently holding her.

Ray sat with me, then asked, "Is Shelly interested in Shaz?"

I replied, "I think so. Jake was on the scene, but I think Shaz is in the running now."

He helped me up so I could assist Shelly back to the lounge. The doorbell rang as Shelly emerged, and I helped her back to the lounge, and sat back down on the other sofa, before Shaz entered.

Ray and Shaz walked into the lounge carrying drinks and snacks. The evening was very relaxing, with Shaz happily serving Shelly all that she desired.

Shaz thanked us for the evening and bid us goodnight, mentioning that the waterproofing guy would be coming early. He then kissed Shelly on the cheek and said, "See you again." Then walked out towards the front door with Ray.

Ray returned to help Shelly up the stairs, and I followed.

Sleep came easily once again, and I didn't budge until the aroma of coffee reached my senses in the morning. It was placed beside my bed, with a gentle kiss and a "Good morning, Princess."

I thought to myself. This is paradise. Why me?

Fifteen

The Magic Spell Book

Ray opened the blinds, letting the sunshine in, and a gentle breeze floated over me. I checked my arm, and it was much better.

After finishing my coffee, I headed to the bubble room. Running the taps, I added my lavender-scented bubbles. Just as I stepped in, there was a knock at the door.

A very sweet voice asked, "Are you okay?" Then popped his head in, and said, "Just needed a visual of my princess in bubbles to make my day!"

He noticed my arm, and exclaimed, "Wow, that is so much better. Must be my tender loving care."

I quietly replied, "It was. How is your other patient, Doctor?"

He chuckled and said, "Sassy already. Miss Bryant was feeling much brighter, and your presence was requested."

I asked Ray if he could escort Miss Bryant to my bubble room.

He bowed and said, "Your wish is my command, my Princess."

I laughed this time, and he shushed me, warning, "You will be put back to bed if you make a noise!"

He closed the door, and I relaxed into the warm water.

Shelly walked in and sat on the edge, saying, "You truly are the princess."

I whispered, "Sorry, but I couldn't get out of my bubbles."

Shelly replied, "I'm washed out again. I think I used too much strength, zapping that horrific creature. Should we go back to see the doctor?"

I suggested, "Let's see how you feel after a bubble bath!"

Shelly splashed me, as she jumped into the other end of the bath.

Feeling hungry, I asked Shelly, "Will you be okay on your own? I can wait for you. But I'm starving!"

She surprised me by saying, "If that's okay, will you stay up here?" This was not like Shelly, and it made me think that the recent events had shaken her. I thought I might ring her doctor later and ask if there is something we can give her, to help her with that.

I assured Shelly, "I will leave the door open so you can hear me." Then I threw on my robe and headed out to the kitchen.

When I went to check in on Shelly, I noticed she had her eyes closed and seemed at peace.

I said to Shelly as loudly as I could, "I'm back!" But she didn't move. So, I shook her gently, and she opened her eyes. I helped her out of the bath and dried her. She was so weak. I called out to Ray as loudly as I could, and luckily Ray heard and came running. He checked her pulse, then called for an ambulance.

We followed the ambulance, and called Shelly's mum, to explain what was wrong. She said that she would get Shellys dad to come and get her, and then head straight up.

The doctor examined Shelly and started her on a drip right away. He said that this happens sometimes, and that she will just need more of an immune booster.

Shelly's mum and dad arrived. Shelly was conscious and explained that she felt weak and tired. I hugged her, and apologised for not realising that her strength would be drained.

Feeling terrible, Ray took me out for a walk, and told me that I needed to let them take care of her. I wanted to ask Esmeralda if this had ever happened to her and Margaret before.

Afterwards, we had coffee and food. Then went back to see if she wanted anything. The nurse had already given her a tray of high-protein foods though. Ray suggested that we go home so I could rest. I kissed Shelly, her mum, and her dad goodbye. I was difficult not being allowed to talk.

As we got in the car, Ray asked if I wanted a driving lesson. I was initially going to decline, but my arm wasn't hurting, so I agreed. He showed me the basics and said we would go on the back road where we would have the road to ourselves.

When It was my turn to drive, I slowly turned into the road and tried to stay in my lane, but there were parked cars. It was a slow and cautious journey, as I went around and up a lane to the back streets. It was much easier than I expected it to be, and slowly, my body relaxed.

I was doing well until we pulled over to practice reversing, which didn't go so smoothly. Ray started laughing and told me to use the mirror instead of turning around. I gave in and said that I had now had enough.

Ray took over and drove us home. He asked if I needed to stop at my Castle House, and I told him yes. When we pulled up, I could feel Esmeralda's presence, and it brought a happy feeling to me.

Ray helped me up the front stairs. Shaz greeted us, and Ray updated him on Shelly's condition. Shaz expressed concern and said that he would like to visit her but didn't want to disturb her. Ray assured Shaz that he would keep him updated.

Shaz then mentioned that the waterproofing had gone well, and the tiler could start tomorrow.

As I quietly snuck away to see Esmeralda, she immediately spoke, "What's wrong?"

I told Esmeralda about joining forces against the demon, and she admitted that they had never encountered such a situation before. With the demons starting to awaken, I asked if she was able to wear the other bracelet instead of Shelly. Esmeralda hesitated and expressed uncertainty, explaining that while she could materialise when she's strong, wearing the bracelet might drain her away completely.

While I was lost in thought, Ray called out, and I pretended to be looking out the window.

Ray asked, "Are you missing this place?"

I replied, saying that it would be lovely when everything is finished, but we haven't even explored the towers yet. Ray understood and suggested leaving it for now. He reassured me that once everyone is healthy, we can assess what needs to be done next. I admitted that I was feeling a bit overwhelmed. So, we decided to head home.

Back at Rays home, Ray asked if I would like to start preparing for my book, to help me focus on something else. I agreed, and he happily set me up, advising me not to open my emails just yet. He wanted me to give my brain a break and indulge in fantasy for a while.

I found it easy to start writing my story. I had already made a list of character names, and knew the setting, and timeframe. I decided to call the story *'Esmeralda'* and as I wrote, my mind took me back to the good times I had spent with her, and how much I loved this house.

The story began to unfold, and with a few extra twists and turns, and an added a splash of fantasy, I found myself laughing.

Ray came in and asked if I needed a break.

I quietly replied, "No, I'm enjoying writing!"

He then asked if I would like something other than water for my thirst, and I requested a hot chocolate. He laughed and said that I'm easy, and he should have some chocolate cake as well.

I went out by the pool to give my eyes a rest. It was there, that Ray brought up the topic of a wedding date. I felt bad admitting that I hadn't given it much thought. Ray explained that if we were to have a traditional wedding, which he was okay with if it was something I had always dreamed of, that it would most likely turn into a big event, with everyone wanting to be invited. Ray understood that this wasn't me at all, and he asked if I would be happy with an island wedding, with just Shelly's mum and dad instead.

I thought about Ray's suggestion, and I asked him where he was thinking of having the wedding. He admitted that he hadn't given it much thought, beyond keeping it from becoming a film production that is. Ensuring it remained private, so no one would be upset about not being invited. I mentioned that I had seen an island getaway resort called the Whitsunday Islands, in a magazine.

Ray hugged me tightly, and expressed how proud he was to be marrying me. I felt incredibly happy that he felt that way. A big wedding was never something that felt like me, and I realised that I had blocked it from my thoughts on it. But now, it was in a happy place, and I couldn't wait.

I hugged Ray and told him that he had made me the happiest girl in the world. We went inside, and then decided to go and tell Shelly the good news, to brighten her up.

Ray asked if I wanted to drive, and I agreed. I was doing well, until I ended up in the wrong lane, and we found ourselves on an unexpected adventure. Thankfully, I spotted a turn and took it, which became a great way out.

Ray swapped places with me and praised me for not panicking. After everything Shelly and I had been through, panic was not in our blood.

As we reached the hospital and walked out to Shelly's room, we saw Shaz leaving. He had come to check on Shelly, then mentioned that he couldn't stay focused because they were still waiting for the tiles to dry. We told him we would see him tomorrow, then walked into the room to see a huge bouquet of flowers, and a radiant Shelly, sitting up beside them.

It was so heart-warming to see her awake and full of life again. I gave her a hug and asked why she was glowing. She giggled and said that Shaz had just been and kissed her cheek. She also mentioned that Shaz had asked her out on a date, when she's feeling up to it, and that he had been worried sick about her.

Ray looked at me with a smirk, and I asked Shelly where her mum was. Shelly explained that her parents had met Shaz and decided to give them privacy to chat.

Ray encouraged me to tell Shelly about our wedding plans, so I explained our decision.

Shelly's excitement was contagious as she squealed, and exclaimed, "Wow, that's awesome! When?"

Ray and I both laughed, and said, "When you're better!"

Shelly shared that she was doing much better. Her drip had been changed to an antibiotic, to treat an infection from an unknown source. The doctor had mentioned that her body couldn't fight it initially, but now it was working, and she would likely be okay after another night. It then dawned on me, that the creature must have caused the infection in her.

We gave Shelly hugs and wished her sweet dreams.

As we were leaving, Ray asked me what I thought about whole cause of her infection not be determined. I shrugged.

When we arrived home, Ray asked if I needed anything. I replied that I would check my emails, then go and rest.

He responded, "Good, I'll be in my study writing."

After finishing my work, I went to study more of the magical book. Then realised that I needed to get a book on the Hebrew language, so I called the library to inquire. They confirmed that they had one, and I asked for it to be held for me until a taxi could pick it up. The lady on the phone kindly agreed and asked for my details.

When I provided my name, she brightened her voice, and said, "I hope it helps with your needs. I'll be very happy to help anytime."

I hung up, giggling to myself, and then headed downstairs to wait for the taxi. Ray heard me and came out to see if I was okay. He commented that I should have asked him to go and pick it up for me, to which I responded that I needed to stay independent, so that I wouldn't lose my magical powers.

He laughed and said, "All princesses need those!"

The taxi arrived, and Ray went down to pay the driver, and remarked that it looked interesting. I explained that it was for research.

"That's making this book even more intriguing!" Ray said, as handed me the parcel.

I thanked him, calling him a kind sir, and noting his help. He smiled, melting my heart, and I couldn't help but wonder, why me?

The rest of my afternoon flew by, as I immersed myself in the words of a language so different from ours. Each symbol held a unique meaning, making even a single sentence a monumental task.

I closed up the book and walked out onto the veranda to admire the breathtaking array of colours as the sun set.

Suddenly, a quiet voice spoke, saying, "What a beautiful picture you make against Mother Nature's sky paintings."

Later in the night, the phone rang, and we both looked apprehensive about it.

Ray answered. His face lit up with excitement. Meeting my gaze, Ray explained that Shelly had received her test results, and everything was good. This was a huge relief, because it meant I could go to London without feeling guilty.

Ray must have read my thoughts, and said, "Now you can come and not feel guilty!"

I jumped onto his lap, and suggested making it a longer holiday, so that we could explore the sights of London as a pre-honeymoon, honeymoon.

Laughing, Ray agreed, and said, "Yes, we don't do normal things. We are creators of our destinies!"

I pondered his words and thought about how true they were.

Ray and I had decided to take ten days off, which would be easily manageable. We could use the computers at the library to check our emails, while overseas. The event had been booked for two weeks' time, and we hoped that Mr. Winston would have fully recovered by then and be able to take on some of the incoming manuscripts. Shelly should also be fully recovered by that time.

Ray asked if I was tired, or if I wanted to continue my research. After considering it, I told him that I would continue until he was ready to go to bed.

Ray laughed, and said, "I will join you shortly!"

The words I had written down, with symbols, seemed to convey the message of being stronger together, but they also emphasised the importance of standing alone in strength. It intrigued me, although I was hesitant to try it on my own. The next symbol had an interesting dual meaning. It could either signify counting one's blessings or imply that one's days are numbered.

Perhaps it wasn't about the frequency of usage of the bracelets, but rather how long the symbols retained their power. Maybe Margaret and Esmeralda had been using them for many years. How could we determine which interpretation was correct? I still needed to under-stand if the combination of travel and electricity had the same value, in terms of usage or duration, until their power diminished. It was crucial to grasp this concept before continuing to utilise them.

Ray came up the stairs, and I put my books away. The moonlight illuminated the room as he turned off the lights. I made a wish upon the stars, seeking guidance and assistance.

Waking in the morning, again to the aroma of coffee, and the gentle kisses from angels, had become addictive. Life was starting to unfold, directing the paths of both Shelly and I.

We heard my phone ringing. Both Ray and I exclaimed, "Shelly!" As I grabbed my phone as quick as I could, to answer it. It was indeed Shelly, and she was bubbling with excitement, as she shared the news that Shaz had come to see her again this morning, on his way to the house.

I exclaimed, "My goodness, he is not letting you out of his sight!"

We laughed together, then Shelly continued, saying that this morn-ing he told her that he couldn't find peace of mind amongst his thoughts of her, and wondered if she thought about him too.
I asked, "Do you?"

Shelly replied, "Yes, all the time! But lately, I've been too tired to think straight. My stomach feels all fluttery whenever I see him."

It was clear that she was falling in love. Fortunately, Shaz wouldn't have to wait long for Shelly to answer that question. I asked Shelly if the doctor had released her yet, and she informed me that he would be coming to see her soon. Then asked if I could pick her up, if she was allowed to leave.

I replied, "Of course."

Ray jokingly said, "Doth thou fair maiden need a chariot to bring her to her castle?"

I laughed, and responded, "Indeed, she doth, and our fair maiden might also be losing her heart to a knight in dirty overalls."

Ray and I shared a warm hug, expressing our excitement at the thought. Then headed to the hospital to collect Shelly.

As we arrived, the doctor appeared. He greeted us and mentioned that he wanted to check my arm while we were here. After the examination, he declared it to be fine for the nurse to remove the stitches.

The doctor then added, "You can both return to your normal lives, hopefully."

Ray accompanied Shelly to the waiting room, while the nurse removed my stitches.

I came out to find both of them laughing. My heart filled with happiness, as our lives were back on track, and we had the bonus of two amazing men who loved us. I walked over to them, and we all embraced in a circle of hugs.

Naturally, Shelly wanted to see what had been done at the house and catch up with Esmeralda.

Ray jokingly said, "I guess we're going to Castle House first!"

Shelly agreed, saying, "Yes, I need to check if the work is being done correctly."

I asked, "Is that the only reason?" as I giggled.

Ray chimed in, saying, "Shaz is a great guy, isn't he?"

Shelly blushed, and replied, "He's very sweet. He's taking me out to dinner tonight!"

Teasing her, I said, "Then you don't need to see him now, do you?"

She gave me her teacher's look, and said, "Be quiet!"

Ray chuckled to himself, and remarked, "It won't be long before we're there."

Shelly pretended to hit him, playfully saying, "Stop teasing me!"

We pulled into the driveway of Castle House. Ray went to open Shelly's door, but she was already out of the car, and headed to the front door.

Ray walked over to me, and said, "Now that's a woman on a mission!"

I replied, "I hope Shaz knows the exciting adventure he's embarking on."

We both agreed that he was a lucky guy.

As we entered the house, there was a happy warmth that hadn't been there before. It was as if the house itself was happy. We walked upstairs to see that all the tiles had been finished. The plumber was installing the taps, and the toilet, and Shelly and Shaz were outside on the veranda.

Ray asked the plumber if the bath and vanity had arrived, and he confirmed that they had. He also mentioned that the glass fitter wanted to start with the shower surrounds first.

Ray and I could hear Shelly's laughter coming from outside, but we decided to leave them be, and went back downstairs to check out the laundry. Once again, I was amazed at the size. It really did have room for a powder room! It all made me feel so happy, seeing everything come together the way it has.

Ray suggested, "Do you want to show me the back area that's puzzling you?"

I agreed, saying, "Yes, great idea!"

We walked out the front door, and around to the back, since there was no back door yet.

Ray exclaimed, "What on earth were they thinking!"

Following me, Ray walked up the well-made stairway. The door was still locked, but being taller, he could see through the top.

He said, "It's another kitchen, with doors going off in two different directions. It seems more modern than the front section. Perhaps another family lived in this section!" As he walked back down, now even more intrigued. He said, "There has to be adjoining doors inside."

I laughed and said, "So far, not yet. Seems like you're not too good at puzzles." then asked, "Is it possible for us to break the lock on this door?"

Ray suggested, "Let's ask Shaz to come have a look."

We went to get him and were greeted by two smiling faces.

Shelly exclaimed, "Shaz gave me a friendship ring! We've agreed not to see anyone else, while we get to know each other more."

I responded, "That's wonderful!"

Shelly then said, "Where have you been?"

When I told Shelly and Shaz what we had been doing, Shelly said, "Hannah and I will wait here for you men to deal with that, and to check the safety first!"
It was clear that she wanted to talk to Esmeralda.

Ray and Shaz left, and Esmeralda appeared. Shelly was in tears, and Esmeralda expressed her joy at seeing Shelly well again. I told them both about what the book had said.

Esmeralda said, "That's made it harder. What do you think?"

I honestly replied, "I'm not sure. I'm leaning more toward the length of time. How long did you have the bracelets for?"

Esmeralda revealed, "At least 50 years. We were 15, and the last time we saw each other was in our late sixties."

We heard the men approaching, and Esmeralda disappeared.

Ray announced, "We're going to break the lock. Do you girls want to come?"

Shelly was unsure, but I told her quietly, that Esmeralda can come just in case we have an unwanted guest. Shelly decided to stay in the bedroom.

As I walked to the door with Ray and Shaz, I felt Esmeralda with me, hoping that we wouldn't need her. The men had a sledgehammer and attempted to hit the lock, but it didn't budge. They tried another tool, but still, there was no movement.

Using the hammer again, Shaz gave the lock another hard whack, and this time it bent inward. With both Shaz and Rays combined body strength, they managed to push the door open. Just like before, the stale air hit us.

Esmeralda hadn't said anything, but maybe she was unaware of who was living here. We went inside, and I immediately went to open some windows. The men were more curious to get the doors open and see where they led.

Esmeralda quietly said to me, "I'm not feeling anything."

I thought that was a good thing, but Ray then asked, "Did you say something, honey?"

I replied, "No."

They kept hitting the door, trying to get it fully open.

Esmeralda suddenly said, "Get away from the window!"

I quickly moved just as they pushed it open. It revealed a hallway, but it was nowhere near as smelly as the others. The men walked halfway down, and I started to feel scared for them.

I suggested, "Maybe we should wait."

Ray laughed, and said, "It's okay. If there's another skeleton, we'll call the police."

If only I could tell them that Esmeralda was with me. As they broke through the next door. Holding my breath, I waited.

Shaz exclaimed, "Wow, it stinks!"

Ray decided to stay outside of that room, while Shaz continued exploring.

Shaz described what he saw, "There's a piano and a cocktail bar, and some old chairs and tables. There's even a window. Oh wait!" he yelled out. "Behind the dusty curtains, there is another door!"

I wished they wouldn't go any further, but I knew we needed to know where everything met up in this house.

I held my breath. Then heard banging from inside, and I could hear Shelly calling out, "Hello, can you hear me?"

Shaz yelled back, "Yes!"

Shelly said, "I know where the door is!"

Shaz replied, "Shelly, stand back! I'm going to smash through the door."

Ray went to help, and I followed behind him. It was a door, but it opened into a powder room.

Shelly called out, "Did you get in?"

Shaz called back to Shelly, saying, "Knock on the wall that you're standing at!"

As Shelly knocked on the wall, Shaz said, "Stand back, Shelly!"

Ray and Shaz smashed the wall, making a huge hole. Shaz stuck his head through and said, "Hello, my sweetheart," laughing.

Finally, one of the extensions made sense. I felt Esmeralda's relief, and that made me relax as well.

Ray and Shaz kept knocking through until the fresh air came flooding in, and we all walked through to Shelly.

Shaz said, "Smart thinking, Shelly."

She blushed and said, "I could hear you hitting the doors."

Shaz replied, "Yes, we went through three."

Shelly looked at me with an inquisitive look, and I nodded, indicating that I had not entered through the wall on the second floor.

Shaz said, "That stairway has hidden rooms everywhere! Now I wonder if there is more on the other side."

I suggested, "Let's just work with all these ones for now, to get a back entrance to this house again."

Everyone agreed, that was a great idea.

"That is important," Shaz said, then added. "Having only one entrance is against the building codes these days."

While Ray and Shaz worked on some plans for the back entrance, Shelly and I headed upstairs, into Esmeralda's room. We asked Esmeralda if she had been able to find out why Margaret was asking for help. She told us that the demon we killed in the mirror at Shellys parents' house, was one of the ones that had taken Margaret when she was trying to get back.

Shelly asked, "Did you speak to her?"

Esmeralda replied that she had only communicated with Margaret via telepathy, and continued to say that there were more demons that were keeping so many souls from leaving. We thought about how horrible that must be for them. If only we could make more bracelets, we could fight more of them and help set the souls free!

I told Shelly to lay down, as I could see that the excursion of today had weakened her. I was torn between keeping Shelly safe and helping Esmeralda. I asked Esmeralda if if she knew if the other trapped souls would be able to help fight, and if we could somehow join with them. She replied vaguely, saying that hope could rally them together. Esmeralda also mentioned that these demons feed off the trapped soul's energy, so we couldn't rely on the older ones, but maybe the newer ones would still have enough strength to fight for their freedom. This made me more determined to find what else could be in those books, that might help. I knew that there would be other curses written down, but maybe there was information on demon slaying too.

As the men walked up the stairs, Shelly and I quickly said goodbye to Esmeralda. Shaz got a fright when he saw Shelly lying down, and he rushed to her side. Shelly reassured him though, saying that she was just resting and that they could still go on their date tonight.

Ray looked at me with concern, but I smiled to let him know everything was okay. Ray then said that he was going to do a dump run with Shaz and that he would be back soon. He asked if we girls needed anything while they were out. I told them we were fine. Shelly and I and were told to keep safe, as they walked back out of the room.

Sixteen

The New Extensions
Hidden Evils

As Ray and Shaz headed down the stairs, Ray yelled out to me, "That new area we opened up is now accessible, and the air was flowing in both ways. Grab some tape and mark anything that you girls want to keep, and we will get rid of the rest."

Shelly asked if I would okay on my own, and I assured her that Esmeralda, who had already manifested again, would be with me down there. Then I told Shelly to keep resting.

I headed off to check out the new area, and took some tape, and a notebook with me, to write down what we would need for that area. Luckily, the funds for the upkeep of this house were substantial, as the bills were piling up.

The first section was empty except for a very dusty covered bed. I marked it as something to be dumped. The bath in the bathroom with the two entrances was still in good condition and was only needing a good scrub. The same went for the shower, but I figured a new vanity wouldn't hurt. I marked the shower and bath curtains for dumping though. The window walls had all been repainted, and still looked newish, which was surprising.

Next was the kitchen, and everything in it was to be dumped. I flicked the light switch to see if there was any power, and noticed it was flickering. That's when things started to get eerie.

Esmeralda said that she sensed something in the corner pantry. We were unsure of what to do. Should we lock it in, or let it out? Esmeralda assured me that she didn't feel any anger from it. so, I decided we would let it out.

Esmeralda positioned herself near the back door. I was shaking, but I figured it was better for me to see it, and deal with it, than the men coming face to face with it later. I opened the pantry door and walked backwards, towards Esmeralda. It didn't come flying out, but rather passed by me and followed Esmeralda. It seemed weak. Esmeralda led it to the door, and then left with it. I sat down on the floor, amazed and speechless. Whoever had done that, was truly evil.

I went back to Shelly to tell her what had happened, but she was asleep. So, I headed down to the kitchen and made coffee, and waited for the men to return.

Sitting on the new porch was lovely, with all the flowers still in bloom, and their scents lingering in the soft breeze. This was the house I loved, it just needed to be cleansed of all the wickedness it had suffered. As I sat, I started to wonder about the towers. What could be in them? Surely nothing bad, or Esmeralda would have known.

I realised I hadn't turned off the lights down in the new area, so I walked around the outside to come up the back stairs. The stairs were well-maintained, though I had never seen the gardener around.

The old gazebo could possibly be freshened up a bit though. As I looked around it, I noticed what appeared to be an old rocking horse. It was the size and type for a baby. The thought of a baby who had passed long ago, sent shivers down my spine. I hoped that they had lived a happy life.

Walking up the stairs, I noticed that there was a room sticking out from where we had gone through. But that was a wall, because Esmeralda had stood in front of it. As I walked closer, I noticed that it was hanging out of the window I couldn't see into. Now I wished Esmeralda was here with me.

Seeing that, I decided to go back around to the front of the house and wait for the men. I felt a shiver, but it must have just been the breeze. As I walked around, I heard their car approaching. They seemed to get along well and were joking around. As they reached me on the porch, they asked if we were done. I told them that I had tagged the items to be dumped, and made a list of things to replaced, including a new kitchen.

Ray and Shaz were about to walk inside, but I asked them to come around the back way. They obligingly followed as I explained why.

When they saw what I was talking about, they both exclaimed, "That's weird!"

As we started up the stairway at the back of the house, I felt the shiver again. This time, I knew it wasn't the breeze. I was about to tell Ray and Shaz not to open it, but it was too late. I heard the first kick, then another. I had just walked through the back door, as they were pulling the sheeting off.

The screech was deafening! The men stood there in shock. I had no one with me, but I saw it coming towards them. I went to hold up my arm, and I felt someone grab my hand. It was Shelly!

The creature's eyes were bright red, and we sent a bolt of energy, right into its eye. It dropped and disintegrated in front of us.

Shelly went limp, and I grabbed her, resting her on the floor. I called out for Ray and Shaz to help. They picked Shelly and I up, and Shaz exclaimed, "WTF was that!"

Shaz carried Shelly to her room and Ray followed carrying me. They laid us down. I asked if Shelly was okay. Ray checked her vitals and said that she was slow but stable. Shaz called the ambulance while Ray ran out to grab us some water.

When Ray came back in, I told him to check shelly for burns. Both Ray and Shaz looked at me strangely but did it anyway. Thankfully, she was fine. I breathed a big sigh of relief, as this was the last thing Shelly needed right now.

We could hear the ambulance coming, and Shaz headed down to escort them up.

Ray asked me, "Are you okay? What just happened?"

Before I could answer, the paramedics arrived and started attending to Shelly. They said she was weak, but stable. They checked my vitals as well and asked what had happened, because we both showing signs of trauma. I explained that I was just in a state of shock, and that Shelly had been electrocuted not long ago, and any exertion caused her to become weak. I continued to tell them that she had been helping with some renovations, and had fallen, but I managed to catch her in time.

The paramedics left, and Shaz said that he would go with them, to stay with Shelly.

Ray was still looking at me, as if expecting me to disappear or something.

I asked him, "What do you remember?"

He replied, saying, "I saw a large black thing, with red glowing eyes fly at us! Then I heard you calling me!"

I nodded, and said, "Yes, we saw it too. It knocked us over and went out through the door."

This made me realise that it didn't electrocute the guys, but it did when it hit Shelly. Maybe it electrocuted Shelly because she had the bracelet on. Those bracelets hold the power within them.

Ray pulled me out of my thoughts, asking if I wanted to go and see Shelly. I said yes and suggested we call her mum, but maybe wait to see what the hospital says first, in case she's fine, as I didn't want her mother to be worried again.

Ray agreed, still looking dazed. I asked him if he was okay to drive, and he assured me that he wasn't hurt, he just never believed in supernatural beings. That was, until now.

Ray then looked at me, and said, "Why weren't you scared?"

I lied, saying, "I never saw anything, just a huge wind knocked us over."

I hope I never have to lie to him again. We locked up the house and headed to the hospital again. I thought this had to stop. I am going to take Shelly's bracelet off her. We will never be apart, so she doesn't need it.

When we arrived, the doctor was already with Shelly, asking her what she remembered.

Shelly was being smart, saying, "I don't remember."

As the doctor left the room to get the nurse, I quickly grabbed Shellys arm, and took off her bracelet.

The doctor came back, then said, sounding puzzled, "This time your vitals are climbing back up on their own, slowly." He then said that they would keep her here, until he was happy. Then said to Shelly, "No activities until you're completely well!" Then he walked out.

Shaz hadn't spoken, he was just holding Shellys hand.

Ray gave Shelly a kiss on her cheek, saying, "We will let Mum know."

Shelly said, "No, don't!"

I said, "Ok, we won't." Hugging her to calm her down, as I understood she didn't want her upset.

I sat on the other side of Shelly, holding her other hand.

Ray asked me, "Do you want a coffee?"

I said yes, as did Shelly.

Shaz went to help Ray, and so I quickly explained to Shelly, what I thought.

Shelly said to me, "No more demons!"

I said, "No, whatever walls are there, they can stay there. Now we know why they just added on."

Holding her hand, our tears flowed. We had never thought all this would evolve. We were just two normal girls who wanted a castle-house to live in, to be princesses. Yes, we believed in ghosts, we always had, but fighting for our lives was not what we planned. I asked if she still wanted the house. Shelly said that she did, and that working with Shaz, made her see her beauty, and that the house needs to be given a new life. I agreed, and it's nearly there.

When the men came back, they had a different aura about them.

That's what Esmeralda used to call it, anyway. They weren't their happy selves. We drank our coffee, and Shaz asked if Shelly needed anything.

Shelly hugged him, saying, "No, I can feel my body coming back to normal. Maybe we could still go to dinner, laughing a little bit."

I said, "Better yet, let's get a 'take away' and you can both come to our house." looking at Ray for an okay.

Ray said, "Yes. There is plenty of room, and we can all watch a movie and chill out. It's been quite a day!"

I wondered if Esmeralda was back. I hadn't felt her all day since she left with that ghost.

We had a great restful night, and Shelly said that she was feeling a lot better. The men were very attentive, but still not themselves. Ray noticed Shelly had taken her bracelet off, asking if it wasn't a friend-ship bond. Shelly said that it was, but it was hurting and that her and I aren't apart anymore anyway.

Ray asked me, "Are you still wearing yours?"

I said, "For now, yes, but if it hurts, I will take it off. It is being used in a way, in my book."

Ray and Shaz looked at me weirdly. I told them that I was doing a fiction story and having fun making things up.

Shelly said, "Is someone your worst critic?"

I laughed, saying, "No! He's not allowed to read it!"

Shelly asked, "Can I?"

Laughing, I said, "Yes!"

That followed with a, no fair, from Ray, and laughter from Shaz. The mood lightened. Ray then broached the subject.

He said, "We need complete transparency from both of you girls!"

Shaz said, "We have both seen something we can't understand, but we also know what we saw."

Ray said, "We both saw a bolt of lightning hit that devil-looking creature in the eye, then it disintegrated!" He continued, "You girls were laying on the floor, do you want to let us in on what you girls know? Or did Shaz and I both imagine the same thing?"

I started to tell them, "It's very complicated and we will explain, but there's someone else we need to bring into this conversation. When we find her, we can talk about it then, so that it makes sense!"

They both said, "So there is something?"

I said, "Yes, but don't imagine anything. There's way too much to tell you both, let alone all the questions that will follow!"

Shaz said, "Ok, when you girls are ready."

We hugged our men, and Shelly said, "We are still the same girls you thought we were."

Shaz said to Shelly, "Come on, I will help you get to her bed."

Ray said, "You are welcome to stay. There is a room next to Shellys."

Ray looked at me as Shaz and Shelly walked off, and said, "I will just lock up. Then, I will come and escort you to your bubble room."

I thought he was doing well. Not running away.

Ray came back saying, "Just one question though. Those things won't get in here, will they?"

I said, "No!" Not knowing the answer. I then asked Ray, "Will you and Shaz stick with us, if we do bring you into this?"

He said, "Of course! Shaz is head over heels in love with Shelly. He is just scared to rush her, being so unwell. And as for me and you, even though I do not understand any of this, you have brought something very new to my life."

I said, "I'm so sorry this has exploded into your life as well."

Ray turned, and said, "Our lives."

Again, I felt like I could relax, floating into our happy place. I woke to sunshine, coffee, kisses, and a very big heartbreaking smile, saying, "Good morning! The other princess has been up and has already left with Shaz. They were going to go to his place. They seemed very happy, and Shelly is looking so much better."

I took that last statement in, thinking maybe the bracelet was holding some kind of power from the demon, that kept her unwell. Then wondered if mine was doing this as well. At the same time, I was unsure what would happen if we both had them off. We needed to learn more from the book.

Ray asked, "Are you ok?"

I must have done what Shelly said I do, and blanked out, deep into my thoughts.

Then he said, "I was talking to you."

I said, "Sorry, but that is normal for me when I need to regroup my thoughts. I have done it since childhood."

He said, "Now that I understand!" Then continued, "I took the liberty of checking your emails. I feel your morning will be taken up. If you are ok here, I need to go and sort some travel arrangements out, then get back to the London firm."

I said, "That would be worth leaving me for!"

Laughing, Ray said, "You always come up smiling."

I hugged him, saying, "I always look forward, not back. That's not where we are heading!"

He said, "Perfectly spoken by a true Author! We will sort out this strange problem together, and we will continue to forward." Then Ray kissed me, saying, "Enjoy your bubbles. Brekky is ready to heat up."

I replied, "I am the luckiest girl in the world!"

A very heavy weight felt like it had been taken off my shoulders. Relaxing in bubbles to start my day was the best idea.

Now to eat, then tackle the emails.

The house felt quiet, like it knew not to disturb me. Opening my computer, I saw how many was awaiting my service. I scrolled through, picking ones I knew about first. Some meant that I had a lot of reading ahead of me, and others were originally meant for Mr. Winston. Then I suddenly felt concerned. Should I ring him? Maybe later, I will decide.

After two hours, my fingers needed a break. I went into the kitchen to make a coffee, when the doorbell rang. Standing there was Shelly, with the biggest smile on her face!

She jumped into my arms, squealing, saying, "Shaz asked to marry me. I said yes!"

I hugged her again, saying, "A little birdie said he was head over heels in love with you!"

Shelly blushed, saying, "I am for him too! We love the same things, and he still loves our Castle House!"

Shelly and I grabbed coffees, then headed up to read more of the book. It was wonderful to have Shelly back to normal. We continued studying the symbols, gradually understanding their meaning, as we saw them used with other words.

Shelly asked me if I was going to take off my bracelet. I told her I was afraid that something might happen if I did.

I then asked Shelly, "What do you think would happen if I put your bracelet on Ray? It would make sense since we're always together."

Shelly responded by saying it might not work, as she thought it was only for best friends.

Ray's car pulled in, and we went to greet him. He seemed very excited and had something in his hands.

Shelly couldn't contain her excitement and blurted out, "Shaz asked me to marry him!"

Ray hugged her, and said, "You both deserve each other." Then said to me, "I have our tickets."

I asked when we were leaving, and he said Sunday, so we needed to start packing.

Shelly exclaimed, "Wow, you're finally getting to travel, Hannah!"

Ray asked how I had managed with my workload, and I told him. He offered to call and check on Frank, then headed straight into his study. I asked Shelly what she had planned for the day. She said she had nothing planned, so I thought it would be a good day for a driving lesson.

Ray came out of his study looking a bit off, and I asked if everything was okay. He told us that Frank had gotten an infection but was doing better today. I hoped Frank would recover quickly.

I reassured Ray by saying, "He has never been sick before, so I'm sure he will be fine once his meds kick in!"

I then asked Ray, if he knew anyone who could give us driving lessons.

He laughed and asked, "Don't you trust me?"

I replied, "Of course! But their cars have brakes on both sides, right?"

He looked at Shelly and asked her if she felt safer that way too. Shelly nodded, and like usual, Ray had a guy coming around, within the hour. We quickly made lunch and put on comfortable shoes. Shelly wanted me to go first, and I was okay with that.

My instructor said I was very good for a beginner but needed to learn the road rules a little more. Shelly took my place and started off slowly, forgetting to use her blinker. I laughed to myself as she accidentally turned on the wipers instead.

When we made it back to the house, Ray came out and asked how it went. I told him what happened, and he admitted that when he started, he went backwards instead of forwards. He suggested that we go and get the road rules book.

I agreed, saying, "Okay, I'll drive!"

Ray exclaimed, "Wow, very confident!" Then added that I would have to park between the lines.

I confidently replied, "Already done, and nailed it!"

Laughing, we got into my car and headed to the driving centre. They gave me a book and said that they would give me the test when I was ready. This was right up my alley. I sat in the car, read the book, memorised it, and went back in. The lady at the centre looked bewildered and asked if I had forgotten something. I answered her by asking if I could take the test. She nodded in surprise.

Walking out with a big smile, Ray laughed and said, "You completely aced it, didn't you?"

Driving home was much more relaxing, now that I knew when and where to change lanes. I wasn't as scared of the trucks either.

Shelly was waiting for us at the front of Rays. As I got out of my car, she laughed and said, "Didn't you have enough stress with the instructor?"

I laughed and thought to myself, should I tell her? But before I even decided, Ray said it for me.

Shelly exclaimed, "Wow, you're awesome! And now the nominated driver!"

Ray said, "Next time will be easier," as he handed her the road rules book.

Shelly replied, "That's easy, but those big trucks are scary. They pull in front of you, and then you can't see!"

Ray laughed and asked, "What do you girls want to do now?"

Shelly excitedly said, "Let's go to the castle-house."

Ray agreed, and said, "Okay, climb in. Hannah is driving!"

We all laughed, joking that the poor car would suffer.

As I drove in, there were several cars on the lawn again. Ray mentioned that Shaz was having the bathroom fittings and laundry installed today.

We walked inside, and Shaz came out from the laundry and greeted Shelly with a big hug. Ray and I smirked and followed him back into the laundry.

Shelly and I couldn't help but exclaim, "That's amazing! So much space!"

Shaz proudly said, "You are all plumbed in, just need the power. I talked to Mr. Hays, and he is coming on Saturday. He said that he would be on his own, as Jake and his mate are going dirt bike riding with a group, but my apprentice can give him a hand if he needs it."

I couldn't thank Shaz enough, even though he wasn't really listening. We left Shaz to continue his work, and went up to check out the new bathroom, which was fit for a queen!

I teased Ray, saying, "This is starting to look pretty nice."

Ray looked at me and asked, "Would you still live here?"

Just as he said that I felt a warm hug from Esmeralda. I asked Ray if he would like to invite Shaz and Shelly to join us for a coffee and a chat, in the living room.

Ray agreed, then asked, "Are you going to fill us in on the red-eyed demon?"

I replied, "Yes, just give me 5 minutes to organise myself."

Ray looked at me strangely, then walked off to get Shelly and Shaz.

Esmeralda appeared next to me, and I said, "You had us worried. We had another huge demon after you left with the ghost."

Esmeralda said, "We need to talk. Your men had seen that demon apparition. So, we will go down, and I will stay visible to them. Shelly seems very happy with this Shaz man."

I responded, "They are perfect for each other."

Esmeralda held my hand as we walked down the stairs and into the living room. Shelly jumped up and hugged Esmeralda, while the men looked as if they were ready to run. We introduced Esmeralda, as the lady who had gifted us Castle House.

They stood and said, "Hello, nice to meet you."

Esmeralda spoke, "I am still the custodian of this house, but I will be leaving as soon as some things are sorted. I had a friend, a very long time ago, who became stuck between here and there. We were naughty, young, adventurous teenagers, playing with white witches' books. We learned to materialise toys and other things, which was fun. Then one day, we found a spell for enchanted bracelets."

The men looked at each other but they said nothing.

Esmeralda continued, "After wearing them for a while, we realised that if the other was sad or in trouble, we could transport through our bedroom wardrobes to each other."

Now the men's mouths were open, staring at Esmeralda.

She went on, "What we did not know was that there was a time limit on them. My friend was coming through to me, but never made it. I waited here all my life in case she found a way. Then one day, I opened the kitchen pantry door, and her bracelet was there." Esmeralda had tears in her eyes, but continued, "I knew then that the only way I might be able to find her, was to find two girls who shared the same bonds. As you both already know, I gave them to Shelly and Hannah. When Shelly had to move away from Hannah, who desperately needed her, I made friends with these two beautiful souls, hoping that one day, they could somehow help me find Margaret."

Esmeralda then went on to explain the demons, and why they have come. "If I leave this house, another very angry ghost, who was banished years before I was born, will get back in. I only left for a short time, but she knew, and took residence again. I came back from my quest to find these girls being attacked by her. These girls were able to send a bolt through the dark, hitting this evil creature, without any of us knowing such power existed in their bracelets. Unfortunately, she still wants to be here, and because I came back, she became very angry. We fought and I was losing, but when she heard the girls' voices, she must have thought they were coming to help me, and in anger, she flew herself outside. I doubt she will test these girls again. I was very weak, and it was lucky the girls protected me. I never lived in any other parts of this house with my parents. They just always said, that if a door is locked, to leave it locked, and hide the key should you so find it. Had I have known what had been done in those eras, I would never have brought the girls into this. Unfortunately, I am the only bloodline that keeps the evil out. Unfortunately, I knew nothing about what was locked away. Hannah, the Ghost I went away with, was that of a baby, born out of wedlock. I have been able, this last week, to find the child's mother, and this set them free. As for the demons, the demons these girls have dealt with, they are out in the world, normally unseen and unknown to humans. Back many years before, people trapped them in rooms and built walls around them." Esmeralda then said, "Sorry! I will have to sit for a moment."

Shelly helped Esmeralda sit, while I told Ray and Shaz, the truth about how Shelly and I were really hurt. "Firstly, Shelly opened a wardrobe in the storage room, and this creature flew right through Shelly. I thought then that it had electricity in it. When it flew at me it scratched my arm. I went under the table to get to Shelly, but it came at me again. I held Shelly's hand with mine, and it was enough to kill it." I continued, "Then when we were at Shelly's house, I felt the coldness of someone's presence, but couldn't see anything. Someone had written on the mirror while I was in the shower, the word, help. It freaked me out as at this time, Esmeralda was missing. I went into the kitchen, and on the window, someone had written, Margaret. We didn't know what to do. But then when Shelly was in the bathroom at the time, a demon tried to get her through the mirror. She threw a towel over it and blocked its entrance. When we picked up Shelly from the hospital that first time, we asked you if we could call into Shelly's to get her clothes. Shelly was worried it would get through if her mum took off the towel. Ray, you heard the scream, but it wasn't me, it was the creature. It screeched as we sent a bolt through it. That's why Shelly's health went backwards. We have been reading a magic book, trying to find some way that can help get Margaret back through. Hers, and other souls, are being held by these demons."

Esmeralda spoke, saying that she thinks the demon we had killed in the bathroom, was chasing Margaret, who must have escaped, but felt her connection to the bracelets.

Esmeralda continued, "It is a horrible place where these demons live. They are not allowed in the afterlife, so they live between worlds, trapping souls leaving earth. They drain these souls for their strength. This is now my quest, to free them, and I believe the girls are now safe in this house. I would like to try, with Hannah and Shelly, to go to the world between, and help free all of the souls, especially Margaret."

Shelly looked at me, and I knew she wasn't up to it!

I said, "No", as did Ray and Shaz.

Esmeralda said, "I understand."

I told Esmeralda what we had been able to read, and that Shelly and I thought that it was not the number of times, but the amount of time, that you had in the use of the bracelets. Esmeralda said that it could be true, as her and Margaret were both in our sixties, when Margaret got stuck. I then told her that maybe it depended on how much voltage was used also. The words did not make sense to us.

Ray said, "Where are these books?"

I said, "At our house."

Ray said, "Maybe it could be me that could wear one of those bracelets."

Shaz said, "And me?"

Shelly looked at me. Her eyes read the same as I felt. Our hearts were so proud of these men.

Esmeralda was fading, and Ray and Shaz asked us to try and help her. Shelly and I helped Esmeralda upstairs. As we laid her down on her bed, she faded away. We could still feel her though, and knew she was still with us.

We walked back downstairs, to find the men in deep discussion.

Shelly said to me, "I know they want to do this for us, but I don't want them to get hurt!"

I knew Ray was thinking. What if his parents were trapped there?

As we walked back into the lounge room, Shaz hugged Shelly, and Ray hugged me, saying, "You girls are so amazing to have gone through all of that, and now I understand why Shelly took hers off. But why didn't you take yours off?"

I said, "No one knows what might happen, they could be useless already, from me taking Shelly's off."

We all sat, talking about needing someone who understood the symbols that we didn't.

Shaz asked if Esmeralda was okay on her own.

I said, "Hopefully, as she is wearing out quicker now. We can feel her presence even though we can't see her, but it is weaker."

Shaz said, "That's amazing. How long have you known her?"

I said, "We've known her since before Shelly had to leave. I used to escape from home and sit with her for ages. She loved having afternoon tea parties. Somehow, It was real food! When she knew Shelly was back ion town, she asked her to come over. I was already headed here. She always knew everything about us. She even knew when I was at the front, before I even knocked. She made a beautiful big Christmas dinner once, and had a tree covered in decorations, and the present under that tree, was the book!"

I told Ray and Shaz, that it was Esmeralda who saved me from my mother, who had come through the door with and axe, and was going to kill me.

Shelly said, "She is so evil!"

I continued, "Esmeralda materialised and sent her flying through the door. Then she tried to protect me from my father. Luckily Jake's dad heard the noice, and stepped in. I owe her a lot more than Shelly."

Ray said, "Let's go back home and try to figure out this book."

Shaz said, "I will bring Shelly, and we will grab some burgers on the way."

Ray said, "Oh yeah, I like those."

Laughing, I went up to say goodbye to Esmeralda, but she never answered. I felt her warmth and knew she was just asleep.

I asked Shaz if he had unlocked any other doors, especially any at the back.

He said "No, and now I'm glad I didn't!"

I said, "There is nowhere those demons could hide now."

Ray said, "We haven't gone into the towers!"

That was true. But we only had my bracelet, and Esmeralda was too weak.

Shelly said, "My bracelet is in the sunrise room, but I don't want to go up!" Ray went and brought it down. We then locked up Castle house and left.

Ray said, as we headed home, "Thank you! If I hadn't been able to put things together, I would have gone crazy. I'm so sorry for all you have been through. No one should have to deal with human evil, let alone inhuman creatures."

I said, "Lucky you came into my life. Just in time to balance out the bad."

Ray asked, "Was there anything at the house, when we had dinner on the floor?"

I said, "We didn't know. But I was worried about being there after midnight!"

He said, "You never said anything."

I told Ray, "Up until then, we had only dealt with ghosts," laughing.

Seventeen

Dealing With The Unknown

Ray and I arrived back at his house. We walked upstairs to retrieve the books, and then placed Shelly's bracelet in the safe.

Ray went downstairs to answer the doorbell. I heard Shelly's voice, as she got halfway up the stairway, asking me for her bracelet. I gave her the books, then went back to the safe to retrieve it. As I was headed back downstairs with it, I felt a static charge. I never thought they might zap us.

I got to the dining room, and Ray was enjoying his burger. It made me giggle because he had sauce all over his face, and that was not the look of a millionaire.

He saw me giggling and said, "Come on, dig in."

I did, and then I gave him a big sticky kiss. Shelly laughed, and it was on. Shaz was running until Shelly caught him, and then the bathroom became very busy.

After cleaning up, we put the books on the table. Ray opened it up to the page I had marked, and Shaz had the dictionary.

Ray was just staring at it, and then he said, "This is not Hebrew. I think it's ancient Egyptian."

I said, "Oh! Now we have no dictionary."

Shaz remarked, "I'm not seeing any words."

Shelly added, saying that it wasn't her educational range either.

Ray said, "There was a professor at Harvard, who deciphered some tombs once, and I'm sure he wrote a journal. I will check on the computer."

While he was gone, I told Shelly how her bracelet zapped me.

She said, "Maybe that's why it was hurting me and keeping me unwell. I did feel better once you took it off me!"

We heard a big "Yes!" from the den, so Shelly and I walked in.

Shaz said, "This is my kind of den!"

Laughing, Ray said, "Help yourself."

Shaz said, "Anyone joining me?"

Ray said, "Yes, I'll have a Jack Daniels on the rocks."

We had drinks. Ray was already finding words and signs. I wrote as he called it, but so far, none of it made much sense. After reading and writing them, we still couldn't make much of it.

Then I started to see a pattern. When I read them from top to bottom, it began to make sense.

I said, "I have it! You read top to bottom, not sideways."

Ray said, "You are not just a pretty face, my princess."

Reading it out, we all agreed that it was explaining that the bracelets were used as weapons by the Pharaohs, to keep their slaves in order. It said that they never took them off, as the power seeped out.
Shelly asked Ray to start again.

I spoke aloud as I read what I had written. "One leader hits hands together to send a deadly shot. One armband touches a gem, a smaller shot. To reload, rest on a gold tablet, close to the sun. To shift in time, two minds think together."

Ray said, "Then it's talking about a serpent ring. With poison, tip it into the head, then dip it in serpent blood and tongue. Serpent chair, arrow tips, scorpion blood and tongue. Wine with red vine, balls of poison." He then said, "My goodness, what have you girls been given?"

I was still stuck on serpent blood.

Shelly asked, "Were serpents like our demons?"

Shaz said, "Until tonight, I thought they were all imaginary!"

Ray said, "So all we learned is that it takes two brains to transport. Then to recharge those bracelets, you lay them on gold in the sun?"

Shelly said, "We think mine is leaking as it zapped Hannah."

Ray said, "Hannah, are you game for me to put it on? Now that we know you can recharge them, maybe us men can try it out."

I felt very unsure, but we also needed to know. I picked it up and put it on Ray, waiting to rip it off if it zapped him.

Ray said, "I can feel the tingle, but let's try it outside so we only hurt a plant."

I said, "Let me try a single shot first."

Shelly and Shaz stood behind, to catch us if we fell. I pushed the gem, and a spark flew out at the pot.

Shelly asked me, "Did it zap you?"

I said, "No."

Ray said, "Okay, if it zaps me, don't touch me!"

I said, "Wait! Let me grab something first!" Then I went and retrieved the rubber bathmat from the guest house.

Ray stood on the rubber mat and fired. Shellys bracelet Ray was wearing, fired with only half its power.

Ray said, "Okay, let's leave it at that."

The bolt had hit the tree behind and splintered it.

Ray said, "Damn, I've been growing that for years."

I said, "I can't travel. I'm scared I won't get back now!"

Ray said, "Let's just leave it at that."

I said to Ray, "Yes, they would take out a demon with us working together. We will try and charge Shellys one. I think we need a rubber bracelet under it, in case it keeps leaking," Then I suggested. "We can try tomorrow when the sun is out." I felt safer knowing that Ray could work with me.

Shaz then said, "Maybe I should try it, to see if Ray and I could work together."

I felt strange taking mine off, but it would be great if Shaz could work with Ray to deal with any other demons. They tried my bracelet separately, first, and they created more power than I had ever gotten from it. Then they were ready to try firing, with the bracelets together.

Shelly and I were holding our breath, as Ray and Shaz stood on the rubber mat. Ray called out, ready, thee he and Shaz hit the bracelets to-gether. The poor tree had no chance, it just crumbled! Another hurdle overcome. Now we knew that we could swap them between us.

We walked back inside, thinking about what we had just learned. We can clear Castle House of all its demons completely, I thought. Helping Esmeralda though, was another issue, as well as transporting. When we were, kids we just did it. But now, the risk of getting caught by demons, or not returning was not something that we should take lightly.

While Ray and Shaz headed back to the bar, Shelly and I headed to the bubble room.

Shelly said, "I'll run the bath while you grab our clothes."

I went into the Bahama room and grabbed Shellys clothes.

Shelly laughingly called out, "Too slow, I'm in!" It was nice to hear her laughing again. I went and lay on my bed, looking at the moon. Strange thoughts came into my head. Maybe there are aliens as well.

It was a beautiful evening, so I wandered out onto the veranda to gaze at the stars. Shelly called out, so I went inside, still feeling unsettled. I locked the veranda door.

Shelly raced in and jumped on my bed, saying, "We are free of the ties!" I wished I could think that way, but I owed Esmeralda, and needed help.

I said to Shelly, "You can turn on the TV, if you want."

I was happily floating in bubbles, when I heard Shaz talking with Shelly, then her little giggle. With that, they were gone. I was so happy she was in love.

Ray came in asking, "Where's my princess?"

Morning found us all out on the veranda, taking in the new day. After a good night's sleep, we were ready to conquer the demons. A plan was made as we ate Ray's beautiful cooking.

Shaz said to Shelly, "I am not a good cook!"

Shelly replied, "I was taught enough to keep us fit and healthy!"

Funny, I had never thought about it, but I knew nothing about cooking, just quick easy food or takeaways. Lucky Ray would keep him and I fit and healthy!

I cleaned up while Ray raided his safe, putting the gold valuables on a rock, and the bracelets on top, in the direct sunlight.

He then came in saying, "Our demon slayers are being reloaded!"

As I was checking my emails, I noticed that some had been opened by Mr. Winston, so I quickly answered the rest.

Ray came in saying, "We are doing more reading. Would you like to join us?"

I closed my computer, saying, "Mr. Winton had answered some emails, he must be on the mend!"

Ray smiled, then melted me into his arms, saying, "Together we will conquer!"

We continued to read the book. It was full of more of the hieroglyphics that we were beginning to get a hang of. Shelly was starting to be able to read them as well. We enjoyed working together, and time flew by. We all decided to head to the dining room and compare our notes.

Ray came in with coffees and snacks. Shelly was so excited that we let her read Shaz and her notes first. She read it out. She had decoded the spell on how to make different items appear, like the bike and baby rocker, Esmeralda had told us about. Even the enchanted bracelets themselves! We all took a moment. I knew we were all thinking the same thing. Did we want more? I asked if there was any information on the pages she had decoded, about a way to tell how long the bracelets lasted.

Shaz said, "There is heaps more to read, we can continue after you two share yours."

I read out mine and Rays notes, they were more about the battle between the lords, and a new weapon they used around the slaves' necks. The weapon sent electric waves through them if they stopped working, while they were building their stone kingdoms. It spoke of a large elephant-type animal with long horns, also wearing these chains like zapping things. They recharge continually as they wear them in the sun.

Shelly said, "They were cruel in the old days! Thank goodness we don't have slavery anymore!"

We finished our break, then headed back to the book to seek more information.

The day had been good. Ray had also received a confirmation from London about the ticket sales of the event. It has hit full capacity, with a waitlist, in case of any cancellations!

We had heard Shaz a few times, talking on the phone his worker back at Castle House.

I mentioned to Ray, "Maybe we should go and check on Esmeralda, and the workmen. If you want, we could maybe open another door. Both of us wearing the bracelets, of course."

Ray asked, "Are you concerned there are more?"

I said, "Kind of, but if there are more ghosts, then I would like to free them."

He agreed, saying, "Yes." Then suggested we take our notes with us.

Shaz said, "While we wait in the car, I will wear it instead of Shelly."

I looked at Shelly, who said, "Yes, they are stronger!"

Ray jumped into the car, and Shelly read out the rest of their notes, while we headed to Castle House. "The first one is about time travel using more energy than electric shots. It also says that the bracelets will fall off, when the energy has worn out. Recharging can be done by the sun or being put onto a new body."

So that must be why the guys were stronger. That must also be why Margaret and Esmeraldas work for us.

Shelly continued, "Build a circle around extra bodies, to either protect or travel."

If this was correct, we could take Esmeralda with us. But she would have to stay in body form. Our notes only uncovered more about the invaders, who had slaves that had to swallow some kind of bomb, then they were sent into the warriors. They held families in stone walls and had neck things put on them.

We reached Castle House and went looking for Esmeralda. I could already feel she was well again. As we walked into the dining room, I could feel that that's where she was. Ray and Shaz followed, and Esmeralda materialised as they walked in.

Esmeralda greeted us, saying, "You have good news!"

The men looked gobsmacked, not understanding how she could know that we had news.

To Shelly and I, it was normal for Esmeralda to know what was going on. I said, "We think so, but we could be wrong!"

Esmeralda said, "I need to go soon. Materialising is wearing my strength out."

Ray said, "If you stay invisible, will you be able to wait?"

Esmeralda nodded, yes.

Shelly then said, "We know where you are, so please stay hidden."

Esmeralda smiled and faded away.

Shaz said, "Ray, let's go and open up that room that we can see from outside. I think it is behind a wall."

Ray said to Shelly and I, "We will be back when it is safe for you both to enter." Putting on my bracelet, they both walked away.

Shelly asked, "Should we try and make two more, to help get Esmeralda get through the demons that are holding Margaret with the other souls?"

I looked at her seriously, and said, "This is dangerous, but wherever they are, it could be very bad. We might not be enough to kill them all, on our own.

For that reason, Shelly said, "I want to go. I'll stay with Shaz or go with Shaz! I feel the same way!"

We knew Esmeralda could help with this, so we decided to wait for the men to come back.

We went to the beginning of the hallway but didn't go any further. We could hear the crash of the wall, and then the door.

As Shelly and I waited, we heard the men say, wow, then them calling us in. At least they were safe. We heard banging again, and as we approached, we saw the entrance to the room. It was the one we could see from the window.

The room was dusty and smelly, and there was nothing in it. But the men were hitting through another wall opposite. They told us that it had to join back up to the other hallway that we had previously found. When they broke through, there was yet another room.

Ray called out, "You girls have to see this one!"

Shelly and I climbed through, to see what looked like a fully stocked laboratory with so much weird stuff.

Shelly said, "This must be where Esmeralda and Margaret made their toys, and these bracelets!"

Ray said, "That means there must be another door still."

Shaz tapped on the walls until he found where it might be. Him and Ray began hitting it with their hammers, revealing a door behind it.

Ray exclaimed, "This is it!"

We looked at all the different bottles, and I wondered if Esmeralda would remember what her and Margaret used. We opened some drawers and found what looked like a wand. I had always thought they were just for show, but now, Shelly and I weren't brave enough to touch it.

The door gave way when the men gave it one last push. They were right, we were back at the stairway. So, this must be the way they went to make their magic.

Esmeralda appeared, and said, "Yes, I remember now. When we were little, they changed the walls. We used to enter through the back door."

While the men kept pulling down the wall, Esmeralda said to us, "I could hear you discussing the idea of making another set of bracelets. Yes, I can remember how we made them, even though I'm not sure that you girls should come with me."

Ray said, "Yes!" Another wall was gone.

I laughed at the men who were loving being in this house now.

Shaz asked, "What were you talking to Esmeralda about?"

Ray also looked inquiringly at us. I told them our plan, but they didn't think it would be safe.

Shelly and I both said, at the same time, "Four is better than two."

We went back through the rubble. I heard Shaz call his apprentice, and he asked him to grab another guy to do a huge dump run.

Shaz, still on the phone, said "Yes, bring the truck."

Ray turned to Shaz and said "Great idea! Your guys doing the dump run frees us up some time for us to make these bracelets. We both know there's no use arguing with either of these girls, and they're right, there is safety in numbers."

"Okay." Shaz replied.

We all headed to the lab room and saw that Esmeralda was already collecting what she needed for the bracelet spell.

Esmeralda said, "I should've thought of this. But I never thought to knock through the walls, to get back into my laboratory to do it."

We all stood in perfect silence while she worked.

Esmeralda exclaimed, "Stand back. The force of this spell might be the size of a mountain!" As she spoke the words that we had been deciphering, then waived her wand.

We waited, and then a ball of electricity hit the bench, leaving a bracelet behind. No one moved until Esmeralda tried to wear it, but the spell had zapped her energy and made her too weak to stay completely materialised, and it fell back onto the bench.

"May I try?" I asked Esmeralda.

Being overruled by my protective knight, Ray said, "No, I'll do it."

Ray tried it on, and to my surprise, the bracelet fit him better than mine fit me. A sneaky suspicion popped into my mind, thinking that Esmeralda had made that bracelet specifically for Ray. But he still needed to test it, so him and Shaz headed out the back entrance to give it a whirl, while Shelly and I stayed with Esmeralda. We could see she was weak and tried to help get things ready for her.

The men came back, and Ray said, "This bracelet took a tree out in one blast! It must have something to do with who made it."

I said to Ray, "Maybe you should say the words and use the wand, as you will have more strength going into it."

Esmeralda agreed, as she was fading. He repeated the words and waved the wand. The bolt that followed was stronger and burned the table.

Esmeralda whispered to me, "I'm going to rest until you are ready."

As the truck drove in. Shaz put the new bracelet on, while saying, "We will put a sign on this room, saying 'keep out', just until we are finished everywhere else."

We walked outside to meet the workers, with Shaz giving directions on what to finish pulling down, and what to clean up. He also instructed them to go and get new doors, but not to enter the room that was taped off.

Ray asked me, "Are we okay to leave?" As he wanted us head home to pack.

He was right, time was flying. Shaz said he and Shelly would stay and help. Shelly gave me a nod, indicating that she was okay with that, too.

Driving home, Ray asked, "Should we try and make some of the other weapons from the book?"

I thought about it, then said, "Yes, the more prepared we are, the better!"

Ray mentioned that once we finished packing, that we would take the book back with us to Castle House and see if we could find all of the ingredients and components needed to make them. Then mentioned, "I am a very accomplished archer. I have a collection of bows and arrows, if we can just make the poison for the tips, I would feel more than confident in using them."

We finished packing for the London trip, checked what the weather was like overseas, to make sure we didn't need any extra coats. I thought I'd checked my emails again while we were here too. I had one from Mr. Winton, thanking me for keeping up with the workload. He said that he would be back in the office tomorrow, and that he had a list of clients he would organise to sign contracts with, ready for me to start when we returned. I told Ray, and he was so happy.

Time had flown, but our bags were ready.

Ray teased me, saying, "You will buy new things while you're there, so don't fret about what you've packed!"

We grabbed the spell book and headed back to Castle House. As we were driving, I got excited again thinking about the renovations. Ray interrupted my thoughts, saying that we would stop to pick up burgers for everyone. I think he's becoming addicted to burgers. That thought made me giggle to myself, as I thought about him buying shares in the burger business and wearing burger socks.

When Ray walked back out of the burger store, he had Jake with him. I stepped out of the car to greet him. He was all excited, saying he had been offered a higher position in the electrical company. Jake said that he would have to move, but it was worth it for the promotion. I agreed. I'm so proud to see how far Jake has come. He's overcome so much over the last few years. I guess I could relate in a way.

Jake asked me to say hello and goodbye to everyone, as he was leaving tomorrow. Then asked how the renovations were going, and if we were ready for his dad to finish the remaining electrical work.

Ray said, "Yes, we have knocked through the back area now, which is the last to be checked, and rewired."

Ray and I wished Jake well in his new career and told him to keep in touch. I thought this was a blessing for Shelly, as she wasn't looking forward to telling Jake that she was now engaged. He would find out eventually though, through his dad.

The truck was gone when we arrived at Castle House, but we parked well out of the way, as we knew it would take another trip to the dump before it wasn't needed anymore. As we walked inside, we were surprised to see how much work had been done. Shaz said that they had already finished all the dump runs, and his workers had headed out to get the doors.

Ray handed Shaz and Shelly their burgers, saying, "Time to regroup."

As we ate, Ray told Shaz and Shelly about his ability on the archery scene, and that he wanted to make the poison for the tips of his arrows.

Shaz said, "The more weapons we have, the better!" Then mentioned that he had also competed in archery, and would be happy to use them also, if it came down to it.

We finished eating and headed into the lab room. I wandered around, looking at everything on the shelves. There were labels with hieroglyphics, and I recognised some from the spell book.

Ray collected more bracelet components and picked up the wand. Just as he did, I heard Esmeralda speak, reciting the words of the bracelet spell. Ray repeated the words as Esmeralda spoke and held his arm out so that Esmeralda could guide him with the wand movement. The spell scorched the entire table.

Shaz said, "WOW! Let me try that bracelet out!"

Shelly, Ray and I followed Shaz outside to watch, and the bracelets power was even stronger, disintegrating an entire tree!

"So, the more strength in the person, the stronger the power!" Shaz said, looking back at us in excitement. Then he said, "Let me try that spell too! In case we need something with even more power than this one!"

Shaz did have a good point, as he was the strongest out of all of us. There were enough components left, so we all agreed to to see how Shaz would go.

Shaz held out the wand, and allowed Esmeralda to guide his arm, and repeated the words she spoke. The entire table went up in a large ball of smoke! As it cleared, the bracelet he created was laying on the lab room floor, where the table use to be.

Shaz said, as he picked the new bracelet up from the floor, "Do we dare try this one?"

We all agreed that Esmeralda wouldn't be strong enough to wait until we returned, so the new bracelet wouldn't be tested until tomorrow.

Hopefully, Esmeralda will be at her strongest then, so that we can help her free Margaret, and the other souls.

Shaz said that he and Shelly would stay and help put the doors on, especially the two doors for the lab room, so that we can keep it locked. Ray asked if we should make the poison for the arrow tips, while we were here. I agreed, thinking that the more weapons we had, the safer we would all be.

Shaz, Shelly, and I, went through the spell's ingredients together, to make sure we knew exactly what we needed. We collected the components, while Ray learned the chant. He had brought the arrows with him, and I laid them out on the floor, were the table once stood.

As we added the last, horrific-smelling liquid, to the stone mortar, Ray told us to stand back. He repeated the chant, then lifted the wand, and tapped the mortar with it. The liquid began to bubble, and the smell that filled the room was disgusting.

Shaz picked up an arrow and dipped it into the liquid. It seeped straight into the tips, and looked as though there was nothing on the end at all!

We needed to try it out. But what on? How do you test a poison arrow? Then an idea hit me.

I said, "There are lots of cane toads out back, maybe we could try it on one? Not that I really want to hurt an animal. But we do need to know they work."

Shelly and Shaz decided they would try to catch one. Ray and I headed downstairs to wait. We didn't want to be breathing in that awful smell while waiting.

As Shelly and Shaz walked outside, I could hear Shaz saying, "You can slay demons but not a cane toad."

I yelled out, "Yep!"

Ray and I finally had a moment to ourselves to talk about our upcoming wedding. As Shelly and Shaz walked back inside, I asked Shelly what sort of theme for her wedding she was wanting.

Shelly said, "I always wanted a beach wedding, like in the movie."

I knew exactly which movie she was talking about, then asked her who she would invite. Ray and Shaz headed to the lab with the cane toad, while Shelly and I continued talking.

"My family, and Vala and Francesca, if they could make it. I don't have any other close friends yet, other than you and Ray."

I hugged Shelly, saying, "You and I could have a double wedding, as Ray and I want a small beach wedding too! If Ray doesn't mind, of course. He doesn't want to turn it into a big production of who was invited, and who wasn't. He has asked his grandparents, and he might have asked Mr. Winston. too. Does Shaz have family around?"

Shelly said, "Yes, I have met them. He has his mum, dad, and two younger brothers."

Ray and Shaz appeared, walking in with big smiles.

"One drop, and we said goodbye to the cane toad!" Shaz exclaimed.

Eighteen

Taking Esmeralda To Margaret

Before we left Castle House, we hung the lab doors, and locked the room.

Sleep came easy, and as morning arrived, I felt well rested enough for the day. Knowing that today, anything could happen. I was ready!

After an energising breakfast with Ray, we headed over to Castle House early. Shaz and Shelly were already there, waiting eagerly. I'm so glad that they looked more excited than scared. Especially Shelly. Shaz seems to have a protected feeling effect on Shelly. It made my heart feel so warm knowing this.

Shaz, Ray, Shelly, and I, all had our bracelets on. Ray also brought Shelly's old one as a backup, just in case we happened to need it. Esmeralda had told us the day before that where we were heading, had a putrid stench about it, so we all put on our face masks. We all made sure we wore our rubber sole shoes too, to counteract any potential static or leaks. There were plenty of arrows in Shaz and Rays quivers, and they were ready with their bows, slung over their shoulders.

Shelly and I found as many knives as we could and dipped them in the arrow tip poison as well, then covered them in cloth to avoid poisoning ourselves.

Esmeralda materialised, looking stronger than I had ever seen her. If anyone else had met her like this, they wouldn't even consider her as a ghost!

Esmeralda spoke, "Everyone hold hands, and say together. To the middle world of demons and ghosts we travel!" Then continued speaking, reciting a chant in the Egyptian language.

I practiced her words in my mind, as did the others, then we all spoke it out loud, following Esmeralda's cue. None of us were scared. We all knew that this was for the greater good, and we trusted that we would be kept safe.

We formed a circle around Esmeralda and continued to recite the chant. This experience became very different from mine and Shellys previous travels, through our wardrobes.

The stench hit us, and our chanting stopped. I looked around at the crumbled relics of some kind of structure.

Esmeralda said, "I can feel Margaret."

We started moving in the direction that Esmeralda had pointed, and suddenly found ourselves face to face with three circling demons. Shaz, Shelly, Ray, and I, all raised our arms together, not knowing how much power four bracelets would conjure up. The blast was so bright, that we had taken out all three demons at once!

Shelly and I quickly moved forward towards Esmeralda, while Shaz and Ray walked backwards in our direction, to make sure nothing came up behind us. We could hear the noises of the trapped souls, getting louder, the closer we got.

Suddenly, a scorching hot wind blew past us, and three, larger, red creatures, stood in our way. One of them sent a bolt towards us, but we were all able to duck out of its path.

Ray and Shaz armed their arrows, while Shelly and I struck our bracelets together. We hit one of the creatures straight in the eye, causing it to screech in pain as it fell to the ground. Shaz and Ray disintegrated the other two, with the poison arrows.

We could see a wall ahead, where creatures that had horrific looking bodies, were lurking. They were gnarling and pacing, dressed in what looked to be something resembling alligator skins. Some of the creatures spotted us, and a huge one-eyed creature, sent a fireball hurling our way. We ran, and as I passed Esmeralda, I grabbed her arm, pulling her with me. I felt we had the advantage, now knowing how far they could throw.

Ray confidently said, "My arrows can reach further than these creatures can throw." Then he aimed an arrow at the one-eyed creature, just as another one emerged from behind us.

Shaz swiftly threw a knife in the creatures direction, which twirled through the air and hit the creature in the skull. It fell to the ground, but not before sending a huge fireball towards us.

We managed to dodge it, as Ray turned and leaped into a roll, firing an arrow. As the arrow hit the creature, it let out one final cry, then disintegrated into a ball of foul green smoke.

The path to the wall ahead, began to fill up with even more ugly creatures. Shaz and Ray unleashed a barrage of arrows, while Shelly and I kept a look out behind us. One by one, all the creatures dropped, and quickly advanced to the wall.

Esmeralda became invisible, and slipped through the metal door, to open it from the other side. As the door opened, it revealed the cells below. A guard to our left spotted us, and I swiftly threw a knife at it, at the same time Ray sent an arrow into its head. Shaz and Shelly joined their bracelets together, as more guards approached from behind us.

Ray yelled, "Duck!" as he sent an arrow through another creature's head.

One of the creatures came at me, but Shelly grabbed my arm, just before it reached me, and we disintegrated it into the abyss. Shelly had spotted another one, before I did, coming over the wall behind Ray. She threw a knife but missed. Ray turned just in time to hit it with a bolt.

Shaz was under attack by one of the biggest creatures here and needed Ray's help to kill it completely. I grabbed an arrow from the spare quiver I was carrying for Ray, and tried to see if I could shoot it with the power of a bolt, towards a creature that had jumped the wall and was headed in Rays direction. Being so close, my aim was perfect. I used the arrow to push the gem down on the bracelet, keeping my fingers away from the path of the fletches. It worked!

We couldn't see any more creatures coming for us and made our way through the entrance. Esmeralda reappeared, and we swiftly followed her, down through the hall, towards where the souls where being held.

I was devastated by the cries of sorrow. The souls they had trapped, were all chained by their necks. When the ones that were working started to fade, the demons sent shocks through the part around their necks. We had to find the source of the power that was sending these shocks. Shelly and I checked each of the soul slaves, feeling the zap each time, they faded. It was the worst kind of torture for these poor souls.

I heard Esmeralda call out, saying that she had found it, and followed her voice. A creature approached Ray and Shaz, who had their backs turned while helping Esmeralda. It was a huge green demon, like the one that attacked Shelly through the mirror. Shelly screamed as we shot it with as many arrows as we could, using the gem bolts to fire them. Eventually, an arrow went straight into its eye, and killed it.

Shaz rushed to Shelly and held her. I stood guard over the power room door, while Ray worked on cutting the connection. My bracelet was nearly empty, so I grabbed out the last few knives I had and was ready to use them. Shaz said that he still had power in his bracelet, but Shellys seemed to be empty.

Ray yelled for me to bring a knife over. He wasn't sure if it would hurt the souls or not, but he was going to try cutting the connection. Esmeralda said to do it and told me to have my last arrow pointed at the door. Knowing that it could be the last bit of power left in my bracelet if I used it. There was an earthquake like jolt, as Ray cut through the wiring, and he was thrown backwards.

There was only silence, and darkness...

Then, right before my eyes, the most beautiful thing I had ever witnessed, occurred. The darkness begun to glow, as all the trapped souls floated upwards, and through the ceiling. They were free at last.

Esmeralda walked towards us smiling, and the soul walking beside her, introduced herself to us. It was Margaret. Tears streamed down my face as Esmeralda began fading into the same glow of the other souls. As her and Margaret began to float upwards, Esmeralda put her hands over her heart, and thanked us as she smiled and closed her eyes.

As I wiped the tears from my eyes, and turned to look at Ray, two glowing souls were embracing him. He had the most contented smile on his face.

I walked over to Ray, and he said, "Mum. Dad. This is Hannah, my fiancé."

I felt the warmth, beaming from Rays parents, as he told them about me. It was the same warmth I always felt, whenever Esmeralda hugged me. This moment was truly beautiful.

Shaz was still holding Shelly, and a tiny soul was sitting next to them. I watched as it floated away.

We all took a moment, sitting in silence, and gathering our strength. Then we all stood, with tears of love, and gratitude for what we had just accomplished, still falling from our eyes. Then, we held hands, and recited the chant to take us home.

We found ourselves back in the dining room of Castle House. We sat, huddled on the floor, in each other's arms. No one spoke, as it all felt too surreal in our minds.

It felt like we had sat there for ten minutes or more, before I finally asked Shelly who the child soul was that I had seen with her. Shelly explained that she was the one Esmeralda had helped, but she had been caught by the demons. She said that her mum had been calling out for her, but she couldn't escape no matter what she tried, and wanted to pass on her thanks to us all, for helping free her.

This was a date, and time that I knew we would all cherish in our hearts forever.

"Well, I don't know about you three, but I could sure go for the biggest burger right now!" Ray said, as he dusted the dirt off his arms.

We all burst into laughter and helped each other to our feet. Who would have imagined, that the four of us would come together, let alone live here, in Castle House, married, and cherishing lots of happy children. We've certainly brought life back into this house we all now call home.

THE END...

ABOUT THE AUTHOR

Y'vonne grew up in Chermside, Brisbane. As a child, she loved the book, 'Thumbelina'. At the age of five, her grandmother would give her fabric scraps, with which she enjoyed making dolls clothes from. By high school, Yvonne was creating unique clothing for her friends, and making an income. Then, at age fifteen, Y'vonne had become the manager of the local Newsagents.

At the age of thirty, Y'vonne found pride in single motherhood, and fostered peace, harmony, and happiness in her home environment, with her children. She started working part-time within the Queensland bridal industry, under the wings of a very inspirational man. That very man knew that she had no formal qualifications, but could see her determination to achieve. Y'vonne took the reins of this special opportunity, and never looked back. From a one week intensive training workshop in Sydney, to working throughout Australia with the biggest bridal wholesalers in the world. Y'vonne continued to work along-side her staff, that she refers to as family, until something slowly crept into her life. That something ultimately led to her having to resign.

As time flew by, Y'vonne's health got the better of her, and took her away from her passions within her career. So she set out, determined to achieve something else. That's when, *'Bohemian Dreams'* evolved, and her little crafty hobby took off!

Once again, Yvonne's health began to deteriorate. This time, with a shock diagnosis, But she wasn't ready to give up. The diagnosis propelled Y'vonne forward, and her creativeness took off in a direction she never really thought it would, before now. She had a book she had written, twenty years beforehand, taken on board by a North Queensland, boutique publisher. This had Y'vonne ecstatic!

During chemo, Y'vonne had a new idea for a Teen Fantasy novel, which became the content of this very book. She knew there was no timeframe to write it, but felt there still needed to be a deadline to finish it, due to her health. So, she set her new challenge, and went for it!

Y'vonne feels very blessed to be one of the very few, fighting cancer, yet still achieving her dreams. She continues to hold tight to her passion of writing, and hopes that her story, both of her life, and within these pages, will inspire others to keep strong, no matter what life hurls their way, because we all have the ability to make magic happen!

Y'vonne, with her loving husband Bill